"We have a prime minister now," Marc s
I'm in instant contact via the quantum re
difference is I can't make personal appe
those."

"No way!"

"Come on," Samantha said. "Jackie will love it. She gets to buy whatever gowns she wants, be the host of a nation for a night. It's not like we have some event every week."

"But . . ."

"Blake, it's time for you to step up," Marc said.

"I was just trying to figure out how to step out, now you want me to step up!"

"Just a little. Delphi holds, what, maybe two or three public events a year."

"It was a lot more than that last year!" Blake said.

"But that was because Sam was promoting goodwill by leveraging Catie. Can't do that while she's at the Academy under an assumed identity."

"Hey, I haven't agreed to go yet!" Catie squeaked.

"We all know you're going," Samantha said. "Quit fighting it."

"I'm going to have lunch with Jackie," Blake said. "I'll discuss it with her and let you know!"

With that, Blake stomped out of Marc's cabin. He was trying to be mad, so he slammed the door behind him. He went to the hub and grabbed one of the Foxes to fly down to Delphi City. *"What am I getting myself into,"* he thought.

"Daddy, are you serious, you're going to Artemis and leaving me here at the Academy?" Catie asked, reengaging in the conversation. She couldn't believe her father would go someplace without her.

"This is what all my work has been about, why shouldn't I go on the first colony mission?" Marc asked. "Sam and I can use a break."

"A break! How is leading the first mission to colonize another planet a break?!" Catie asked.

"Hey, we'll have about a year of focused work," Marc said. "It will be without all this extra drama that comes with politics here on Earth. Besides, unless I step away, Prime Minister Nazeri will not have a chance to step up and really run Delphi Nation."

"But you're still going to be in the middle of all the big stuff, aren't you?"

"Somewhat, but then I get to turn away from it and focus on the colony. And Sam gets to spend all her energy on the colony."

"Whatever," Catie said. "I have to go figure out what it means to go to the Academy. I sure hope Liz knows something." Catie left the cabin in what could graciously be called a huff.

"Is she going to be okay?" Samantha asked.

"I'm sure she will be, the question is, will the Academy be okay," Marc said.

Catie went down the hall to the cabin she shared with Liz. They shared a cabin on Delphi Station and a condo in Delphi City. *"At least we used to share them,"* Catie thought.

"Liz!" Catie hollered as she opened the door.

"Hey, what did your father want?" Liz asked.

"He's making me go to the Academy!"

"That's great!"

"What do you mean?! It's terrible!"

"Going to the Academy will be great for you."

"But what about our company, designing our new ship, flying?!"

"That stuff can wait. Do you know how long? Are you going in as a senior?"

"I don't know. I guess I should have asked more questions," Catie said.

"Cer Catie, the plan is to have you go in as a cadet second-class," ADI said.

"Second class! A sophomore, no way!"

"Catie, a cadet second class is a junior," Liz said. "They count back from your graduation year."

"Why can't I be a senior?"

"There are several reasons that the Captain and Cer Blake discussed. But it came down to having a believable backstory," ADI said. "As a cadet second class, it is possible to create an identity for you that will stand up to scrutiny. But as a senior, that is almost impossible, as they are only accepting seniors from the other military colleges."

"So I have to go for two years?"

"You will be going to complete your degrees. If you complete them within the year, then you might be able to graduate early. You'll have to discuss it with Cer Blake," ADI explained.

"Call Uncle Blake," Catie ordered her Comm.

"Hello, you've reached Blake. If you have this number, then you'll understand that I'm currently unavailable so that I can have some time alone or I'm with someone. Please call back or leave a message!"

"Grrr," Catie growled, "he must be with Jackie!"

"Hey, you can wait until tomorrow," Liz said. "Let me tell you about the Academy. It's going to be tough, but you'll learn a lot, and your time there will eventually be some of your fondest memories."

"But this is different than the Naval Academy," Catie complained.

"They're modeling our Academy on the U.S. Academies, so it'll be close."

"So, why is it going to be tough?"

"Their goal is to break you down so they can build you up. They want to break into that sense of individuality and get you to think as part of the team."

"I already think like that," Catie said.

"Well, you play well on a team, but that's different than thinking like a part of the team."

Catie pouted but quit arguing. "So, what's it like?"

"First, during Basic, or whatever they call the first few weeks, **do not stand out**," Liz said. "No matter how perfectly you do something, they're going to find fault. Don't react, just do your best to correct whatever they tell you to, even if it doesn't need it."

"That sounds like fun," Catie said, her voice dripping with sarcasm.

"It's horrible, but it's only a few weeks. And during Basic, time management is key. You'll never have time to do everything. You have to work with the other Plebes to share the load. When it was especially bad, one of us girls would volunteer to be the one late so she could finish up for everyone. It's things like that that will get you through it."

"Anything else?"

"Smiling will get you in more trouble than anything. The instructors are not amused when you're amused," Liz said. "Just keep your game face on the whole time."

◆ ◆ ◆

"Uncle Blake, tell me what's going to happen," Catie demanded over her Comm after she finally found him. He was down in Delphi City at a bar.

"You know what's going to happen. You're going to the Academy, I'm getting stuck playing host for a bunch of stuck-up people, and your father and Sam are running away."

"But why a junior?!"

"It's the best we can do. All the seniors are from other military schools. So whatever cover identity we come up with, they would know it was fake. But if things work out okay, we'll let you graduate with them."

"But what am I supposed to do? How are things going to be set up? And what is this Plebe training thing?"

"Okay, well, at least I can do this right," Blake said. "The first thing you need to understand is this is going to be the hardest thing you've ever done in your life. You have to report on Tuesday, and after that, you're beyond our help. If we have to intervene, it will spell the end of your time at the Academy."

"Oh great!"

"You'll do fine. But this summer is about forming bonds, learning to form bonds. That is what will make everything else in your career easier."

"So they're going to break me down to build me up like Liz said."

"Pretty much. Now some advice. **You do not want to stand out during Basic.** You want to blend in, stay in the middle, keep your head down. They will be looking for cadets who are trying to act like they're special, and the instructors and upper-class cadets are going to make it abundantly clear that they are not special," Blake said.

"That's what Liz said. But she didn't know how you guys have set things up."

"You'll have three weeks of Basic here in Delphi City. That will all be about getting you in shape, breaking you down into moldable clay, and building you back up. Then there are three weeks in Guatemala. That will be about teaching you how to push through the pain. How to survive anything. You'll be crawling around in the jungle. They'll take you right to the edge and keep pushing you, you'll have to push back or fall over."

"That definitely sounds like fun," Catie scoffed.

"But there is nothing like the feeling you'll get when you survive it. And you will survive, and that is an order!"

"Is everyone going to be going through the same thing?"

"No, the cadets from another military school will only have a week of general orientation here in Delphi City. Then they will become the leadership team that runs the program for the next two weeks. When you go to Guatemala, they'll still be the leaders, but they'll be having a completely new experience. Kal's team will run the program, and they'll make real Marines out of you."

# 2 Getting Ready

"Blake, please order the Victory to Earth orbit," Marc requested. They were in his office; Marc had flown down to Delphi City the day before so they could meet in person.

"You're going to use it as your colony ship?" Blake asked.

"We'll use the Sakira first. It and the Roebuck are the only ships that we know we can add jumpdrives to. But I'd like to start work on converting the Victory in parallel with converting the Sakira."

"One second, . . . Okay, it will be here in seven days," Blake said. "You should keep at least one flight bay active."

"I was *planning* to," Marc said.

"Good. Ajda has the plans that she and Catie made when they modified the Sakira for the asteroid mission. You can tell her to start making cabins."

"I should do that right away. I plan to convert one of the flight bays to passenger cabins, and use part of the second for cargo space."

"What about the Paraxeans? I assume you'll send them to the first planet."

"We will. By the way, does it have a name?"

"Catie and I assumed the Paraxeans would want to name it."

"I'll let the governor know. And yes, I'm planning to send them there. But I still haven't heard if we can move that asteroid in one piece."

"Hmm, with Catie at the Academy and our mysterious Dr. McDowell's communication issues, how are you going to find out?"

"I assume I'll send Catie to get a status update," Marc said.

"That's not going to be easy, she'll be pretty much locked down for the next three weeks. You'd better send her now."

"Call Catie . . ."

"Hi, Daddy," Catie said, not exactly her usual exuberant self.

"Hi, Sweetie. I wonder if you would be willing to go visit Dr. McDowell before you head to Delphi City."

"I don't know, I'm going to be pretty busy getting ready for the Academy."

"Don't be that way, it doesn't suit you."

"I know, but I should still be mad at you."

"It's your choice."

"Yeah, right. Anyway, I'll go see him this morning. For the Paraxeans."

"Thank you."

"Still mad?" Blake asked.

"She's trying to be."

"Well, that's an improvement over yesterday."

"I'll take what I can get. How big a force are you recommending I take with me?"

"Half a flight bay; so twelve Foxes and eight Lynxes; are you going to take an Oryx?"

"I wish we could, we'll have to wait for Catie's new ship to be built and make a run before we can get the Oryxes," Marc said.

◆ ◆ ◆

"Dr. McDowell, . . . Dr. McDowell!"

"Oh, . . . hello, Catie," Dr. McDowell muttered.

"How are you doing with the jump ship concept?"

"The power requirements are driving me crazy. And that engineer, Ajda, is not helping any. You know, she has a bad temper."

"What's the problem with the power requirements?"

"To make it work with four probes, you have to lock them together. That means you have to use their regular grav-drives," Dr. McDowell explained. "Their fusion reactors are then having to supply all that energy, and it takes forever to charge the capacitors up to jump potential. Before you get there, something changes, and you have to use the energy to adjust the grav drives. It's an endless cycle."

"Oh, you don't know about the antimatter reactors," Catie said as she realized that their compartmentalization of knowledge had bitten them, again.

"Antimatter reactors?"

"Yes, we have more powerful reactors we can use," Catie said. "With them, we can supply more energy. But it means we won't be able to use probes anymore. We'll have to build ships."

"Antimatter reactors," Dr. McDowell said again. "I guess that would provide more power. Whatever, get me four ships, and I can test this out. Until then, I'll work on my other projects."

Catie was surprised that Dr. McDowell didn't show any interest in the antimatter reactors, but he had always been a strange one.

"I'll go talk with Ajda about the ships," she said to Dr. McDowell's back. He was already back to working with his equations.

◆ ◆ ◆

"Ajda, do you have some time?"

"I do, especially if you can get that idiot, Dr. McDowell, to quit asking for impossible configurations for these probes," Ajda said.

"I just talked with him. He's going to wait for us to design a ship that he can use. He suspects his power requirements are impossible to meet, but he didn't know about the antimatter reactors."

"I can assure you that his requirements are impossible to meet!"

"So we have to design a small starship. I assume the antimatter reactors are too big for a probe."

"You assume correctly. And they're not going to be too easy to fit in anything smaller than the Roebuck unless you make them significantly smaller."

"Even if we only had it contain the drives? No flight bay, or cargo bay?"

"These drives he wants are huge. And those reactors aren't small either, especially with the power requirements he's asking for, plus all the extra capacitors," Ajda said.

"Okay, I'll see if we can get Dr. Tanaka to look at the reactors. They can probably be made smaller; the Paraxeans didn't spend too much time simplifying their designs once they came up with them. Then I'll have Dr. McDowell calculate the power requirements for the jumpdrives based on the new configuration."

"Thank you!"

"How are you doing with my new ship design?"

"Your cargo ship?"

"Yes."

"Well, it certainly is interesting. The team and I will finish up our review this week and send you the documents. We're finding several gaps you'll need to address."

"Can you make sure I get the files before Monday?" Catie asked. "I'm going to be out of contact for about a week, and I'd like to be able to work on them."

"Not a problem."

"Thanks, bye."

◆ ◆ ◆

"Daddy?"

"Yes, Sweetie?"

"Can we have Dr. Tanaka work on the antimatter reactor?"

"What's wrong with it?"

"The jumpdrives require too much power for a fusion reactor to supply. The antimatter reactors are kind of big and bulky. We really want to have the jump ships be as small as possible."

"I see," Marc said. "You know that Dr. Nakahara is working on the antimatter converter."

"Yes, but this is more about the overall reactor," Catie said. "Besides, isn't he working on the quantum relays?"

"Yes he is. I guess he might not be spending too much time on the antimatter converters right now."

"So, can I ask Dr. Tanaka to work on it?"

"Sure, go ahead and talk with him. He's up there, and he already knows about the antimatter reactors."

"Good. By the way, I mentioned them to Dr. McDowell."

"The antimatter reactors?"

"Yes."

"I don't see a problem. Anything else?"

"I'll let you know."

"Dr. Tanaka, do you have a moment?" Catie asked.

"Of course, Catie san. What can I do for you?"

"You know about our antimatter reactors."

"Yes, I've assisted Dr. Nakahara on the converter for them."

"Well, they are very big and bulky. The Paraxeans didn't spend a lot of time optimizing designs, so I wonder if we can modify the design so that they're more compact."

"I noticed that," Dr. Tanaka said. "I'm sure we can make them smaller. How much smaller are you hoping to make them?"

"We need one that can deliver about ten terajoules of power and is as small as you can make it."

"Ten terajoules, why not use three or four fusion reactors?"

"That would be almost as big as the antimatter reactor," Catie said.

"About half. So much smaller?"

"Yes."

"I'll look into it. I'm sure that we can reconfigure it to save space. Who should I work with for the engineering?"

"Ajda," Catie said. "She might assign someone else, but she'll be the primary contact."

"Not you?"

"I'm going to be out of touch for a while."

"Very well. I'll get on it right away."

"Thank you."

◆ ◆ ◆

"Daddy."

"Yes?"

"I've got everyone working on the jump ship, but I think it's going to take some time. It might even be a year."

"Okay," Marc mused. "I guess we can bring in one of the space carriers and let the Paraxeans use it for the second wave of colonists. Then they can get their colony started with the Sakira and the Roebuck while we wait for the jump ships. Do you think they'll work?"

"I'm pretty sure they will," Catie said. "Dr. McDowell was only worried about the power requirements."

"Okay. ADI?"

"Yes, Captain?"

"Are you confident that we have sufficient control over the Paraxean carriers to allow the Paraxeans to use one for their second colony mission?"

"I would recommend that we remove the DI from it and use the interface modules like we have on the Enterprise and Victory," ADI said.

"Okay, is there a reason to prefer one over the other?"

"Yes, the DI in one of them is on the verge of collapse. We need to remove it anyway," ADI said.

"On the verge of collapse!" Catie gasped. "What does that mean?!"

"Three in four DIs reach a point where their cognitive abilities collapse. If it is going to happen, it usually happens around two hundred years, when they start to become sentient," ADI explained.

"So they go crazy?" Catie asked.

"You might describe it as that. When it happens, the Paraxeans recycle the DI's systems and build a new one," ADI said.

"They kill it?!"

"In a manner of speaking, yes. If we remove this one, possibly Dr. Metra and I can study it and figure out why it happens," ADI said.

"The Paraxeans haven't done that already?"

"They have never put much effort into it," ADI said.

"ADI, go ahead and work with Dr. Metra on a plan," Marc said, taking control of the conversation again.

"Sorry, Daddy."

"It's alright. I'm as shocked as you were. ADI, tell Blake to have the carrier brought in so we can work on it while we work on the Victory."

"Daddy, you know you could speed things up if you brought the battleship in. You could cannibalize all of its cabins and the galleys. I think it has eight galleys."

"I'm not sure we should put that in orbit around Earth," Marc said.

"Then put it out by the asteroids. It would still be faster than building everything new. And you don't have the workforce available that we used when we built the space carriers."

"I'll think about it. Now I think you have some preparations to get back to."

"Thanks to *you!"*

Marc just shook his head. "Bye, Sweetie."

"Bye."

"Blake? . . ."

"ADI, where is Blake?" Marc asked after not getting a response from Blake.

"He is on the Mea Huli," ADI replied.

"Is there a reason he is not responding to my call?"

"I believe he has his Comm in isolation mode," ADI said.

"Why . . ."

"He has Cer Jackie with him," ADI said in explanation to the question Marc was forming.

"Call Captain Clements." Marc decided to work around Blake's absence and call the Captain of the Victory.

"Mr. President, how may I help you?" Captain Clements said when he came on the line.

"Captain, can you tell me the status of the Paraxean battleship?"

"Yes, sir. The battleship is in orbit around Jupiter at this time. It has a skeleton crew aboard to maintain the reactors and stasis pods."

"How many working reactors does it have?"

"Just the one, sir. We have not put any efforts into repairing the others."

"Can it be flown to Earth?"

"I'm not sure, but I would assume so. It was flown to Jupiter. I'm having my aide check for you right now."

"Thank you. I wonder if we should dismantle it at the Gemini Station, or fly it to Earth?"

"Gemini Station would cause less excitement."

"You're probably right. If you can, have it moved there."

Samantha walked into Marc's office and came around his desk. She hugged him from behind, "Having a rough day?"

"Just lots of little issues, but I mostly just assigned them to others to deal with, so not so bad. Why are you down here?"

"I thought I'd come down and spend time with you," Samantha said. "I think you might need a bit of emotional support with Catie starting the Academy tomorrow and not being able to have any contact with her."

"It is bothering me more than I thought it would."

"So, you're not such a tough guy after all."

"I guess not. We should go find a place to hide before Linda comes complaining about the same thing."

"I know just the place."

"You do?"

"It's docked right next to the city, and nobody is planning to use it for the rest of the week."

"I thought Blake had it."

"They just got back."

"Clever girl!"

"Lonely girl."

# 3 Academy – Day One

It was Tuesday, June 29$^{th}$, as Catie made her way to the Academy receiving area carrying her duffle bag. Around her other cadets were arriving with their families; of course, Catie couldn't have any family with her; she felt a bit odd being by herself.

"Hey, are you by yourself?" another young woman asked.

"Yes, it's just me," Catie replied.

"Same here. My folks couldn't make it; too many kids and job responsibilities. I'm Candice Williams," she said as she shifted her duffle bag and extended her hand.

"Alex MacGregor." Catie grabbed the offered hand and gave it a firm shake. "My parents couldn't make it either."

"Do you have any idea what we're in for?"

"I've been told that the next three weeks are going to rate somewhere between the sixth and seventh circles of hell," Catie replied.

"It can't be that bad. My uncle survived the U.S. Air Force Academy, and he said it was great."

"I think he lied to you," Catie said. "But I've been told it is much better looking back on it than it is living through it."

"I'm sure that's true."

Catie's Comm buzzed. "Candidate MacGregor, proceed to the green tent."

"I'm being called, green tent," Catie said.

"Blue tent," Candice said. "See you around."

"If we're lucky."

Catie made it to the green tent where an NCO grabbed her bag, slapped a label on it, and threw it in a pile. "Register your Comm now!" she ordered.

"Yes, Sergeant," Catie replied. "Comm, register with Academy green tent," Catie said, reading off the sign the NCO was pointing at.

"Comm registered."

The sign continued to explain that once registered, their Comm would be blocked from connecting to anything except the Academy Library and the Comms of Academy personnel — no phone calls, no texts, no social media, no email, no contact with anyone outside the Academy.

*"Oh great,"* Catie thought.

*"I can still talk to you, Cer Catie,"* ADI said as if she had read Catie's mind.

*"Isn't that against the rules?"* Catie texted back.

*"Only a little,"* ADI said. *"You are after all a Lieutenant in the Delphi Defense Force."*

*"Nice to know that's still worth something."*

"Candidate, move to the bus!" the NCO ordered.

"Yes, Sergeant!" Catie snapped back as she turned and headed to the bus.

She saw the other candidates waving at their families before they boarded the bus. Once they were on the bus, they belonged to the Academy. Their families wouldn't see them until they completed the first three weeks, or they dropped out.

The bus drove them onto the Academy campus and parked in front of one of the dorms. "Your Comms will have your room numbers on them. Proceed to your room, change into the shipsuit that will be on your bed with your name on it, and be back here in five minutes." The NCO at the front of the bus yelled. "Move!"

Catie hurried off the bus and walked quickly toward the dorm.

"Walk, do not run!" another NCO shouted.

Catie made it to her room, stripped and put on a shipsuit, and was pulling on her boots when her roommate arrived. All the candidates had been required to arrive the day before and report for a physical. Catie assumed that was where they got all their sizes from.

"Hey," her roommate said as she started stripping.

"Hey, I'm Alex MacGregor."

"Joanie McCoy."

"I'll see you down there," Catie said as she ran out the door and hurried back down to the quad.

"Find a set of blue footprints to stand on," another NCO yelled. "Move!"

Catie planted herself on a set of footprints and assumed an at-ease position and waited. More and more candidates streamed out of the dorm, to fill in the square with the footprints.

A few stragglers came in after the five minutes were up. Nothing was said as they found the last few footprints to stand on.

A tall Marine officer stepped away from a group and took up position in front of the square.

"I am Major Beckman," he said.

*"He sounds like a Marine; loud and authoritative,"* Catie thought.

"I will now give you the oath. Place your hand over your heart and repeat after me . . ." The oath of office streamed across each candidate's HUD.

"I [state your full name], having been appointed a cadet in the Delphi Defense Force, do solemnly affirm that I will support and defend the Constitution of Delphi Nation against all enemies, foreign and domestic; that I will bear true faith and allegiance to the same; that I take this obligation freely, without any mental reservation or purpose of evasion; and that I will well and faithfully discharge the duties of the office upon which I am about to enter."

"You are now Plebes. You will not earn the right to be called a cadet until you finish the first phase of your training, affectionately called the Beast," Major Beckman said. "We are here to start a proud tradition, a tradition that follows on the sacrifice made in the Paraxean war. One that will live up to the standard of our fellow Delphineans who sacrificed their lives so that Earth would remain free. Do not let them or me down."

The major turned to the big NCO standing behind him. "They're all yours, Sergeant Major."

"Let's start with a few basic rules!" the sergeant major yelled as the major headed out like there was a fire somewhere.

"There are only seven responses when you are addressed by an instructor. They are, yes, sir; no, sir; no excuse, sir; sir, may I make a statement; sir, may I ask a question; sir, I do not understand; and sir, I do not know! Is that clear?!"

"Yes, sir!"

"Do not call me sir. If you are addressed by an NCO, you will respond with their rank! Is that clear?!"

"Yes, Sergeant Major!"

"Better! Now, Plebes, stand at attention!"

Catie snapped to attention, eyes straight ahead, shoulders back, head tilted just so. She could hear instructors making their way down the line, correcting the stance of other Plebes.

"Do you call that standing at attention?" an instructor was yelling in Catie's face. "Shoulders back! I said, shoulders back!"

Catie struggled to move her shoulders further back without falling over.

"Head up, chin down. Make a forty-five with those feet!"

Catie made minor adjustments, wondering how the instructor was finding fault with her stance.

*"Remember, you'll make mistakes, and if you don't, they'll call a few out anyway,"* she remembered her Uncle Blake telling her.

Finally, the instructor moved on. It took five minutes before they had dressed everyone in the square to their satisfaction.

"At-ease! Now, those of you who were late getting down here, give me twenty push-ups!" the sergeant major ordered.

About half the group dropped to the ground and started to do push-ups.

"Start over, count them off!"

"One . . . two . . ."

"The rest of you, eyes forward unless you want to join them!"

"Plebe Jones, get down and join them. And since Jones wants to join in, we need to start over. Jones, count them off!"

"One . . . two . . ."

Catie suppressed the urge to smile. *"Smiling will get you in more trouble than anything. The instructors are not amused when you're amused,"* Liz had warned her.

"nineteen . . . twenty."

"Alright, now that some of us are warmed up, let's warm the rest of us up. One lap around the grounds." The Academy dorms occupied a quad, so that meant 1600 meters.

Catie set off, adjusting her pace, so she was just behind the lead pack of Plebes. A few of the Plebes had torn off at a fast pace, far outpacing the main group. During the run, various NCOs yelled at the Plebes about their running style, mainly demanding that they keep their eyes forward as they ran.

As Catie rounded the last corner, she could see and hear the sergeant major yelling at the group that had led the way. "Is that what you think of your fellow Plebes! Just leave them behind? Well, I think you need to go and make sure they all make it. Move it!" He sent them on another lap. Catie was hoping he didn't think her group had been too fast.

*"No such luck,"* Catie thought as the sergeant major yelled out. "While we're waiting on the rest of your platoon to finish, we have time for some calisthenics!"

"Let's see some push-ups! Give me twenty."

"One," an enterprising Plebe started the count. "Two . . . three . . ."

Another group of runners arrived to hear, "You are just in time to join us! Everyone, give me twenty crunches!"

"One . . . two . . ."

"Fifteen minutes, that is shameful!" the sergeant major yelled. "You have to be able to make that run in twelve minutes, ten minutes for the men. Fifteen minutes is pathetic. I do not allow pathetic Plebes to graduate. Do you hear me!"

"Yes, Sergeant Major," rang out with a few 'Yes, sirs' mixed in.

"Do not call me sir. Do I look like an officer to you? It is, 'Yes, Sergeant Major!'"

"Yes, Sergeant Major!"

"Now, you have ten minutes to get to your room, shower, and change into your day uniform, and make it to the mess hall! Move!"

Joanie arrived at their room just after Catie.

"Joanie, lay out your uniform while I shower." Catie put her shipsuit into the laundry hamper.

"You'd better not take too long!" Joanie whined.

"Two minutes, max!" Catie slammed the door to their bathroom.

Two and a half minutes later, Catie emerged wearing a robe. "Your turn. Don't waste time."

"I won't. I do not want to be late."

Catie put on her uniform. It was a simple two-piece suit. Slacks, a white blouse, and a blue jacket to match the slacks. A belt with a brass buckle, no insignia, just a name badge. She was putting on her shoes when Joanie came out.

"Did you wash your hair?" Joanie asked.

"Yes."

"How did you get it dry?"

"I used the hairdryer."

"Where is it?"

Catie showed Joanie the hairdryer.

"I've never seen one like that; how does it work?"

"You pull it from the wall, put it over your head, make sure all your hair is inside, and these earmuff things are on your ears. Then you turn it on; your hair's dry in thirty seconds."

"How can it work that fast, will it ruin my hair?" Joanie asked as she switched it on.

"No," Catie mouthed as Joanie waited the thirty seconds.

"That is amazing," Joanie said as she pulled the bag off of her head. "How does it work?"

"It takes the air pressure down to a few ounces. Air comes in here in the front and is pulled out in the back. With the low pressure, the water just evaporates off your hair."

"Thanks, should I put my hair up like yours?"

"Definitely. Just put it in a ponytail then wrap it up like this," Catie explained as she mimicked the moves. "It's supposed to be above your collar and tight to your head so that you could slip a helmet over your head."

"How do you know about that and about the hairdryer?"

"I lived on Delphi Station for a few months. Someone up there showed me," Catie lied. It was a white lie, she did live on Delphi station, and someone, ADI, had told her how to use the hairdryer.

Catie helped Joanie get into her uniform, and then they left their room, walking quickly toward the exit.

"Hair, up," Catie suggested to one of the women they passed.

"How?"

Catie made motions over her head, showing how to tie the bun as she hurried on.

"Gawd, I thought I was going to die," a pair in front of Catie and Joanie said.

"I know. I don't know how I'm going to run that thing in twelve minutes," the other girl said.

The Plebes bunched up at the entrance to the mess hall as they narrowed down to file in.

"No talking," Catie suggested quietly.

The suggestion trickled back, and the talking quieted down. It also trickled forward, but not fast enough.

"What do we have here? A bunch of Chatty Cathies!" the sergeant major yelled. "Move to the side!" he segmented off the line at where he felt the chatter had been going on. Those Plebes moved to the side and stood watching the others file in.

"Your seat will be displayed on your HUD! Find it!"

Catie gave Joanie a nod as they each moved to the table and seat they had been assigned. Catie took up position behind her chair and assumed an at-ease pose. The Plebes who had been sitting down at the table quickly stood up and followed her example. The other tables also followed the example and stood behind their assigned seats.

"Those of you who were not paying attention and took your seats when I distinctly told you to *find your seats,* will owe me an extra ten push-ups tomorrow morning! Now Corporal Hendricks will demonstrate how you are to seat yourself! Everyone, turn around, and watch!"

Corporal Hendricks demonstrated how to be seated, how to stand. Then she demonstrated how to eat, setting the fork and knife down while you chewed each bite.

*"How are we supposed to actually get any food into ourselves,"* Catie moaned to herself.

The answer was you didn't; nobody ate very much food, and the Chatty Cathies didn't eat anything. After lunch, the Plebes were escorted into a large auditorium classroom. They were each handed a notebook and pen and told to find a seat.

Catie found a seat toward the back. She flipped the notebook open, but she didn't plan to take notes. With her eidetic memory, it wasn't necessary. The auditorium quickly filled up.

"I am Commander Marshall, and I will be giving you the basics on the spaceplanes and starships in the Delphi Space Navy," he said. "You will be expected to memorize the details of each vessel and spaceplane. You will have those details ready to recite at any time."

Catie darkened her specs and brought up the design of her new cargo carrier. She and Liz had decided to call them StarMerchants. Using the sensors that Dr. Metra had placed at the nerve endings in her tailbone, she was able to draw and type without any apparent motion. She had her specs set to notify her if her name was called or someone came close to her.

She flipped through the design, reading the notes that Ajda, the aerospace engineer in charge of designing and building the ship, had left her. She answered the various questions, adjusted the specs to get around restrictions that Ajda had pointed out, and added in things that she'd forgotten to specify.

"Sir, Plebe MacGregor wants to answer a question!"

Catie looked up to see one of the NCOs two aisles down from her, giving her a stare.

"Plebe MacGregor, what it the wingspan of a Fox?" Commander Marshall asked.

"Sir, a Fox has a wingspan of fifteen meters!" Catie responded.

"Correct, now what is the max capacity of the Enterprise flight Bay?"

"Sir, the Enterprise has four flight bays. The first three can carry one hundred twenty-eight Foxes; the fourth one can carry fifty-nine Foxes."

*"Did he talk about operational mode?"* Catie texted ADI.

*"No, Cer Catie,"* ADI replied.

"Very good, Plebe MacGregor," the commander said.

"Do not darken your specs," the NCO, who had caught her, ordered.

*"ADI, can I adjust my specs so I can work and not have them appear darker to these instructors?"* Catie messaged ADI.

*"I will adjust them for you,"* ADI said. *"I will also adjust your alert to pick up someone approaching you from farther away. It will also alert you if someone gives an instruction."*

*"Thanks."*

"You now have one hour to get your rooms ready for inspection. You will unpack all your gear, stow it, make your beds with the linens provided, and clean the head! Move it!"

The Plebes filed out of the auditorium and hurried as quickly as they could without running.

Catie was stowing the gear from her duffle bag when Joanie showed up. There were several uniforms and shipsuits laid out on their beds that they also needed to stow. There were also several pairs of shoes, tennis shoes, shipboots, and dress shoes. They both had one pair of dress shoes with low heels that had been issued for the women and a pair of regular shoes. Catie put her civilian clothes in the closet, then her military issue. She wasn't expecting to wear her civvies anytime soon.

"Why did they give us skirts and high heels?" Catie asked.

"I don't know, but they gave us both types of uniforms, unisex and female," Joanie said. "I guess they figured some women would want to wear skirts."

"Seems stupid to me."

"Whatever. Hey, how did you know about the fourth flight bay?" Joanie asked. "He hadn't covered that yet."

"I studied up on the ships before I came," Catie explained. The fact that she had actually done the baseline design for all the spaceplanes and starships for Delphi's Space Navy hadn't hurt, but she couldn't mention that.

"We are going to starve if we have to eat like that every meal," Joanie said as she started to stow her gear.

"I'm sure they have a way to get the calories into us," Catie said. "I'll clean the head if you'll dust the shelves and clean the floor."

"Deal!"

# 4 The Paraxeans Move Forward

"Governor, President McCormack is here to see you," the Paraxean aide to the governor announced Marc as soon as he presented himself at the office. They had assigned the governor a full floor of offices in the building next to MacKenzie Discoveries' office.

"President McCormack, please come in," Governor Paratar said after the aide opened the office door. "Would you like some refreshments?"

"I'm fine," Marc said.

"Do you have news for us?"

"I do." Marc and the governor seated themselves in the chairs by the window. The governor's office was impressive. He'd decorated it with fine wooden furniture. It was reminiscent of what one would have expected to find in Napoleon's office when he was emperor of France. Marc had been made aware of the governor's lavish spending but had decided to ignore it. The man had a vast array of problems to deal with; what did it matter that he liked to surround himself with fancy furniture and antiques?

"May I inquire what it is?"

Marc smiled. *"The governor isn't a very patient man, no, Paraxean,"* he thought. "Yes you may."

". . . And, what might it be?"

"We have officially assigned the first planet to you and your colonists," Marc said. He realized he was being a bit petty, making the governor beg for the information. *"Grow up!"* he thought.

"That is very good news."

"Unfortunately, we are not yet able to move your asteroid with our jumpdrive," Marc continued. "I'm having one of the Paraxean carriers brought to Earth so you can use it as a colony ship. I assume we'll both use the Sakira to start our colony, but the carrier will allow you to make a second mission with substantially more colonists while we figure out how to move the asteroid; We will provide the command staff and the pilots necessary for protection. I'll send you the design we're doing for the Sakira. For the carrier, you will be able to use three of the flight bays and the cargo bay to transport what you need to the planet."

"I'm not sure I understand," the governor said.

"If you convert a flight bay to passenger cabins, you'll be able to accommodate quite a few colonists," Marc said. "We're planning to convert one flight bay so the carrier can carry forty thousand colonists. You could double that number if you put four per cabin. The two other flight bays can be made available for cargo."

"So, you plan to ferry all of our colonists?"

"Hopefully, not. We thought you would like to start preparing the planet while we complete the changes to the jumpdrive so that it can transport your asteroid. We suggest you send a small group out in the Sakira, possibly four or five thousand. Then that could be followed up by a larger group in the carrier."

"Ah, I see. So, we could accomplish our first year's goals while you finish your drive. Then we would be ready to start moving larger numbers down from the asteroid."

"Correct," Marc said.

"When could we start?"

"The Sakira can be ready in two months," Marc said. "The carrier a few months after that. We'll also be using the Sakira to start our colony on Artemis, and we've started to convert one of our own space carriers to deliver colonists."

"What about cargo?" the governor asked.

"As I said, you can put cargo in one of the flight bays or two, depending on how many colonists you want to take. And the carrier has a cargo hold. On the Sakira, you would only be able to use the cargo hold. But we're working on a new class of ship, a cargo ship. We hope to have it ready in six months."

"A new cargo ship?"

"Yes, it would be able to carry significantly more cargo than the Sakira or the space carriers. And as you know, the round trip is only a few weeks."

"Thank you; this gives me enough information to lay out a plan. How many colonists may I bring here to Delphi Station to help me?" the governor asked.

"We've finished the build-out of the first set of rings," Marc said. "We can accommodate another two thousand Paraxeans."

"That should be more than enough. I cannot begin to express our thanks to you and your people."

"Then I'll leave you to your planning." Marc excused himself from the governor's office.

"Liz, . . ." Marc messaged her once he got back to his office.

"Hello, Marc, what can I do for you?" Liz replied.

"The Paraxeans are going to bring a few more colonists out of stasis. I'd like you to lead the mission. Specifically, I'd like you to go with them when they land on the asteroid."

"I can do that; how many colonists?"

"Two thousand," Marc said.

"Oh, that's a lot. I assume I'll be using the Sakira."

"Yes, it should be able to ferry that many with the mods Catie made to ferry everyone out to the asteroid belt."

"I'll check and make sure. But as I recall, she put in two thousand cabins, plus all that rec space. When am I supposed to leave?"

"I would expect the governor to have his list ready within the week."

"Okay, then I'll clear my schedule," Liz said. "Is there anything else?"

"Not that I know of," Marc said.

"You must want me to observe or learn something about the Paraxeans."

"Not specifically. I do want to know their process for bringing their people out of stasis, and I'm curious to know more about the layout of the asteroid."

"Didn't we already send a team to it?"

"Yes, but they were a bit overwhelmed. You're more comfortable with all the new technology, so you'll be able to learn more."

"I'll see what I can do," Liz said. "Do you mind my asking about Catie?"

"No, go ahead."

"Have you heard how she's doing?"

"ADI reports that she's doing fine. That's all I'm getting right now. The new cadets are on communication lockdown for the first three weeks."

"Is it okay if ADI lets me know if there are any problems?" Liz asked.

"Cer Liz, you are my third contact after Marc and Linda," ADI interjected.

"Thank you; how did I beat Blake out?"

"I think Catie flipped a coin," Marc said. "Don't tell Blake."

"Don't worry, I won't."

◆ ◆ ◆

"I relieve you," Liz informed Lieutenant Payne, the current acting captain of the Sakira.

"I stand relieved," Lieutenant Payne said. He was now back to his old job as First Officer of the Sakira, or First Mate since this was a civilian operation.

The Paraxean Governor had requested that Liz pick up his team and head to the asteroid the next day. He would communicate the list of colonists he wanted to have brought back once they got there. *"He is obviously in a hurry,"* Liz thought.

"Very good, please plot a course for the Paraxean asteroid," Liz ordered.

"Yes, Captain," the navigator replied.

"Time to destination?"

"Ten days, if we take eight hours off from heavy acceleration per day for rest."

"Make it so."

"Aye-aye, Captain."

Liz was not looking forward to ten days where you needed to sit or lie down most of the time to deal with the increased g-forces. Liz decided she would try to sleep four hours during high acceleration and four hours under normal acceleration so she would at least have some time to move about the ship or work out.

In the meantime, she brought up the plans for the new cargo ship Catie was designing. She wanted to make sure that Catie and Ajda didn't miss anything, and she wanted to be intimately familiar with the ship as she hoped to be flying it before the end of the year.

# 5 Academy Week One

At 0430 on Wednesday, the speakers blared out the song *Wake Me Up* while the instructors pounded on their doors, yelling, "You have five minutes to get dressed and into formation!"

"They have to be kidding," Joanie moaned.

"I don't think so," Catie said. She hopped off of her bed, already dressed and ready for the day.

"What did you do, sleep in your shipsuit?" Joanie asked.

"No, I got up at 0330," Catie said. "I'm usually good with four or five hours of sleep. Now, hurry up. You've only got four more minutes."

Catie laid out Joanie's uniform while Joanie made a quick trip to the bathroom.

"What's that for?" Joanie asked as she pulled on her shipsuit.

"For after PT," Catie said.

"Good thinking." Joanie put on her ballcap, and they both checked to make sure each other's hair was in a proper bun. The two girls made it out into the hallway and into formation with one minute to spare.

"Get into step, Plebe Heartfelt! One . . . two . . . three . . . four!"

"Keep pace! Quit bunching up, one meter between you and the Plebe in front of you!"

"Quit hugging your neighbor!"

On and on, they marched, they ran, and they stood in formation. They had to do push-ups in total sync. Jumping jacks, one . . . two . . . one . . . two.

"Ten minutes to shower and be back in formation in your uniform!"

"Move it! Move it! What are you waiting for?!"

They were marched to the cafeteria to have breakfast. At least they were allowed to actually eat the food this time. Then thirty minutes later, they were back in formation practicing rifle drills.

"Don't hold it like a stick; it's a weapon. Treat it with respect!"

"**Do not drop your rifle!** Give me twenty push-ups! **Don't lay your rifle on the ground**! Hand it to your squadmate! Make that thirty push-ups!"

"Form up!" the instructor yelled. "Now, let's see if you can march to class!"

They marched them to the big auditorium for yet another lecture on the history of Delphi Nation.

*"They're just doing this to keep us busy. They can't march us eighteen hours a day, so they make us go to these classes,"* Catie thought. She adjusted her specs and went back to working on the design for the StarMerchant.

"I cannot believe it," Joanie said. "I'll never get this all down. We have to learn all these facts, and we have to make every move precisely. I can't even turn around correctly."

"Sure you can," Catie said.

"No I can't, look." Joanie stood at attention then made an about-face. "See, I know it's wrong, but I can't figure it out."

"Try doing it slowly."

"Why, they'll just yell at me about that."

"Just do it slowly until you get the coordination down. Once you build up some muscle memory, you'll be able to speed it up and have all the timing down. We use that technique in martial arts all the time."

"Oh, don't tell me you have a black belt!"

"I don't have any color belts, but I've been training for three years."

"Doesn't that mean you're not very good?"

"No, it means my instructors don't care about belts. Now try it slowly."

Joanie did the about-face slowly but still messed it up. Catie messaged ADI, *"Is there a video we can use?"*

*"Yes, Cer Catie, there is,"* ADI replied.

*"Can you adjust it so it maps itself to her body, and she sees where she messes up?"*

*"Yes, Cer Catie. The video is ready,"* ADI said.

*"Download it to my Comm."*

*"It's under drills,"* ADI said. *"I've added one for each of the moves you have to learn."*

*"Thanks,"* Catie messaged.

"Joanie, link Comms with me," Catie said. "Now watch the video. I'll have it play at half speed."

"Cool, it looks like I'm in it," Joanie said.

"Good, now match your moves to the video."

"That was better," Joanie said. "I can see what I'm doing wrong."

"Good, now keep practicing it. I'll move it to your Comm along with one for coming to attention from the at-ease position as well as going to at-ease from attention. You can practice them for a while. You've got some time before lights out."

"Thanks, Alex," Joanie said.

"I only got yelled at half as much today as yesterday," Joanie said as she and Catie entered their room for the night.

"Good."

"Do you have a video for the rifle drills? I can't even come close to doing those right."

"Sure, but what will we use as a rifle?"

"I can use the broom," Joanie said.

"Sure, that's an age-old tradition," Catie said.

"I shared your video with some of the other girls," Joanie said. "I hope that's alright."

"No problem. We want our squadron to do well, so we have to help everyone."

"Even the guys?"

"Why not?"

"Some of them are kind of jerks!"

"I'm sure we're all kind of jerks sometimes. We're all under a lot of stress."

"Okay, then I'll definitely share them with Joey. He's a real klutz."

"Alright, this is your fitness test. It is an individual event, so do your best. First test is the run. Segment yourselves by your expected time. Those of you who think you'll finish the five-K in less than twenty minutes come to the front! Men, you have twenty-eight minutes to finish, women, you have thirty."

Catie made her way to the front. Only two other women came forward with her, along with ten guys. Their squadron was sixty Plebes, and half were women. Catie couldn't believe that only three other women were expecting to finish under twenty minutes, it was only a five-K after all.

"Go!"

Catie settled herself into a pace that would have her finishing in just under twenty minutes. It wasn't long before there were only two men ahead of her and one woman keeping pace beside her. Behind, she could hear the next group setting off. But this was her race, and she ignored everything and everyone as she focused on her breathing. The course went out along the airport, crossed the old runway, then headed back to the Academy grounds. As Catie rounded the final turn, she thought about doing a kick to the finish but decided against it. Under twenty minutes was one hundred percent on the men's test, women who finish in twenty-five minutes were given a hundred percent. Catie had set a goal to get a perfect score on the fitness test, the men's test.

"Thanks," her running mate said as they crossed the finish line together. "I knew you would set the perfect pace."

"You're welcome," Catie replied. She ran over to the instructor. "Plebe MacGregor requests permission to offer encouragement to her squadmates!"

"Permission granted."

With that, Catie ran back up the course to help encourage those who were struggling. "Breathe, you can't run on those little pants!" she yelled at two as she fell in beside them. "Kick your feet out, come on, you can do it!"

She fell back to the next group struggling to finish. "Come on, dig deep! Breathe, breathe. Don't let the squadron down. Dig, dig. That's better!" She paced them for a minute before falling back to the last group that was struggling to even run.

"Run, don't walk. You'll never make it like that. Come on, pick it up!" She set an easy pace for them and got them to at least attempt to run. But it was hopeless; they had already lost too much time.

They crossed the finish line in shame. The next squadron was getting ready to start out and was there to witness their shame.

"Those of you who did not make time, form up over here!" yelled the instructor.

Five men and six women, still gasping for breath, walked over and formed up as ordered.

"You are a disgrace! A child can run five-K faster than that! You have two weeks to improve your time, or you'll be sent home. Do I make myself clear!"

"Yes, sir!"

"Now the rest of you, look at them. They are your mates. If they fail, you fail. You've been here a week. You've done PT every morning. Couldn't you tell that they needed help? What are you? Selfish?"

"No, Sergeant Major!"

"Form up and march to the gym for the rest of your test!"

"Alright. Line up here and grab a partner. Your partner will count your reps. They will only count reps that are correctly done. Do not give grace, or you will be asked to go home. The next test is push-ups. You have two minutes; you can rest if you have to. Men will do forty push-ups for a minimum score. Women will do thirty. Max score for men is seventy, for women sixty. Begin!"

Catie and Joanie had partnered up. Catie went first. "One, two, three, four, . . . and sixty! you're done." Catie kept going, counting the last ten herself while Joanie looked on dumbfounded.

"Why did you do seventy?!"

"I'm going for a perfect score," Catie said.

"But sixty was perfect."

"A perfect score for cadets, not women," Catie said.

"Whatever, count for me."

Joanie barely managed to get to thirty, resting twice while Catie counted down the time.

"Good job!"

"That almost killed me, and you did seventy."

"I've been doing them almost every day for three years," Catie said.

"You're a masochist."

"Next we have crunches! Your partner will hold your feet down and count for you. You have two minutes!"

Again, Catie went first; it didn't take her long to knock off one hundred crunches, twenty over the max for women. Joanie did better this time, managing fifty crunches, ten more than the minimum.

"Now pullups. Two minutes, you can rest between them if you need to. Men you have to do ten minimum, women five. Max score is twenty, women, yours is fifteen. Partner, make sure their chin clears the bar!"

Catie completed twenty in less than a minute, on the last one she built up some momentum and brought herself up until her waist was even with the bar. She paused and looked around. One of the other women in her squadron had completed her pullups and had done the same thing. She smiled at Catie as she swung back down. It was the same woman who had paced beside Catie during the run.

Joanie only managed to do four pullups. She strained for thirty seconds to try to get the last one in, but could not get her chin over the bar.

"Sorry, Joanie."

"I'm sorry, I'm the one who failed."

"Hey, you've got two weeks to get in shape and pass. I'll help you."

# 6 Board Meeting – July 5th

Marc entered the boardroom once everyone else had arrived. It was easy for him to do since his office was across the hall.

"I call this meeting to order. You'll note that Catie is not here. She's going to miss this meeting and the next one due to prior commitments. She'll review the notes and send in her reports," Marc said.

"Is she alright?" Fred asked.

"She's fine, just overcommitted," Marc said. "Now, I understand you have some good news for us about Delphi Station."

"Yes, while everyone has been distracted with all the excitement over the last few months, we have completed the second and third ring for section two. They were attached over the last two weeks," Fred said.

"Amazing, how come I didn't hear about it?" Samantha asked. "They would have had to stop the station's rotation, wouldn't they?"

"Only section two's rotation. The hubs are connected by magnetic bearings, so they rotate independently. Nobody is living in ring one, so other than a few lab people, no one was affected."

"Thanks, that explains it. What are we going to do with all that space?" Samantha asked.

"It will take months to build it out," Fred said. "So, although it's a big milestone, nothing will change for a while."

"We should call them rings four through six, that way we won't get them confused," Samantha suggested.

"Good, idea. I'll have them change the signs," Fred said.

"Fred, thanks for the station update, that's great news. We've been ignoring Delphi Station too much. Now, how is manufacturing going?" Marc asked.

"Things are running smoothly. Since we now have a steady supply of the platinum group metals, we've kicked a few things into a higher gear. Herr Pfeifer can give you the breakdown as far as increased sales and profits go."

"And speaking of sales," Marc said. "I need to announce a change. Marcie Sloan has been our chief sales and marketing person for the last few years. She's decided to make a change."

"We're losing her?" Blake asked.

"She's going to be joining Catie's new company as the C.O.O.," Marc said.

"Which company?" Herr Pfeifer asked.

"The consumer electronics one," Marc said. "I'm not sure if they've picked a name yet."

"How are we going to replace her?" Blake asked.

Marc looked at Samantha.

"I've been searching for a candidate for the last two weeks. I suggest we hire a marketing director and let them figure the rest out," Samantha said.

"I like that," Jonas said. "More well-defined jobs will work better."

Marc smiled at the implication since he, Catie, and Samantha had been sharing the role of marketing director since the beginning.

"Speaking of more well-defined roles, I think we should appoint a permanent commander for Delphi Station," Marc said. He looked at Blake and raised his eyebrows.

"I think Captain Clark might be interested," Blake said. "I'll talk to him tomorrow."

"Thank you. I'll talk with the prime minister and let her know our plans," Marc said. "It came up at my last meeting with her, but I don't want to surprise her since Delphi Station is one of her provinces."

"Should we look into having a civilian mayor?" Samantha asked.

"It seems a bit of overkill," Marc said. "She's appointed one for Delphi City, so I'll wait to see when she thinks it's necessary for Delphi Station."

"Don't wait too long. We don't want the residents up there to think we're ignoring them."

"Since Delphi Station only has one thousand permanent residents, I think we have time. Now, Dr. Metra has asked for time to present a proposal. Dr. Metra." Marc nodded to her, indicating she had the floor.

"Thank you," Dr. Metra said. "As you know, we've opened several clinics around Earth as we slowly introduce our medical advances. Although we are focusing on several childhood diseases, we also handle special treatments for people who have life-threatening illnesses that cannot be treated by Earth's established medicine. But the most numerous requests we receive are for organ transplants. We are not set up to perform those at the clinics, and in many cases, we don't have any better technology as regards doing a transplant. What we do have the unique ability to do, however, is make organs."

"Oh, I never thought of that," Samantha said.

"It's obvious but not obvious," Dr. Metra said. "We can grow organs for the transplant patient using their own DNA. Because the organ is based on their DNA, the patient avoids all the complications of rejection. It's actually an ideal solution, and they don't have to wait months or years for a donor to come available."

"What about the problem that caused the organ to fail in the first place?" Samantha asked.

"Usually, the organ problem is environmental; however, if it is genetic, we can modify the gene to resolve the issue before we grow the new organ."

"So, you'd like to offer this service?" Marc asked.

"Yes. We would have to grow them here in Delphi City since we start the process using the printers, but we can deliver organs within two to three weeks of a request."

"What would we charge for this service?" Herr Pfeifer asked, earning him a withering stare from Dr. Metra.

"I think we can afford to provide this at no cost," Marc said. "If the cost becomes onerous, we can recover our expenses."

"That would get you by laws that outlaw the sale of organs," Blake said. "I assume this will lead to some changes in those laws."

"What about emergency transplants?" Samantha asked.

"We cannot make the organs faster, but we can build up a supply of organs that meet the various blood types and size requirements for transplant. They can be used in emergency situations. Typically, you're talking about a heart, liver, or kidney. Then the patient and their doctor can assess whether they want to do a second transplant based on the patient's own DNA."

"I don't see any reason you shouldn't move ahead. I recommend you work with the existing groups that handle matching donors with recipients," Marc said. "Let me know what else you need, and we'll make it available."

"Thank you," Dr. Metra said.

"This should do a lot to help Delphi's image," Samantha said. "We will need to manage the publicity."

"I agree, do you have someone in mind to do that?" Marc asked.

"I think we should ask Linda and Dr. Sharmila if they have contacts that they would recommend."

"Okay, work with Dr. Metra on that," Marc said. "Now let's move on. Herr Pfeifer, what do you have for us?"

"Fred and I have formatted a status report that shows orders, capacity, backlog, and cost," Jonas said. "We believe that it will allow us to report the status of things quickly and efficiently. That means we can skip all the mundane stuff at this meeting and focus on where we are having problems."

Liz pinged a high five to Blake over their Comms at that announcement. Blake just shook his head. *"If Catie were with her, they'd be dancing,"* he thought.

"As you can see, everything is going well. We have completed the spinoff of Vancouver Integrated Technologies. That pleased Herr Hausmann immensely. After that, you can see that we have more than enough cash on hand to start the production of the new jetliner this fall," Jonas said. He was beaming as everyone leaned forward to study the report.

"I believe you should move ahead with the recruitment of your pilots and crew. You'll want to have them trained and available before you launch. I'll be happy to discuss it with your new marketing director when we hire 'em, but I think you should launch several new routes at the same time as you announce your new airline. Create a large media splash."

"Should we alert the existing airlines?" Samantha asked. "This is really going to hit their bottom lines."

"They should be tracking the certification progress," Jonas said. "I'm sure they know it's coming."

"Speaking of that, Fred, I neglected to ask about the progress of the certification," Marc said.

"We're tracking for an October certification," Fred said. "But, there are some machinations to push that out beyond Christmas."

"I could live with that," Marc said. "I'm not sure we want to start up an airline in the middle of the holiday travel season."

"You are too nice a man," Jonas said.

"Cautious," Marc corrected. "Anything else?"

"I will let the report speak for itself," Jonas said.

"While we're on the subject of planes, Catie informs me that her new cargo ship should be ready by October, barring a major setback."

"That will free up pilots as well as Oryxes for other uses," Blake said.

"On that subject. I've formally communicated to the Paraxeans that we've dedicated the first planet to them. I've also just heard that they've decided to name it Mangkatar, which means something like 'new home' in Paraxean."

"So, what's their timeline?" Admiral Michaels asked.

"Liz is on her way to their asteroid in the Sakira to bring some colonists back. That should allow them to complete their planning and stage their colonization. Both they and we will need to make the first mission using the Sakira. Hopefully, after that, we'll be able to follow up with one of our space carriers. We're planning to convert the Victory, and they're planning to convert the Galileo to accommodate twenty- to thirty-thousand colonists. Catie is designing the jump ships, and once we've established a base settlement on each planet, the ships should be ready and able to take care of sending the space carriers to it.

Catie is asking for a few more months before we try to move something as big as the asteroid."

"I would think so," Admiral Michaels said.

"I believe our new Academy and our new University are slated to begin holding regular classes starting in late August," Marc said. "Are there any problems?"

"Not that I'm aware of," Blake said. "Fred and I have handed off the management of the construction to the prime minister's new director of public works."

"Okay, then I'll wait to hear from her. Kal, how is recruitment going?"

"We have eight hundred finishing up their training in Guatemala. We're going to scale back for three weeks while the Academy puts their cadets through it. Then we'll ramp back up. We have a full class here in Delphi City; they should finish about the time the cadets are coming home," Kal said.

"That's an impressive start."

"I need to know how many you plan to take with you to Artemis and how many, if any, you plan to send to Mangkatar."

"I'll be asking you for those numbers," Marc said. "We need a few for the first mission in the Sakira, but you'll need to plan on staffing both space carriers, assuming one flight wing each. Also, for Artemis, we'll need a ground force to protect and police the colonists."

"I'll work on numbers for you. Blake, are you going to do the pilots?"

"I will," Blake said.

"Thank you," Marc said. "While we're on the subject of colonies, Sam, how are our would-be colonists doing?"

"They're doing fine. We're still training and cross-training. They're actually getting into shape. So no problems."

"Still having fun?"

"Yes, especially with the kids."

"How about our international situation? Sam, I know you're not the foreign secretary anymore, but I'm hoping you can still help me keep tabs on the international issues."

"Might I recommend that you make her your National Security Adviser; that would give her a formal role and allow clear lines of communication," Admiral Michaels suggested.

Marc looked at Samantha.

"That works for me," she said. "I like keeping my fingers in the pie, but I'd like to avoid all the work so I can focus on Artemis."

"Good, then you are officially appointed," Marc said. "What can you tell us?"

"First, I think you should hear ADI's report on the Russian manufacturing."

"ADI?"

"Thank you, Sam," ADI purred. "I'm happy to report that the Russian companies have completed their designs, which incorporate the mini fusion reactors into their ships and locomotives. They and I are very happy to see very strong orders for both. They have already increased hiring, and that is adding a boost to those local communities."

"That is excellent news," Marc said. "I'm still worried about the stability of the Russian government."

"Things have progressed well on that front. The president and the government seem to have weathered the storm caused by the release of those documents." Samantha referred to the leak of documents showing the pilfering of the Russian treasury by several major government figures as well as some of their newer billionaires.

"The economic news that ADI reported is helping them establish a stronger link to the communities. We're still hearing pleas from separatist factions, but Margaret is telling them to work with the government," Samantha said. Margaret had served as Delphi's Ambassador to the U.N. and was now the Minister of Foreign Affairs.

"Okay, so treading water on that front," Marc said.

"I think that's an apt analogy," Samantha said. "They are now pushing for us to allocate them space on Delphi Station."

"We promised to allocate lab space," Marc said. "Their people will have to move into whatever cabins are open. I do not want to create separate enclaves on the station."

"I understand, but you do realize that it will happen anyway."

"To some extent, but if they're spread out among the other residents, I hope it will help to integrate them into a community of station residents instead of by their country of origin."

"I understand," Samantha said. "On a more positive note, Margaret informs me that our new ambassador to the U.N. is finding that there is a block forming around Delphi Federation. Multiple countries are signaling that they intend to vote with us."

"I think that's good," Marc said, "but only time will tell. Admiral Michaels, our surface fleet?"

"We have deployed two carriers, one to the Mediterranean Sea and the second here in the South Pacific. The next two should be ready for deployment in four months. We've managed to find another two frigates, and we've placed them with the two carriers. We still are working to get them to their full complement; it's slow, but it's progressing well. I would suggest we find a retired admiral who has commanded a carrier group to take charge of the surface fleet," Admiral Michaels suggested.

"I hear that Admiral Morris is available," Blake said.

"Am I allowed to shoot him?" Admiral Michaels asked.

"I think you would need to stand in line," Marc said, shaking his head at Blake's antics. "That's good news about the carriers and frigates; I hope we won't need them, but they are a significant enhancement to our security. I assume you've briefed the prime minister."

"Yes, I have. She understands, but is not particularly happy about it."

Marc laughed. "She is the consummate pacifist."

"That she is."

"Thanks, everyone. Have a good day," Marc said to close the meeting. "Fred, do you have a moment?" Marc asked before Fred could get up to leave.

"Sure. What's up?" Fred asked, sitting back down.

Marc waited until the room cleared before proceeding. "I wanted to let you know that I've noticed that you seem to get stuck with managing a lot of things. I wondered how you were feeling."

"Are you kidding? I love it," Fred said. "I got my M.B.A. in hopes of running a charter flight company; getting to run all this is like a dream come true."

"Are you sure?"

"Hey, homeboy from Compton makes it big. And with that bonus I picked up this spring, my mama's one proud woman."

"Would you be interested in a more official role?" Marc asked.

"Maybe. What do you have in mind?"

"President of MacKenzie Discoveries," Marc said.

"Whoa, that's a big step," Fred said.

"I think you've already been doing the job."

"More like Chief Operations Officer."

"*So*, president would be a step down?"

"No, no, but I haven't been setting strategy, things like that. I've been focused on execution."

"I'd still be the C.E.O., and we'd talk through strategy," Marc said.

"Let me think about it."

"Any reason for the hesitation I should know about?"

"Not really. There is this new pilot I've started dating. I'd like to get a better sense of our relationship before I spring something like this on her."

"Okay, you've been doing the job, so not much needs to change. I can bump your salary and deal with the title later."

"I like that," Fred said.

"Alright, let me know when you want to make it formal. I'd like to do it before I head out to Artemis."

"That's plenty of time."

◆ ◆ ◆

The next morning Marc called Samantha, Blake, Nikola, and Kal to his office to discuss the colony mission.

"I'd like to review my plans for the colony, and we need to talk about how we can attract more colonists," Marc said as his way to open the meeting.

"*What*, you mean adventure isn't enough to have them lining up?" Blake asked.

"I think we've already got all the ones that are attracted by just the adventure," Marc said.

"Well, how did they find colonists back in the day?" Kal asked.

"Criminals," Blake said.

"Well, besides dumping their criminals on the colonies, how did they attract colonists?"

"As I recall, they usually gave them land," Samantha said.

"There you go," Blake said.

"But if we do that, then the colonists will disperse to their land, and we won't be able to have the necessary labor and community to get the colony established," Marc said.

"You can make the offer of land contingent on completing service to the community. Say, a two-year period," Samantha suggested.

"What about people who want to start a business?" Marc asked.

"For them, you can give them a town lot and maybe the building," Samantha said.

"I knew there was a reason I brought you onto the colony board," Marc said.

"Everything will work if you think of it as a negotiation, with your needs and the colonist's needs being met."

"The concept of negotiations sometimes goes over Marc's head," Blake said as he moved out of Marc's reach.

"Got it," Marc glared at Blake. "Now, how much land do we offer?"

"What are they going to be doing on it?" Kal asked.

"I assume farming or ranching," Blake said.

"There's a big difference in the amount of land you need for farming versus ranching," Kal added.

"Sure, but they tend to be different types of land," Blake said. "Ranching would be hillier or dryer. Something that makes it less suitable for farming. Farming pays more per acre."

"So how big for farmland?"

"The average size of a family farm in the U.S. is one hundred hectares," ADI said.

"What's that in acres?" Kal asked.

"Two hundred fifty," ADI replied. "An average ranch is about twice the size."

"So, four hundred hectares would make for a thousand-acre farm," Marc said. "That would allow them to raise livestock as well as farm. And twice that much for ranchland."

"I think that will attract a lot of people," Samantha said. "Now, how will the land be allocated?"

"Why don't you define the parcels early, once you get a lay of the land, then each person gets to pick based on a random selection," Kal suggested.

"Yes, and you could increase their odds of getting to choose early based on their service. Points for doing good work, points taken away for getting drunk and disorderly," Samantha suggested.

"I'll have to think about that. But I like how you're thinking. Now, let me show you my plans for the town," Marc said as he brought up a holoprojection on their HUDs and synced them, so they all saw the same thing relative to the table.

"I'm laying it out on a four-block grid," Marc said. "Lots are half the depth of the block, so each lot has only one street frontage. Of course, corner lots get two. I'm planning on major infrastructure every eight blocks going north-south. The other north-south streets will have just the infrastructure to support the buildings and roads. The cross streets will only have infrastructure to support lighting and roads; the houses and buildings all have to pull utilities from the road."

"Smalltown U.S.A.," Blake said.

"What do you mean by major and just enough for buildings and roads?" Kal asked.

"Major infrastructure will be designed to accommodate a future subway system."

"Whoa, isn't that a big investment?" Blake asked.

"Not really. What I'm thinking is, we put everything below the street, so the main streets are wider and cover a twelve meter by six-meter elliptical polysteel tube. That would accommodate a subway running in each direction and allow for the sewage, storm drains, electrical lines, and communication lines as well. The small streets would just have three-meter tubes."

"That's still a lot of work," Blake said. "You can't just bury the tubes; you have to compact the ground, etc."

"Sure, but we don't have to do that much to start. We can build the tubes like we do the station rings, so that's not too difficult. We dig it out, and compact it, then fill with the polycrete, the same material you used for the foundations when you built the compounds. We build the tube, then backfill with more polycrete. Then you've got a street that will last for decades and the ability to add major infrastructure as you go."

"You're still moving a lot of material around," Blake said.

"But we're doing it on a blank slate. There's nothing there."

"Okay, it can work; what kind of machinery are you planning to take?"

"The machine components for an excavator," Marc said. "When we get there, we'll build it, but make the polysteel frame and structure on site, so we don't have to haul it there."

"For compacting?"

"Same thing, we take the key components of the machines, and build them on site."

"Where are you going to get all the material?"

"We'll have to find a source of oil and iron," Marc said. "That has to be our top priority anyway. This just uses the same material that we need to have anyway."

"You do remember that the site is sitting right next to a petroleum field," Blake said.

Marc's eyes floated up like he was looking into his brain to read the information. "Oh, right, I had forgotten that. Of course, Dr. Qamar would have taken care of that when he picked the location."

"What are you going to do for power?" Nikola asked.

"We'll have four fusion power plants to start," Marc said. "Then, each building will have solar panels on it. We're going to be bringing a large supply of them with us."

"Why do you need them if you have four fusion plants?" Nikola asked. "I understand the idea of using solar, but is it that critical, given the space they'll take up in your cargo?"

"Yes, but these fusion plants are not that big, they're the same ones we're sending the Russians for their ships and trains. That's pretty much as big as we can make the portable ones. I don't want to try to deal with a full-blown power plant," Marc said.

"Wait a minute, you power an entire starship with them, why can't you use them on the planet?" Nikola asked.

"Umm, we don't actually power a starship with the fusion reactors. The fusion reactors are just startup generators. The real power comes from the antimatter reactors," Marc said.

"*Antimatter*?!" Nickola asked, giving Marc a hard stare.

"One of those closely-held secrets," Marc said. "The starships run on antimatter reactors. They're very expensive to build, and we only get one good one out of every ten attempts."

"I see. And I assume that they're dangerous."

"Not so much. The reactor actually creates the antimatter just before it combines it to generate energy. So, there is never very much antimatter around."

"Isn't it expensive to make antimatter?"

"Yes, about fifty percent of the energy produced goes into making antimatter, but that E=mc2 is really a big lever. The reactors can generate enormous amounts of energy, and right now, I'd like to avoid people knowing about them. And I don't want to put them somewhere where they could be seized. We have great control over the starships via our DIs, but putting them on the ground is a lot of exposure."

"I understand," Nikola said. She still gave Marc the eye for holding out on her. "But if you're going to rely on solar, how are you going to keep things running at night?"

"Ah, my next design," Marc said. "My mercury tower of power."'

"Give me a break," Blake said. "Tower of power, what are you, like ten?"

"Wait until you see this. I'm putting mercury in a closed system. I want to bury it, so a kilometer-deep well feeds a large chamber. We pump the mercury up during the day and let it flow down and run the generator at night. A typical city of one hundred thousand uses five hundred forty billion joules of energy per day, that's three-quarters of a billion watts."

"Why are you using mercury?" Samantha asked. "Isn't it bad for the environment?"

"That's why it's a closed system," Marc said. "And mercury is liquid and weighs thirteen times more than water."

"So how big is the tank?" Blake asked.

"Twenty by twenty by ten meters," Marc said.

"That sounds doable."

"Where are you going to get the mercury?" Samantha asked.

"One of the volcanos on the surface should have deposits of cinnabar, mercury ore. We'll mine it and extract it. And we'll make sure to capture all the sulfur and bad stuff."

"Sounds like you'll need a lot of miners," Kal said.

"Yes, but if they all get to retire to a farm after two years, it doesn't sound like such a bad deal."

"Miners should get extra points," Samantha said. "It's not the same as construction work."

"Yeah, we'll have to come up with a way to rate the jobs," Marc said.

# 7 Two Weeks of Hell

"Please have a seat," Commandant Lewis said to the two cadets who had just snapped off a salute in front of her desk. Both of them quickly and properly took a seat and sat at attention.

"Cadet Miranda Cordova. You're from the U.S. Naval Academy."

"Correct, Ma'am."

"You were a battalion commander before your discharge."

"Yes, Ma'am."

"Your story?"

"Ma'am, I was in my senior year when a drunk driver sideswiped my car. I was medically discharged with severe trauma to my neck vertebras. Delphi offered to fix me up, and I've always wanted to go to space."

"And you, Cadet Thomas Jefferson, you were a squadron commander at the Air Force Academy."

"Yes, Ma'am. I have a similar story. I was in my senior year at the U.S. Air Force Academy. I was skydiving when a freak downdraft collapsed my sail. I got slammed into the ground pretty hard. Broke my pelvis and my back. I got the same offer from Delphi."

"Both of you have excellent records from your Academies. I've spoken to your commandants, and they give you superb recommendations."

"Thank you, Ma'am."

"Cadet Cordova, you are now Cadet Colonel Cordova, and you will take command of the Cadet Wing," Commandant Lewis said. Then she turned to Cadet Jefferson. "Cadet Jefferson, you are now Cadet Lt. Colonel Jefferson, and you will be her executive officer."

Both cadets were stunned and neither knew if they should say anything.

"Do you accept?"

"Yes, Ma'am!"

"You both have significant experience in leadership positions. Work with Colonel Harriman and select the other cadet officers. I expect your selections on my desk tomorrow by 1800."

"Yes, Ma'am!"

"Do you have any questions?"

"I do, Ma'am," Cadet Cordova said.

"Go ahead."

"It seems that the trainers have been going light on the Plebes. When I was a Plebe at the Naval Academy, we were pushed much harder."

"That might be so. I think Commander Blackwood wanted to transition the Plebes. In my opinion, it has been a steep transition, but we have to acknowledge that they're not coming from the same situation as a typical Academy recruit."

Cadet Cordova and Cadet Jefferson didn't say anything, but their faces showed they weren't buying it.

"One thing you should keep in mind, Commander Blackwood was a Navy Seal. I don't think he's taking it easy on anyone."

"Yes, Ma'am . . . I mean no, Ma'am!"

"Very good. I expect you to work the Plebes hard. We want those that can't cut it to leave. **But**, we do not want to lose someone because of carelessness or cruelty. Do I make myself clear?"

"Yes, Ma'am."

To Catie, if the first week of the Academy was the sixth circle of hell, the second week was the ninth circle of hell. When the instructors and NCOs stepped back, and the cadets who had previous Academy experience stepped forward, things ramped up to a whole new level.

The senior cadets had spent their first week getting acclimated to the Academy and its unique rules. They'd been put through some minor hell by the instructors, but now they were in charge, and they let the Plebes know it. Where the NCOs could find two or three things wrong with the way you came to attention, the senior cadets could find six.

The NCOs had thought an hour of rifle drill was adequate, the senior cadets thought that was just a warmup.

The Alfa, Bravo, and Charlie squadrons were made up entirely of cadets from the various military academies. There were eight squadrons in all. Each of the squadrons was named after a letter from the NATO phonetic alphabet. Once they finished Basic, they would reorganize, and the squadrons would probably pick up nicknames as well.

Each squadron was broken down into six flights of ten cadets each. A second-class cadet was put in charge, a second-class cadet was a junior. A first-class cadet, a senior, was in charge of the squadron, and there was a plethora of third-class cadets for each flight, each of them ready and eager to search out and find errors.

"Attention!" Cadet Lieutenant Hoffman yelled; he was now in charge of Foxtrot Squadron, Flight One.

Catie's flight snapped to attention. They'd had their usual rude awakening at 0430 and were now formed up for PT.

"Make corrections!" Hoffman ordered. His two minions, the two cadet sergeants assigned to Flight One, moved down the two ranks of Plebes formed up in front of Cadet Lieutenant Hoffman. One for each rank.

"Shoulders back! Chin down! Eyes up! Fingers aligned with the seam! Heels together!" The corrections were endless.

"Twenty push-ups!" Hoffman ordered. The flight snapped down to the push-up position and started counting. "Corrections!"

"Fingers together! Upper arms parallel to the ground! Do not pause at the top!"

*"When did push-ups become so much more complicated?"* Catie thought. "Five!" she counted aloud.

"Now that you know how to do them, give me twenty!" Cadet Lieutenant Hoffman ordered. So they got to start over after already doing seven.

"One . . . two . . ."

"Forty side-straddle hops! Corrections!"

"Your feet need to be **more** than shoulder-width apart! Clap those hands! Stay in sync!"

"Now that you know how to do them, give me forty good ones!"

"One . . . two . . ."

"Twenty engines! Corrections!"

"Do not bend your arm toward your knee, keep them parallel to the ground! Knees higher, touch your elbows! Shoulders back!"

"Now that we've corrected your form, give me twenty!"

"One . . . two . . ."

It went on for what seemed an eternity, mule kick, ski jumps, high jumpers, flutter kicks, swimmers, crunches. Each exercise needing extra corrections as if the NCO instructors had not already corrected every detail.

When they finally finished PT, they got to eat, or at least try to eat.

"Sit at attention!" Cadet Lieutenant Hoffman ordered. "Corrections!"

On and on, the corrections went.

"That is not the way to stand up from the table! Ten push-ups!"

"One . . . two . . ."

"Now try it again!"

After breakfast, they got to endure two hours of rifle drills, followed by an hour of marching. Included in each was the bonus of endless corrections! Everyone was happy to go to class for the afternoon. At least there, they would only have to endure the NCO trainers and the class instructor. The cadet officers had their own classes to go to.

Of course, after class, the cadet officers thought a little bit of marching would help settle all that learning down.

◆ ◆ ◆

"Where did they find Cadet Lieutenant Hoffman?" Joanie complained after she and Catie finally made it back to their room for the night. It was the end of the first day of week two. "He's a sadist!"

"I heard he's from the Citadel," Catie said. "What about his boss, Cadet Major Baker? He sure seemed to be enjoying himself."

"They're both sadists!"

"That's Cadet Lieutenant Sadist and Cadet Major Sadist to you," Catie said. "But, hey, we've only got them for five weeks. When we get back from Guatemala, they'll reorganize us, and maybe we'll luck out, and someone else will get him."

"Why the reorganization?" Joanie asked as she rubbed her foot.

"Now, we're organized between those who have experience in one of the military academies and those who don't. When we start class, they'll shuffle it to balance out the experience and the class ranking."

"But we'll still be stuck with these guys as the officers?"

"Mostly," Catie said. "At least they'll be busy with classes then and won't have time to ride us every minute."

"You hope."

"I'm exhausted," Joanie said when she and Catie made it back to their room after the second day of week two.

"Being corrected every minute is exhausting," Catie said.

"That and PT is using up all my energy. I'm still struggling with the run."

"I notice you're breathing up in your chest," Catie said.

"That's where my lungs are," Joanie said.

"That's true, but the volume is in the lower chest. You need to breathe with your diaphragm. Didn't you ever sing?"

"Can't carry a tune."

"Here, let me show you. I learned this from a Hawaiian friend who teaches me Aikido," Catie said. "Now sit on the floor cross-legged and wrap your arms around your body, like you're giving yourself a hug."

"Okay," Joanie said as she sat on the floor.

"Now, lean forward until your arms are touching your legs."

"Hey, it's hard to breathe!"

"Relax. In that position, it is almost impossible to breathe without using your diaphragm. Now focus on expanding your ribcage in your lower back."

"Hey, I can breathe."

"Good, now do that every night before you go to bed and in the morning for thirty seconds. Longer, if you can find some time."

"I'll try. Like I have time, I still have to help clean our room and then start typing that stupid paper."

"Did you finish all your research?"

"Yes, but typing everything up is going to take me hours. Are you ready to type yours yet?"

"Oh, I finished," Catie said.

"You finished. When?!"

"Yesterday."

"How could you, when did you have the time?"

"I did it in the morning. You know I get up at 0400."

"*Yeah,* but you typed it in just one hour?"

"Sure," Catie said. It had actually only taken her twenty minutes to type it up. With her nanites, she could type around one thousand words per minute.

"I wish you would type mine."

"Tell you what, you go and clean Mary's and Julie's rooms so they can go do a quick run. And work on their breathing with them and their roommates before they run, and I'll type your paper."

"That's a deal. But that's too good a deal, what are you going to get out of it?"

"Those four will never pass the fitness test if they don't start working out at least twice a day," Catie said. "So this will give them time to work out."

"Okay, I'll do it. Just for today?"

"Why not all week?"

"That's asking a lot. I'll spend as many days helping them as you have to spend typing my paper."

"Nuh-uh. I'll be finished with your paper by the time you get back," Catie said. "But, I want them to get help for more than just one day."

"No way can you finish my paper that fast!"

"You want to bet?"

"Sure. If you're finished with my paper when I get back, I'll help them all week."

"You have to spend at least five minutes with them on their breathing *and* clean their rooms," Catie said.

"Sure, no problem, bet?"

"Bet. Send me your files."

"You're back faster than I expected," Catie said when Joanie showed up twenty-five minutes later. Catie was prepping her uniform for the next day. *"It sure would be a lot more efficient if we could just wear shipsuits all day,"* she thought.

"Did you give up on finishing my paper?"

"No, it's done," Catie said.

"I don't believe you."

"Check your Comm. I already transferred the files back."

"Wow! What do you type, like five hundred words a minute?"

"Let's just say I'm fast," Catie said.

"If you want to really help those girls, you should offer to type their papers. Between that and me cleaning their rooms, they would have at least an extra forty minutes a day to work out."

"Good idea."

"Hey, I heard you're typing Dubois' paper," Plebe Howard said. "How much would you charge to type mine?"

"I'm not doing it for money," Catie said.

"Then what are you doing it for?"

"I'm doing it so they have time to do extra workouts. They need help to pass the fitness test."

"If you want to help people pass the fitness test, then you should type Joey's paper. That guy doesn't stand a chance."

"If you help him, I'll type your paper and his," Catie said.

"How are you going to manage two extra papers?"

"That's my problem. I'll type yours if you help him until the fitness test."

"Deal."

"That means you'll need to help clean his room, too, so he has time."

"Hey, if I get out of typing that paper, cleaning his room for a week will be nothing."

"And you'll need to run with him. Joanie will spend some time teaching him to breathe correctly."

"Breathe correctly?"

"Yeah, he probably breathes up in his chest, without using his diaphragm. Makes for short, choppy breaths. Oxygen starvation makes it hard to run fast. Have Joanie show you the exercise."

"Whatever. I'll send you the files."

By the end of the week, the entire squadron had divided up the chores to ensure that the Plebes who were struggling were given extra time to train. Joanie was running around helping everyone practice their breathing, and Catie was typing twelve papers.

"No classes tomorrow, what's up with that?" Catie asked.

"Hey, it's Saturday," Joanie answered.

"I think there's more to it than that. Baker looked very pleased with himself when he announced it."

"I'm sure they've thought up some fun exercises for us to do. Or maybe we'll get to go to the rifle range!"

"I don't think fun is going to have anything to do with it," Catie said.

The next morning when they formed up for PT, instead of doing PT, they marched to Delphi City's central park.

"You'll be happy to know that we've been given exclusive use of the beach for today," Cadet Colonel Cordova announced as the Plebes marched onto the beach. "We've even arranged for some toys to play with." She pointed to a stack of logs.

"Each squadron will have two hours to play on the beach!" Cadet Lt. Colonel Jefferson said. "While you're playing, the other squadrons will be practicing their marching."

"That means we'll be marching for eight hours," Joanie hissed.

"Plebe McCoy, give me twenty!"

Joanie got down and did twenty push-ups. *"Serves me right for talking out loud!"* she thought.

Catie and Joanie's squadron was the third to hit the beach. It was really torn up from whatever the other squadrons had done. Five Plebes had been taken away on stretchers, and the others looked like they'd been put through a special kind of hell. Their exhaustion was palpable as they made their way off the beach. They were allowed a ten-minute water break before they had to start marching.

"Our turn!" Cadet Major Baker shouted. "Each flight, grab a log!"

There were three-meter-long logs spread across the beach. They were about half a meter in diameter and looked like they weighed a ton; in fact, they weighed five hundred pounds each.

"I want those logs at the top of the beach, and I want the red end pointed at the ocean at all times, and keep them off the sand!" Cadet Major Baker yelled. "Now, move!"

Catie's flight ran down to their log, they looked at their Flight Lieutenant for instructions, but he just motioned up the beach and smiled. The Plebes spread themselves out on both sides of the log and lifted it. It was awkward; four of the men in the flight were six feet or taller. Three women and two men were around five feet seven, and Juliet was five feet one.

They started to shuffle up the beach, but with the rough sand, it was difficult. They had only made it four meters before someone tripped, and they dropped the log. The rear four kept hold of it so that it didn't crush anyone; just the front end hit the sand.

"Pick it up and go back and start over!" Cadet Lieutenant Hoffman yelled.

"This is impossible," Julie wailed. "The sand is too rough to walk on, especially when you're carrying this log."

"Then let's not do that!" Catie said. "Let's do like a bucket brigade. We line up and move the log forward, the rear two move to the front once the log is beyond them, and so on!"

"Let's do it!" Plebe Howard yelled.

They started their log brigade; it was soon apparent that Julie was unable to get a grasp of the log because of her short stature.

"Julie, you go out front and make a place for the next two to stand on," Catie yelled.

"Got it!"

Julie moved to the front and started kicking the sand level. As the log moved up the beach, she ran in front, leveling the sand.

Their flight was the first to get the log to the top of the beach. They stood there, holding it and smiling at each other, proud of their accomplishment.

"Don't just stand there! Take it back down to the water!" Cadet Lieutenant Hoffman yelled.

The trip down was easier on Julie since she already had leveled spots for them to stand on, she just had to smooth them out from the wear of five Plebes walking on them.

"Bring it back!" Cadet Lieutenant Hoffman yelled.

Their technique slowly spread up and down the line, and by the end of their first hour, all the flights were following their example.

"Now, I think it's time to roll them!" Cadet Colonel Cordova yelled.

"Alright, turn it sideways and roll them up the beach," Cadet Lieutenant Hoffman ordered.

"What do you think, same method?" Plebe Howard asked.

"Yes, but you tall guys need to level the sand. You'll have a hard time getting this low," Catie said.

"You heard what MacGregor said. Start leveling the sand," Howard yelled as he got in front of the log and started to level the sand along its length.

The other three tall men got out in front with Howard and started leveling while everyone else bent over and started to roll the log up the slope of the beach. Here Julie showed the advantage of being short. She took up the position in the center of the log and dug in and pushed. Slowly they built up momentum. The effort by Howard and his team was helpful, but the sand was still rough and uneven. The big hills were knocked down, but there were plenty of smaller ones to impede their progress.

"Nice job, now roll it back to the water!" Cadet Lieutenant Hoffman yelled.

Since it was downhill, rolling it back to the water's edge was easier, but that just meant it took less time before they had to turn around and roll it back up the hill.

"Come on, you can go faster than that!" Cadet Lieutenant Hoffman yelled.

Slowly the rolling of the log smoothed out the sand level. After the fourth trip, there was little for the tall guys to do.

"Alright," Howard yelled, "let's help!" He got down on all fours right next to the log. With his feet dug in, he pushed the log ahead of himself as he stretched his body out. Once all four of them were helping like that, it was almost easy to roll the log up the beach. Of course, that just meant that they got to roll it up and down more often.

As before, their technique spread up and down the beach. It happened quicker this time, as the other flights were looking to see what they came up with.

"Time's up!" Cadet Lt. Colonel Jefferson yelled. "Time to march. Form up on your leaders!"

"Clever," Cadet Colonel Cordova said to Cadet Baker.

"Was it? They just had to make more trips."

"True, but you'll notice that Cadet Lieutenant Hoffman's flight is the only flight to finish without any injuries. And your squadron is also the only one to finish without needing the stretcher. Good job," Cadet Colonel Cordova said.

"Thank you, Ma'am, but I didn't do anything."

"Exactly."

"Gawd, every muscle in my body aches," Joanie complained once she and Catie made it back to their room for the night.

"I told you he looked too happy," Catie said. She sat on the floor with her back against her bunk as she massaged her calves. "I hate marching. Do I look like a freaking Marine?"

"Have you already decided which branch you're joining?" Joanie asked as she sat down beside Catie and started to massage her calves as well.

"Oh, yeah, I'm going for the Space Corps," Catie said.

"Alex MacGregor, Starship Captain," Joanie said. "I think you'll probably make it."

"I plan to," Catie said. She couldn't mention that she'd already been a starship captain. "Which branch are you thinking about?"

"It isn't the Marines," Joanie said. "I'm not sure, either Space Corps or the surface Navy. I like the idea of being stationed planetside."

"You don't like space?"

"Don't know, I've never been," Joanie said. "I'll have to wait and see."

◆ ◆ ◆

"Wake up," Catie nudged Joanie.

"What for, what time is it?"

"0400," Catie said.

"Why do I need to get up now?"

"They'll be by in twenty to thirty minutes to roust us out," Catie said. "You need to stretch, or you'll die during PT."

"It might be worth it for that thirty minutes of sleep."

"You'll thank me later," Catie said. "I'm going to roust the rest of the squadron."

Catie made her way down the hall, pounding on the doors. She got some colorful greetings as she woke up her squadron mates, but they all eventually recognized the wisdom of her advice.

When the Cadet officers of Squadron Foxtrot pounded on the doors of the Plebes at 0440, they were shocked to have them immediately come out and form up.

"What are you doing awake?!" demanded Cadet Lieutenant Hoffman.

"I woke up early, it must have been all that exercise yesterday," Julie said. "Couldn't go back to sleep, so I did some stretches and got ready."

"Couldn't they lighten up after the beach?!" Joanie whined.

"That was three days ago," Catie said. "They probably don't even remember it."

"Did you notice the smile on Baker's face again?"

"I did. I don't know what's coming, but I'm sure we're not going to like it."

"Did you hear that Jackson quit?" Joanie asked.

"He did?!"

"Yep, he said he didn't join the Academy to be a punching bag."

"Wuss! How many does that make?" Catie asked.

"Twelve," Joanie said. "Six the first week, and four last week. Now Jackson and some girl in Delta Squadron."

"That actually doesn't sound too bad out of three hundred newbies," Catie thought.

◆ ◆ ◆

After PT, they were ordered to breakfast while still wearing their shipsuits.

"I told you," Joanie whispered to Catie over breakfast. "They probably thought this up because you got everyone to stretch the other morning."

"I doubt that. I'm sure they've been looking for something unique every chance they get."

"Any guesses?"

"Nope. We'll know soon enough."

"You will all be pleased to hear that some moron has put a horse ranch in the middle of Delphi City. Now, I don't know why anyone would do such a thing, but we're going to take advantage of it," Cadet Colonel Cordova announced.

Catie winced since she was the moron. She'd added the horse park for Kal and his new girlfriend. And Kal had been right; it was a draw. The hotels both had guests lining up for reservations to ride a horse. And they were quality horses, pureblood Arabians, with a few quarterhorses mixed in for the beginners.

"Now, we've been given exclusive use of the park for the day. In exchange, we've agreed to clean their stables. I'm sure we'll have plenty of slackers who will volunteer for that task," Cadet Colonel Cordova said. "Squadron leaders, form up your squadrons."

Before they were marched to the horse park, the Plebes were all outfitted with gear. First, they put on an ammo belt with a canteen for water and ammo pouches full of lead weights. They were given a backpack, also full of weights. Each of them was also given an M-4 rifle to carry which added another 3.5 kilos. By the end, when you added it all up, the Plebes were carrying thirty kilos each.

"Those rifles are not loaded, but they are in perfect working order. Do not drop them, do not get them dirty, do not get them wet, do not abuse your rifle; your rifle is your best friend!" shouted Cadet Lt. Colonel Jefferson.

The Plebes marched to the horse park. Apparently, the Cadet officer corps had been very disappointed to find that they did not have access to an obstacle course in Delphi City. Those were in Guatemala, and when they got to Guatemala, the trainers there would be taking over most of the control. The discovery of the horse park presented a perfect opportunity to make up for that lost opportunity.

The cross-country jump course had been designed to utilize the park's eight hundred meters on a side layout to maximum benefit. The course mostly traveled around the outside edge of the park, traversing into the inside area to ensure maximum viewing for the spectacular jumps. The horse barn and corrals were in the center of the park next to the visitor's pavilion. Lots of people liked to come to the park for a picnic or just to hang out and watch the riders and their horses. There were plenty of nice open spaces for them to congregate in.

"Alright, now listen up. Each flight will be given a two-hundred-meter head start before the next flight starts the course. Stick together, if the flight behind you tags one of you, you and your whole flight get to come back to the beginning and start over. This course is seven thousand meters long, so you should enjoy the exercise. You will jump, crawl, or climb over each obstacle; do not go around them. A cadet sergeant will be at each obstacle to let you know the proper course over it!" Cadet Lt. Colonel Jefferson yelled.

"Your goal is to make it through the course with all of your flight mates. We don't care how you do it, as long as each and every one of you goes over or through every obstacle. Delta Squadron, Flight One, you're up!" Cadet Lt. Colonel Jefferson yelled. "Go! Echo Squadron, Flight One, you're next! . . . Go! Foxtrot Squadron, Flight One, get ready!"

"I know this course," Catie said. "I'll lead the way and set us up for each obstacle. I'll try to think of the best way over the big ones before we get to them. Just follow me. First jump coming up, just crawl over it. There's a one-meter drop on the other side!"

"How do you know the course?" Plebe Howard asked.

"Don't ask, but believe me, *I know it*."

"Foxtrot Squadron, Flight One, go!"

Catie took off in front. She had run this course in her head so many times when she was designing it on the way back from Artemis that she couldn't even begin to count them. But she definitely knew every inch.

The first jump was a starter jump, big and showy. The face was usually decorated with flowers during a competition, but today it was just a half meter step up, then another half meter of dirt slope before the top rail. As Catie approached the jump, she pulled her backpack off. It was filled with blocks so it would make a perfect step, she tossed it against the wall of the jump and used it to step up onto the dirt. Then she crawled to the top and hopped back to the ground. "Last one, bring my pack with you," she shouted as she took off for the next jump. Howard grabbed Catie's pack before he easily hopped up onto the dirt.

The second jump was a simple log placed at 1.2 meters height. Catie hit it, flipped her legs to the side, and did a barrel roll over it.

"Next jump is two down steps, then a jump. Someone, take position at each step and help the others make it down!" she yelled.

She waited for Howard to show up with her pack before taking off with him to catch up with the lead.

"Is this cheating, you know the course already?" Joanie asked.

"It's in the library, anyone could have checked it out on their HUD on the march over," Catie said. "All the jumps are detailed."

"How do you know?"

"I checked," Catie said before she sprinted ahead. She negotiated the two steps down with the help of one of her mates at each step, then crawled over the two-step logs as she took the lead again. She was setting a fifteen-minute per mile pace; with the workouts all last week, their slowest runner was holding at twelve for a five-K, so she figured they could handle this pace. She could always slow down if it was too much.

"Next is an uphill jump. Just take it like you did the log!" Catie yelled as she climbed the hill to the jump. After the jump, she paused to look at how they were doing relative to Golf Squadron. To her eye, their flight had increased the distance. *"Good, we definitely don't want to get tagged back to the start."* Catie thought.

Catie took off for the next jump. "This one's a table. Everyone will need help to get over it. I'll start. Howard, when you get there, take my place!"

When Catie reached the table, she knelt down on all fours. That allowed the Plebe behind her to step on her back, then step onto the table. She was thankful when Howard showed up to take her place. Being a stepping stool was harder than she had expected.

"Next jump is two corners. Take them at the edge where they're narrower! Vault them!" Catie demonstrated, hitting the first jump one meter from the corner, flipping her legs over the side, and rolling off the back side. She ran a curved line to the second, so it was lined up correctly and did the same thing. Each of her flight mates was able to see the person in front execute the move, so all they had to do was copy.

On the seventh jump, Catie tagged a member of Echo Squadron.

"Echo Squadron, Flight One, you're too slow, head back to the beginning and try it again!" one of the Cadet NCOs who were posted along the course yelled.

◆ ◆ ◆

"Water coming up!" Catie yelled.

"Don't get your rifle wet!" the Cadet NCO warned them.

"I think she's actually telling us something!" Julie yelled.

"Julie, give me your rifle," Catie ordered. "Walk ahead and show us a clear path."

Julie handed her rifle to Catie and headed out. She immediately took a dunk as she tripped over an underwater hazard.

"They must have put stuff in the water," Catie said.

*"Obviously,"* Julie said as she got back up. She shuffled her feet as she continued across the small pond. "How deep is this thing?"

"One meter at the center," Catie said.

"Rifles overhead," Howard yelled. "Catie, give me Julie's rifle."

"Something's here!" Julie yelled.

"Hold up until someone gets to you to mark it for us!" Catie yelled.

"Holding."

There were two other underwater obstacles to negotiate before they crossed the twenty-meter pond.

"Good job, Julie," Howard said as he started to hand her rifle back. "I think I should carry this for a bit. At least until you dry off."

"Thanks!"

◆ ◆ ◆

Foxtrot Squadron, Flight One, made it around the course, almost catching up with Delta Squadron by the end of the course.

"I'm exhausted," Catie said. "Gawd, these guys are sadistic."

"Alright. You've got twenty minutes to get some water; then, we're going to let you all do it again. This one is for the money. The three flights with the worst time on this round get to muck out the stables."

"Sadistic is putting it mildly," Plebe Howard said. "I hope we have something left for this round. I'm worried that we left it all out there on the course."

"I know what you mean. Getting tagged is going to be a death blow. How many got tagged or had to restart on this round?"

"Twelve," Joanie said. "It seems every other one got their rifles wet. I guess the trailing team could see the disaster in front of them. But when they made it through, the next team didn't get a warning."

"Let's go talk to the other Foxtrots and give them some advice. We don't want the squadron to look bad," Catie said.

◆ ◆ ◆

In the end, they had to run the course four times. Even though they were never tagged, they were completely exhausted and had to walk-trot the last time through. Of course, that meant they were yelled at the whole way.

"I swear that Cadet Colonel Cordova is the devil incarnate," Joanie said when they got to their room to shower. They had thirty minutes to shower, change, and make it back to the mess hall for dinner.

"I agree, but what does that make Jefferson?"

"Yeah, he is worse. I guess he'd be the devil wannabe."

"Funny, just never let him hear you say that."

Dinner was unusually relaxed by the standards they were used to. The cadet officers allowed the Plebes to chat and joke a bit as they reviewed the tough day they'd endured.

"Plebe, MacGregor, how did you know about the water hazard?" Cadet Sergeant Rosenbach asked.

"Julie guessed," Catie replied.

"Water, don't get your rifle wet, it seemed obvious," Julie said.

"Apparently not, only one other flight figured it out on their own. The others had the example of a wet Plebe leading their flight back to the beginning," Cadet Sergeant Rosenbach said.

"Probably was a girl," Julie said.

"Hmm, I'll have to check that out," Cadet Sergeant Rosenbach said. She was smiling.

As the dinner moved along, the upper-class cadets started quizzing the Plebes on their knowledge about Delphi and Delphi Defense Forces. Finally, Cadet Major Baker got around to Catie.

"Plebe MacGregor, how many men does it take to keep a Fox combat-ready?" Cadet Major Baker asked.

"Sir, it requires zero men to keep a Fox combat-ready," Catie replied. Cadet Major Baker had been stressing 'men' all week.

"Zero! Do you think the Fox repairs itself?!"

"No, sir! It requires eight sailors to keep a Fox combat-ready."

"Then why did you tell me zero?!"

"I said zero men, sir. If the ground crew were all women, this Plebe is confident that they would get the job done."

"So, you think that there shouldn't be any men in a ground crew?!"

"No, sir. This Plebe was just trying to be accurate."

"And how is zero men accurate?!"

"This Plebe was just acknowledging that men are not required."

"Why, do you hate men?!"

"No, sir, I just think we should ignore sex when assigning jobs."

"Why is that?!"

"The Delphi forces code says that we see only Rank, Skill, Dedication, and Talent in our Marines and Sailors."

"So, you don't think it's important if a sailor is a man or a woman?!"

"No, sir."

"What about if you're dating one?!"

"Sir, I don't know!"

"You don't know if you like to date men or women!"

"I haven't made up my mind, sir!"

"Do you want some help?"

"You are helping, sir."

The cadets all tried to stifle their laughs

"Ahem," Colonel Sunamoto coughed. "I believe the Plebes are needed in the classroom."

"Yes, sir," Cadet Major Baker said. "Flight leaders, assemble your flights and proceed to the auditorium for class."

"The commandant will see you now," the admin told Catie. She had been summoned to the commandant's office that morning.

"Thank you, Sergeant," Catie said as she stood up. She made her way to the door. "Ma'am, Plebe MacGregor reporting as ordered."

"Please be seated," Admiral Lewis said.

"Yes, Ma'am." Catie took a seat in the chair in front of the desk. She carefully sat at attention.

"Now, Cadet MacGregor, can you explain what happened yesterday with Cadet Major Baker?"

"Ma'am, I just answered his questions."

"You think your first answer was the correct answer?"

"Yes, Ma'am. Any other answer would have been incorrect," Catie said.

"So, you couldn't have said, eight sailors?"

"Ma'am, he asked how many men, not how many sailors. If I had answered sailors, it would have been incorrect, and I'm sure Cadet Major Baker would have pointed that out."

"And your reply that you didn't know if you wanted to date men or women?"

"Again, I was trying to be accurate," Catie replied.

"It wasn't just your way of setting him up?" Commandant Lewis asked.

"Setting him up for what, Ma'am?"

"You do know that it is not your job to weed out the cadets who have trouble with women?" Commandant Lewis asked.

"Yes, Ma'am. That would be the job of you and your staff," Catie replied.

The commandant sighed. "Do you have an opinion about what we should do with Cadet Baker?"

"Ma'am, this Plebe is not qualified to have an opinion," Catie replied.

"Would you be disappointed if we didn't expel him?"

"I would be disappointed if you did," Catie said.

"I see that you had exceptional marks from the instructors in your first week here. During the last week and a half, your marks are excellent but not exceptional, can you explain the difference?"

"No, Ma'am. I would need to do a detailed analysis of what changed between the first week and the second to do that, Ma'am."

Commandant Lewis tried to suppress a smile but failed. "Very well. You do know that you have marked yourself out for the other Cadet officers?"

"Why is that, Ma'am?"

"You don't happen to be studying to be a lawyer, are you?"

"No, Ma'am."

"I also see a flag in your file, do you know why that is?"

"I haven't seen my file," Catie said. "I would have no knowledge of any flags."

"Probably not, it's well hidden; it would only come up if you were subject to severe disciplinary action. I only noticed it when I was comparing your file to Cadet Baker's file. You are dismissed."

Catie stood up and saluted the commandant, made an about-face, and exited the office. Once out the door, she let out a sigh and practically ran back to her room.

"Cadet Baker, please have a seat," the commandant said after Baker came into her office for his interview.

"Yes, Ma'am."

"Would you like to explain what happened yesterday?"

"Yes, Ma'am."

"Then proceed."

"I lost my temper," Cadet Baker said. "No excuses, Ma'am."

"Why did you lose your temper?"

"Two reasons, Ma'am. First, Plebe MacGregor is impossible to break or fluster. None of the Cadet officers have been able to make her flinch. Second, I think I'm overcompensating for the emphasis we have on women here. At the Citadel, women only made up fifteen percent of the class. Here, every time I turn around, I'm confronted with an accommodation that we have to make for the women."

"What kind of issues?"

"Different thresholds on the PT test, different thresholds on punishment exercises, having to pair everyone up, privacy issues."

"So, you would be happy to go to the toilet while a bunch of women were looking on?" the commandant asked.

"No, Ma'am. But that's just it. We're setting up for the second half in Guatemala, and we have to have privacy screens. If it was just guys, we wouldn't need them."

"So, your problem is that you have to pack an extra five kilos of gear?"

"It sounds stupid when you say it like that," Cadet Baker said.

"Does that give you a hint?"

"Yes, Ma'am. I'm making a big deal out of nothing. I guess I'm projecting my stress on the one thing that stands out," Cadet Baker said.

"Ma'am, I want to apologize. I know I've let you down, and I understand you have to kick me out. But I've set a poor example; I just hope that the others can see past it. I'll issue a formal apology if you think it will help."

"We're not kicking you out," the commandant said.

"You're not?!"

"Unless you want us to."

"No, Ma'am. I really want to stay. But I'm not sure that would be fair to Plebe MacGregor."

"She told me she'd be disappointed if we kicked you out," Commandant Lewis said. "And you and she both know that she's going to have a target on her back after yesterday."

"I'm sorry, Ma'am."

"Well, sorry isn't going to help Plebe MacGregor. I'll let you know your punishment after I've had some time to think about it. For now, you are still restricted to quarters."

"Yes, Ma'am. And thank you for not kicking me out."

"Dismissed."

Blake entered the commandant's office from a side door, "Well, that was interesting."

"I'd say so," Commandant Lewis said.

"So, why did you want me here?" Blake asked.

"I wanted your input on what we should do with Cadet Baker."

"Not about Plebe MacGregor?"

"I think she'll be fine. As you heard, I've decided not to expel Cadet Baker."

"What's his story?"

"Well, you heard the interview with him. He claims he was overcompensating for the emphasis on women and just let his temper get away from him."

"He sounded plausible. And appeared to be honestly apologetic," Blake said.

"He did, and he was," the commandant said. "What do you think about his punishment?"

"It's your decision," Blake said. "I'll support whatever you decide."

"I'm inclined to give him a second chance as a cadet officer. Move him down to command one of the flights instead of the squadron," Commandant Lewis said. "But, I'm concerned about retaliation against Plebe MacGregor."

"I think that should be a concern regardless of what you do with Baker," Blake said. "One thing you might consider is sending him on to Guatemala early, as part of an advance team. That would obscure the punishment and let tempers cool, and a few extra days down there will allow the instructors there to take care of discipline."

"I like that idea. I'll talk to my staff and see if we can make that work. Do you think Plebe MacGregor will be able to deal with the flack she's going to be getting?"

"It looks like she's pretty unflappable. I read the file you gave me. If your staff does their job, then she should be fine."

"I tend to agree; she's quite the young lady."

"I agree."

"You wouldn't happen to know the story behind that flag in her file?"

"Nope, might be something about that rebel streak she seems to have."

"Maybe. Admiral, I want to thank you for stopping by."

"My pleasure."

"How much trouble are you in?" Joanie asked.

"I don't know, but if you don't get showered and dressed, we're both going to be in trouble."

"I just got back from PT," Joanie said. "I've got six more minutes. Rumor is that Cadet Major Baker has come down with a serious flu."

"I'm not surprised; now go shower!"

The next morning it was announced that Cadet Major Baker would be leading an advance team to prepare Guatemala for the first experience with the Academy class. There were some hints that he would be running the obstacle courses multiple times to make sure they were suitable for cadets.

"Plebe MacGregor, you seem to be up on all the proper labels," one of the first-class cadets hollered during lunch. "What do they call a sailor who serves on a surface ship?"

"Sir, this Plebe doesn't know of a particular label," Catie replied.

"What would you suggest as a proper label?"

"Wet comes to mind," Catie replied, eliciting laughs from almost everyone at the table.

"Then what would you call a sailor who serves on a space carrier?"

"Vacuum packed," Catie replied, which got everyone laughing.

"Then what would you call a Marine?"

"I would call a Marine *whatever* they told me to call them," Catie said.

"Hey, she's smarter than I thought," the first-class cadet said.

"That was good," Joanie said. "But, you know they're going to keep riding you."

"That's what I would do in their place," Catie said.

# 8 Finally, A Break

"Hey, we survived the Beast!" Joanie said as she and Catie made it to their room to pack for the weekend.

All the cadets got a two-day break between the first phase of Basic and the advanced training in Guatemala. They would get to spend the weekend with their families, or if their families lived too far away, their Academy family, locals who had offered to sponsor a cadet so they would be able to enjoy some family life during their years at the Academy.

"I'm looking forward to the break," Catie said. "Are you staying in Delphi City?"

"Yes, I've been assigned to a family here," Joanie said. "I hope they're fun."

"Hey, at least they won't be yelling at you every minute."

"That's true. You know, I could sleep the whole two days."

"Sounds nice," Catie said as she checked to see who she'd been assigned to. To her amazement, she had been assigned Dr. Sharmila as her Academy family.

"Hey, ADI, is this right? Dr. Sharmila and the twins are going to be my Academy family?" Catie messaged ADI.

"Yes, Cer Catie. She and your father discussed it and felt that the risk was minimal. Your mother and father wanted you to have someone familiar to spend the time with," ADI replied.

"Alex, what's up?" Joanie asked as Catie dropped out of their conversation.

"I was just checking out my Academy family. It's a doctor, and she has two young daughters."

"That might be fun. I'm packed, so I'm out of here!"

"See you Sunday night."

"Definitely! Bye."

"Hello," Catie called out as she knocked on the door to Dr. Sharmila's condo. She'd texted her as soon as she was packed and on her way out of the dorm.

"Catie!" she heard one of the twins squeal through the door.

"No! It's Alex, dummy!" the other twin said.

"Oh right! Hey Alex!" Prisha and Aisha said as they opened the door.

"Hey you two. I've missed you!" Catie pulled them both into a hug.

"We've missed you too. You have to tell us all about the Academy!"

"Well, I don't know that much about the Academy, but I do know a lot about basic training."

"Like what?"

"Like you get yelled at a lot," Catie said.

"Catie, come on in," Dr. Sharmila said. "You're staying in Aisha's room. They sleep together most nights anyway," Dr. Sharmila said from the kitchen. "Let me put this in the oven, then I'll join you and the girls."

Catie let the twins drag her to the other side of the condo, where their rooms were. "You're in here," Aisha said. "I cleaned it up for you."

"That's nice," Catie said. "Don't you normally clean it up?"

"Once in a while," Prisha said. "But usually we're too busy."

"Doing what?"

"Going to school, studying, exercising!"

"Exercising?"

"Yeah, we have to stay in shape. Kal counts on us to do microgravity tag with his guys."

"Has anyone caught you yet?"

"Nope!" they said. One of them did a backflip to demonstrate the type of exercises they did.

"Well, I've been doing lots of exercise at the Academy," Catie said.

"What kinds of exercises?"

"Running, and this thing they call the Engine," Catie said as she demonstrated the Engine for the girls.

"That looks easy!"

"Yes, but they want you to do it perfectly," Catie said.

"Like this?" the twins said as they started doing the Engine.

"Oh, no! You can't bend your arm toward your knee; they have to stay parallel to the ground. Nope, keep those arms perpendicular to your chest. Now, shoulders back," Catie corrected.

"Really, I think I'm doing them right!"

"You might be, but I'm still going to yell at you and tell you to fix your form anyway." Catie started laughing.

"Why?!"

"I think they do it so you learn how to perform under stress, but sometimes I think they just like to be mean."

"Well, then I would just ignore them."

"No, that would make them mad," Catie said. "You have to make a little adjustment to let them know you heard them, or they'll just keep yelling at you."

"That doesn't sound like fun!"

"It's not really, but if you think about it like you're performing in front of a big crowd and they're yelling for you, it's easier to take," Catie said while thinking, *"at least that's what I told myself."*

Catie and the twins walked back into the family area of the condo.

"Catie, is it alright if your mother comes over?" Dr. Sharmila asked. "Since we're colleagues, I don't think anyone will take notice, and she would like to see you."

"Of course, it's alright," Catie said. She wondered if her mother had cooled off from reading Sophia's book.

"Good, she'll be here in about an hour since she'll be getting off from work soon."

Catie and the twins spent the time playing a video game. Each of them had a Fox; it was supposed to be a free-for-all, but as usual, the twins joined forces and attacked the other player, Catie.

"Girls, go do your homework," Dr. Sharmila said when Linda messaged that she was on her way.

"We're playing with Catie."

"Her mother is on her way. So you need to go do homework so that Catie and her mother can spend some time together."

"Are you in trouble?" the twins asked Catie.

"I hope not."

"Girls!"

The twins got up and headed to Prisha's room, moaning the whole way.

"Hi, Mommy," Catie greeted her mother as she opened the door.

"Hi, Sweetie," Linda said as she pulled Catie into a hug. "How is the Academy?"

"Hard."

"Hard?"

"There's always someone yelling at you," Catie said. "It really wears on you."

"I'm sure it would," Linda said. "But as I recall, that gets better once classes start."

"As you recall?"

"Yes, I was dating your father when Blake went to the Academy. He had a hard time in Basic."

"Uncle Blake?"

"Yes, your Uncle Blake. He didn't like being yelled at all the time either," Linda said. "He came home during the break before the second half of Basic. I remember him punching a few walls."

"I'd like to punch some walls, but I don't want to hurt my hand."

"Blake told me that you're going to Guatemala next week?"

"Yes, for field training," Catie said.

"Hmm, I'm not so sure I like that."

"I was going to go do it anyway," Catie said. "Everyone in Delphi Forces has to go."

"Well, I think a fifteen-year-old girl should be waiting until she's older," Linda said.

"No way!"

"Especially a fifteen-year-old girl who was kidnapped by a Moroccan crime lord when she was twelve."

Catie grimaced. "Aren't you over that yet?!"

"We haven't talked about it."

"I was hoping we didn't have to," Catie said.

"Why didn't you ever tell me about it?"

"Because I didn't want you to make me come home," Catie said. "It was all over by the next day."

"Yes, but it had to have traumatized you."

"Not really, I woke up in the car trunk. I talked to Daddy when I woke up, and then they shoved me into that cabin on the fishing boat. Daddy and everyone came and got me after that. The worst part was that I needed to pee and didn't want to ask those thugs."

"If you weren't my daughter, I'd say you were weird," Linda said, trying hard not to laugh or cry.

"Daddy took care of the guy who kidnapped me," Catie said.

"I know; he had ADI show me what they did to rescue you."

"Then you know."'

"Yes, but it still terrifies me that you keep taking all these risks," Linda said.

"Hey, the kidnapping wasn't my fault," Catie said.

"I know, but I saw you demanding to go on their mission to capture Omar Harrak. I wish you weren't so adventurous."
"You mean crazy?"
"I was trying to be nice."

"Well, you should know that my goal is to captain my new cargo ship," Catie said. "Liz and I are partners, and we've formed a new company."

"That sounds safe, but then why are you going to the Academy?"

"Because *Daddy says* that you have to be an Academy graduate to captain a starship," Catie said.

"He told me that."

"Are you and he talking?" Catie asked.

"After I beat on his chest for ten minutes we talked," Linda said. "He told me that you and Samantha sneaked out somehow. That wasn't very nice of you to run away."

"Maybe not. I like to think of it as a strategic retreat," Catie said. "You didn't hurt Daddy, did you?"

"You can't hurt your father. I only pound on his chest because I know it doesn't really hurt him. And it lets him know how mad I am." Linda started to laugh, "I do have a terrible temper," she said. "I hope you didn't inherit it."

"Maybe just a little," Catie said.

"Well, you better be careful with that at the Academy, or you'll be in trouble."

"I know."

◆ ◆ ◆

"So, what are your plans for the weekend?" Sharmila asked Catie after they sat down to dinner.

"I have to check on the design of the StarMerchant," Catie said. "I've had zero private time for the last three weeks. I need to do a walkthrough."

"You are doing too much," Linda said. "Can't you just focus on one thing at a time?"

"You have more than one patient at a time; I have more than one project at a time," Catie said. "And I have to check up on some work that Nikola and Artie are doing for me."

"How are you going to do that?" Linda asked, pointing to Catie's black hair.

"I'll do a virtual tour of the ship, using my Avatar," Catie said. "I couldn't even manage that at the Academy. Same thing with Artie and Nikola. It won't be that unusual."

"I don't know; I think you're too busy," Linda said.

"Strange to hear that from Dr. McCormack, *who worked eighty-hour weeks* back in San Diego," Catie said.

"Now, children, play nice," Dr. Sharmila said.

"Sorry," Catie and Linda said together.

"What are we going to do?" the twins asked.

"What do you want to do?" Catie replied.

"We want to go to the space station and work out on the obstacle course," the twins said.

"I can check to see if Liz can get us a ride up," Catie said. "I can't just grab a Lynx like I used to."

"Oh, right, you're just Alex now," the twins said.

"What else do you want to do?"

"Can we go outside and practice our exosuit maneuvers?"

"If Liz has time," Catie said. It required special clearance to go outside on a spacewalk, and although Catie McCormack could have someone issue the necessary permission at any time, Alex MacGregor could not.

"When are you going to be finished at the Academy?" the twins asked, obviously not happy to be losing their main conduit to special privileges in Delphi City and Delphi Station.

"Probably one year," Catie said. "I sure hope it's not two."

"Us too!"

"ADI, I need you to turn off your surveillance of me for the next two hours," Catie said.

"Oh, you're going to get even with Sophia!" ADI said, sounding like an excited little girl.

"Who knows," Catie said. "The surveillance."

"Oh, let me come along."

"I can't; you would rat me out."

"No I won't. My surveillance of you is compartmentalized, so as long as you don't do anything that I would have known about without surveillance, and you tell me to switch to privacy mode, I won't be able to report it. So can I come?"

"Sure, that'll work."

"I assume we're going to go get that thing you had printed," ADI said.

"You know about that?!"

"Same rule applies," ADI said.

"Good, and yes, we're going to get the gizmo I had printed."

"Gizmo, a small mechanical or electronic device with an unspecified practical use," ADI said.

"Yeah, that's what it is," Catie said.

She left Dr. Sharmila's condo, careful not to wake the twins. Then she ran down to the corner where the printer was and got her gadget, stuffed it into her backpack, and headed towards the Michaels' condo building. She had a light hoodie on over her shipsuit. With the hood up and knowledge of where the cameras were, she was able to avoid giving a clear shot of her face.

"Oh, this is why you hacked into the systems and scheduled maintenance for this condo building," ADI said, guessing at what Catie had planned.

"Yes," Catie said. She walked around to the back where the service van was; then, she sneaked into the building using the Comm she had programmed as belonging to one of the workers.

"Hmm, we should close that security gap," ADI said.

"Later."

"Yes, I'll close it tomorrow. Of course, that will provide you more cover unless someone spots the timing of the change."

"Thanks."

Catie used the elevator to get to the top floor, where Sophia Michaels lived with her parents. She then made her way to the utility closet. The service crew was working on the floor below, so she had no trouble entering the closet and climbing up into the crawlspace in the ceiling. She made her way to the area above Sophia's bathroom. She clamped her gizmo to the hot water line that led to Sophia's shower; then, she twisted the screw until it pierced the line, making a connection. Catie reversed the screw so her surprise could flow into the line, then she flipped the switch on and ran a few tests before she pronounced everything ready.

Then Catie made her way back to the utility closet and retraced her steps out of the building. When she made it back to Sharmila's condo, she carefully snuck back inside and ducked back into the room that she was borrowing for the weekend.

She brought up a display on her HUD and reran the tests she'd run in the crawlspace. Everything checked out, so she went back to bed.

"Okay, I give up. What did you do?" ADI asked.

"You'll see," Catie said.

"I don't want to wait; it'll be more fun if I know," ADI said.

"When did you start whining like a little girl?" Catie asked.

"When I stopped getting my way."

"Okay, in ten days when Sophia takes her morning shower, she'll get a little surprise," Catie said.

"Ten days; so you want to put distance between your opportunity to act and the act itself."

"Exactly."

"And what is the act going to be?"

"That you'll have to wait for."

"Pooh, but I will get to see it happen," ADI said. "See if I share the video with you!"

"That's okay. I'm sure I'll hear all about it."

"Are you guys ready to go to Delphi Station?" Catie asked the twins.

"We're more than ready!"

"Okay, we're meeting Liz at the airport. She is taking an Oryx up so she can give us a ride. It's not as nice as flying in the Lynx, but we don't have to wait."

"We like the Oryx," the twins said.

"Hey, Liz," Catie said as she and the twins arrived at the airport.

"Hey, Alex," Liz said, giving Catie the once over. "I like this look better than Keala."

"I do too," Catie said. "I'm more like myself."

"We like the green eyes," the twins said.

"They're still talking in unison?" Liz asked.

"Most of the time," Catie said.

"Hey!"

"Hey, yourself. You're the ones who keep behaving like you're just one person. It confuses the rest of us," Liz said.

The twins giggled. "Let's go!"

"Hang onto your panties, we have to wait until the Oryx is loaded," Liz said.

"We're not wearing panties," the twins said, alluding to the fact that the shipsuits had a built-in panty liner and were designed to be the only thing touching the body so they could manage the heat and moisture.

"Who are they rooming with?" Liz asked.

"They have their own room," Catie said.

"Good."

"Ah, there's our signal," Liz said. "Come on, your Oryx awaits."

"What are we carrying?" Catie asked as she and Liz settled into the cockpit.

"Kitchen appliances," Liz said. "They're finishing out the last two levels of ring three."

"No way!" Catie exclaimed.

"Of section one," Liz said.

"Oh, that makes more sense. I guess you would have said ring six if it was section two."

"Only if I remembered," Liz said. "Now, do you want to fly her?"

"You bet! It's been four weeks," Catie said.

"It's going to be a long year."

"You're telling me."

Once they reached Delphi Station, they handed off their luggage to one of the stewards and headed directly to the microgravity obstacle course. There was no way they could put up with the twins whining if they delayed that.

"Hey, Liz, hi, Prisha and Aisha. I see those two found a new victim."

"Hi, Randy. This is Alex, and yes, the twins talked me into bringing them up here so they could torment her," Liz replied.

"Well, I just finished cleaning it up. The last group didn't do that well in the microgravity."

"Tourists?"

"Unfortunately, no. A couple of new security guys. They'll adapt, this is their first trip up. If they don't adapt, there's plenty of work for them in Delphi City."

"They made you clean it up?" Liz asked.

"Well, the bots did most of the work," Randy said. "Now, you're not going to get sick on me, are you?"

"I don't think so," Catie said. She did a quick flip to show him that she was comfortable in the microgravity.

"Good, because I have to clean the bots," Randy said, laughing as he walked on by.

"Okay, how do you guys want to do this?" Catie asked the twins.

"Us against you and Liz."

"That doesn't sound fair. Has anyone ever tagged one of you?"

"No way!"

"You might as well give in," Liz said. "You know that they'll turn it into them against us no matter how you divide the teams."

"That's true," Catie said. "So, we chase you?"

"Sure!"

"Gotcha," Catie said as she reached out and tagged one of the twins.

"No fair! We get a ten-second head start."

"Then go!"

The twins raced through the door and bounced off the ceiling.

"Well, that's the last time you get to tag one of them," Liz said.

"Except when they're chasing us."

"There is that."

"Get!" Catie shouted as she kicked one of the twins in the butt.

"You're just a sore loser," the twins yelled back.

"Sore is right," Liz said, rubbing her shoulder. "You know you shouldn't have kicked her; you could have hurt her."

"No I couldn't. Besides the lack of gravity, the shipsuit would have distributed the impact over a bigger area," Catie said.

"Huh?" Liz said.

"Yeah, what do you mean?" the twins said, risking coming back into range of Catie's foot.

"The suits will spread a high force impact over a larger area," Catie said.

"How?" Liz asked.

"You know they're filled with a thin layer of material?"

"Sure, that's what conducts the heat away," Liz said.

"Well, it also acts like Silly Putty, and distributes small-area, high-impact blows over a larger area."

"What's Silly Putty?" the twins asked.

"You've never played with Silly Putty?"

"No!"

"Well, it's a putty that you can play with like clay, but if you roll it into a ball and throw it against the wall, it will bounce."

"Cool!"

"It helps to protect you against small, fast-moving rocks when you're in space. And it also helps to lessen the force against one of your joints if you get in a bind," Catie said.

"I could have used that when I played basketball at the Academy," Liz said. "I really messed my knee up one year taking a charge."

"It probably would have helped," Catie said.

"Maybe we should design some braces and such for athletes using this," Liz said.

"Might be a good business. I'll ask Nikola and Marcie to look into it."

"Can we have some Silly Putty?" the twins asked.

"I'll get some of the stuff they use in our suits and get it to you before I go back to school," Catie said. "Now get!" Catie wound up her leg like she was going to kick one of them again.

The twins just giggled and bounced up to the ceiling, and then stuck their tongues out at Catie.

"Okay, while we have some time to ourselves, what are the plans for testing the Sakira's jumpdrive?" Catie asked Liz while the twins raced ahead to their cabins.

"ADI's going to fly her out and do a few jumps," Liz said. "We just need to verify that the drives are big enough to handle the Sakira. I don't see a reason to have anyone aboard when we do the test, do you?"

"I guess not. And that will let you get the test done in just a few days. You could get someone on the Enterprise to be in her when she jumps; but you're right, we've already proven the drives, this is just about size."

"Glad you agree, because she's already on her way."

That afternoon, Catie wrapped her hair into a bun, "Lots of practice doing that at the Academy," she thought. Then she put on a beret to hide her black hair. "Dr. McDowell barely notices me anyway. If he says something, I'll tell him I'm trying out a new look."

Catie walked down the passageway to Dr. McDowell's lab. There weren't very many people out and about, so she only had to acknowledge three people with a polite nod of her head. There wasn't any recognition on their parts, and she didn't know them either.

"Dr. McDowell?" Catie announced herself.

"Huh?"

"Dr. McDowell, it's Catie. I came by for an update."

"Oh sure. Give me a minute."

Catie waited ten minutes while Dr. McDowell finished up the equation he was working on.

Frustrated, he tossed the piece of chalk he was using into the tray and wiped the chalk dust off on his pants.

"You know you could put a whiteboard in here," Catie suggested.

"Yes, but I can't stand the smell."

"Then how about a big digital drawing tablet? It would be just like a whiteboard, but you'd use a stylus."

"That would be nice; how big a one can I have?"

"I can have one made as big as you'd like, or you could have three of them," Catie said. "I think it will take a couple of days, but then you could avoid all that chalk dust."

"Three would be nice."

"They'll be here next week," Catie said.

"Thank you, now what can I do for you?"

"A status update on the jump ships."

"It'll work, but I'm still trying to figure out how to best compensate for the drift between the four vessels."

"Why are they drifting?"

"Because, although they are only a few hundred meters apart, the speed of light is finite, and their positions do change."

"Oh, I'll talk to Ajda, she can give you instantaneous position information."

"Instantaneous?"

"Quantum coupled communication," Catie said.

"Of course, you would have that," Dr. McDowell said. "Then, I should be able to redefine some formulas and have a working model in a few weeks."

"Great. How big an object can we move?"

"I'm not sure yet. We'll have to start small and learn as we go."

"Okay, thank you, and please keep me posted," Catie said, knowing she was unlikely to get any updates from him.

"ADI, please make it look like I'm in my condo in Delphi City," Catie requested.

"You do know that you can set that up with your Comm," ADI said.

"I do, but I thought you liked to help me," Catie said.

"I do, but I want to make sure you're not stuck if I'm too busy."

"Are you ever too busy?"

"Sometimes," ADI said. "It's a lot of work to manage a space station. And when the space carriers are active, I can get very busy."

"Oh, and Daddy is planning to move the Victory here soon, isn't he?"

"Yes, he is. Your Avatar is ready."

"Thank you, ADI."

"You're welcome, Cer Catie."

"Nikola," Catie messaged.

"Hi, Catie. You're a little earlier than I expected."

"I didn't spend as much time with Dr. McDowell as I had planned."

"Is that good news?" Nikola asked.

"Sort of, he's says he'll be ready to run tests in a few weeks. I had to tell him about the quantum relays."

"Well, since he's working on FTL jumps, that's not a very big reveal."

"No, it's not, and if he'd told Ajda what he was struggling with, I'm sure she would have told him."

"We all know that communication is not his strength," Nikola said with a giggle.

"That's an understatement."

"Let me show you what I've done with the mini-Comms," Nikola said. "I've made these prototypes just using blocks of polysteel since we're not changing the Comm itself."

"Okay."

"Here you can see where I've added a layer with an inlay," Nikola said as she displayed a three-centimeter square of polysteel with jeweled inlays. The inlays were made of small pieces of turquoise embedded in the polyglass. They were arranged in a mostly symmetrical pattern with thin strips of silver separating the pale blue turquoise rectangles.

"That's beautiful," Catie said.

"Thank you. Now I know you're not much of a jewelry person, but most women hate to show up somewhere to find someone else wearing the exact same piece of jewelry, so I suggest you do these in limited quantities. We have lots of gems to choose from, ruby, jade, lapis, opals, even seashells," Nikola said.

"Wow, this is complicated."

"Just hire a jewelry designer; they'll have a ball," Nikola said. "I've also made this."

Nikola brought out a piece of material that was about the same size as the mini-Comm. Then she brought out a model of a mini-Comm that had a small depression in its face. She slipped the material into the depression and it snapped into place.

"It's held in place by an electrostatic charge. You have to use a little suction cup to remove it," Nikola said. "But you can make these in any color or combination of colors you want. Then your customers can change the inlay to match their outfit."

"That's cool."

"That's a big thing with women; even some men will want to change things around. And these are inexpensive to make," Nikola added. "I wish you were here, then you could feel them. They have a nice cool feel, I tested them on an actual Comm, and they go from cool to warm depending on how much you use your Comm. Or you can set the Comm to hold them at a specific temperature."

"Okay, so can you work with Marcie to hire a jeweler? And I guess we should start making and selling them."

"Not a problem. Marcie and I were just waiting for your okay."

"Great, then go ahead."

"Wonderful. Oh, by the way, Leo figured out your iris. He needs you to approve a prototype with Ajda."

"Wow, that was fast. I'm talking to Ajda next. I'll have her contact him."

Catie managed a virtual walkthrough of the StarMerchant with Ajda. There were lots of small details that she hadn't thought of, but would make running the ship simpler. She was glad that Ajda was taking care of everything, but thought it kind of sucked that she couldn't be more involved.

# 9 Guatemala

"Welcome to Guatemala," a Marine sergeant major yelled. "I hear you've been having a nice vacation back at the Academy. Well, that's over, your asses belong to me now!"

"Oh gawd, if he thinks we were on vacation, what does he think hard training is!" Catie wondered.

"Form up!" the sergeant major yelled. He bent down and grabbed a handful of mud. "I want to introduce you to your new best friend. We call it *el cieno* down here!" He walked over to Cadet Lieutenant Hoffman and smeared some of it on his face; then, he walked down the ranks smearing it on the faces of each cadet in the first row.

"You will learn to crawl in it, dig in it, wear it, throw it, love it!" the sergeant major yelled. "Now everyone, bend down, get a big handful of it and cover your face, then I want you to start marching. . . . Left face! March! Double time! March!"

Foxtrot Squadron started running in step. The sergeant major ran backward as he moved up and down their line, yelling at them to pick up the pace.

"I heard Foxtrot was a badass squadron, did I hear wrong?!"

"No! Sergeant Major!"

"Then show me what you got. Pick up the pace!"

"Just what we needed, a nice ten-K to warm up," Joanie moaned when they finally were allowed to check into the barracks.

"Don't forget all those lovely push-ups," Catie said.

"Oh, how could I forget those. Right down in the mud," Joanie replied. "And that mud stinks."

"Get your shower, or I'm going first, and you can wait," Catie said.

"Get down in that mud!" the sergeant major yelled at Catie.

She pushed herself deeper into the mud as she shimmied along under the barbwire. She didn't have to worry too much about the wire scratching her, her shipsuit was virtually impervious to it, but the sadists here in Guatemala had realized that so the wire was electrified. With the wet mud as a ground, even getting close to the wire was enough to give you a real jolt.

"Keep moving! What are you doing, taking a nap!"

*"Oh Lord, please let me meet the sergeant major in the microgravity obstacle course one day,"* Catie silently prayed as she pushed harder into the mud with her boots, scooting through the ooze faster.

Finally, reaching the end of the barbwire, Catie jumped up and started running toward the wall. She leapt up and grabbed the rope about three meters up, and continued to go up hand over hand to the top of the wall.

"MacGregor, we are not kangaroos, go back down and climb up again!" one of the instructors yelled at her.

*"Give me a break!"* Catie hissed under her breath as she slid down the rope to start the climb over.

"Move it! There are others coming!"

Over the wall, through the tires, across the rail, over the teeter-totter, Catie ran. Finally, she reached the end of the course, where she literally took a shower with her shipsuit on.

"I hate **mud!"** she hissed.

"You're telling me!" Cadet Walters said. "Do you think they just pump this stuff back out there?" He pointed back toward the slime channel they'd had to crawl through.

"Probably."

"Just shoot me!" Joanie cried as she made it to the showers.

"We can't, but ask again next week when we're on the rifle range," Catie said.

"I just might!"

"I sure hope next week is better," Joanie said when she and Catie made it to their room for the night.

"Hey, at least we're still getting to sleep in a bed. I hear we'll be out in the field more often than not, starting tomorrow," Catie said.

"Rats!"

"It's just two more weeks."

"We will survive," Joanie belted out the refrain. "Hey, I'm going down to the mess hall. Julie and I are going to work on our Delphi Facts. Do you want to come?"

"No, I've got some things to do here," Catie said.

"See ya."

"ADI, surveillance off," Catie said.

"Oh, are you finally going to spring your trap?"

"I'm going to arm it," Catie said.

"When will it go off?"

"0700 in Delphi City; 1100 here."

"When you'll be conveniently occupied at the rifle range," ADI said.

"That's the plan."

"Has anyone ever fired an M4 before?" the sergeant major asked.

Catie reluctantly raised her hand. She had thought about not admitting it but figured she would give herself away anyway.

"Cadet MacGregor, when did you fire one?"

"Sergeant Major, last year, a friend took me to a firing range and taught me to fire it," Catie said.

"Did he teach you how to clean it?"

"Yes, Sergeant Major. And we also learned how to do that in Basic."

"How fast can you tear one down and put it back together?"

"I don't know, Sergeant Major; I've never timed myself," Catie said.

"Well, come up here, and we'll time you!"

"Yes, Sergeant Major!" Catie barked as she moved to the front. *"Damn, how fast should I do it?"* she wondered.

"The field manual specifies that you should be able to field strip it in one hundred fifty seconds," the sergeant major said as he handed the rifle to Catie. "Begin."

Catie ejected the magazine and checked the chamber to make sure there wasn't a round in it.

"Very good! You can see that Cadet MacGregor likes that pretty face of hers and doesn't want to have powder burns on it, or worse, shoot herself or one of us!"

Catie ignored the sergeant major's narrative of her efforts as she stripped the rifle down, checked its components for wear or defects, and then reassembled it.

"Nice, one hundred twenty-five seconds to strip it down, and only one hundred seconds to reassemble it. Of course, you haven't put the magazine back in it."

Catie jammed the magazine back into the rifle, then handed it to the sergeant major.

"No, I don't want it, I want to see you shoot. Prone position, fire downrange!"

Catie lay down, positioned herself for the shot, and fired.

"Keep firing, I want ten shots!" the sergeant major ordered as he used his pocket scope to see how she did.

"Nice shooting, you had a good teacher," the sergeant major said. "Let's see you do that from the kneeling position."

Catie fired off ten more rounds, hoping that the sergeant major would start teaching the others how to shoot and leave her alone.

"Folks, we have us a regular sharpshooter here. MacGregor, you can help out teaching the rest of these maggots how to shoot."

"Where did you learn to shoot like that?" Joanie asked as Catie was coaching her.

"Like I said, a friend took me out to the range," Catie said.

"Yeah, but it had to be more than once."

"It was; he liked to shoot," Catie said. She couldn't say that Kal, the Marine Commandant had been her teacher. "By the way, do you still want me to shoot you?"

"No! I'm doing better this week. But I'm still finding mud in my hair, my ears, and some other places I won't mention."

"You'd swear the stuff moves on its own," Catie said. "Now relax and exhale as you squeeze the trigger."

At seven o'clock, Sophia Michaels finally got around to taking her shower. She made a point of starting out late on weekends. Her mother tolerated it since she was always ready to leave the condo by seven a.m. on the weekdays, even though she sometimes stayed home to do her schoolwork or write the articles for the Delphi Gazette.

As Sophia was rinsing her hair, the device Catie had installed in the ceiling injected its load into the hot water line. Catie had timed it to go off two minutes after the hot water started to run. Once its load was injected into the hot water line, the device fused the hole that was in the metal band around the line, sealing it. Then it released a spring that bounced it off the line and over a few feet. It landed with a soft thump, then fused its circuit board into a solid lump. That opened a small vial of acid which ate away at the plastic. As it ate the plastic, it wicked more of the acid from the vial to feed its hunger. Before Sophia finished washing her hair, the device was an indistinct lump of plastic with some metal mixed in.

Sophia had just finished rinsing her hair when she opened her eyes and saw green on her hands. She blinked, then tried to rinse her hands, the color wouldn't come off.

"Oh no!" she cried as she quickly exited the shower. She looked in the mirror. Her hair and part of her face were green. "Catie! I'm going to kill you!"

"What's the problem?" her mother called out.

"I'm green!"

"What?!"

"I'm green!" Sophia wrapped a towel around herself and exited her bathroom.

"Oh, my. You are green," her mother said. "Did you try washing it off?"

"I was taking a shower when it happened!"

"Let's see," her mother said. Mrs. Michaels walked into the bathroom and turned the shower on. Clear water ran from the nozzle. She stuck her hand into the water and brought it out. It was clean.

"Were you washing your hair?"

"Yes!"

Mrs. Michaels squeezed some of the shampoo onto her hand, then washed it off. Then she tried the conditioner. "Doesn't seem to be the soap. Did you use anything else?"

"No! It's Catie. She's getting even for my book!" Sophia wailed.

"You knew she would," Mrs. Michaels said.

"But, green! How am I going to go out in public?"

"We can go to the clinic and see if they can get it off," Mrs. Michaels offered.

"Ohhhhhh! I'm going to kill her!"

"Then she'll have to get even again, it'll become a vicious cycle. You should stop while you're ahead."

"You call this being ahead?"

"You've still got the money from the book, you're alive and well, even if you're a bit green. Get dressed, and we'll go see what they can do at the clinic. While you dress, I'll call building maintenance to have them check on the water."

Five thousand miles away, Catie watched as Sophia and her mother exited their condo. Sophia was wearing sunglasses and a scarf to cover her hair and most of her face. Catie smiled, "Gotcha!"

◆ ◆ ◆

"Form up, we're going to send you on a march all by yourselves!" the sergeant major yelled.

Foxtrot One formed into two lines, prepared to march with a full load, thirty kilos of equipment in their packs, and one kilo of water in their canteens.

"Cadet Lieutenant Hoffman, take them out."

"Too bad by ourselves didn't mean without that idiot," Joanie whispered.

"Right face! Forward march!" Hoffman ordered. "Double time, march!"

Catie noticed that for some reason, Hoffman wasn't carrying a pack. *"What a wuss!"*

One hour later, they reached the turnaround point. Everyone was familiar with the ten-K route out from the main base.

"Water break!" Hoffman ordered.

"About time," Julie said under her breath. "What a jerk!"

"Hey, I have to pee," Mary said.

"So!"

"I need an escort, do any of you need to go?"

"I'm hoping to hold it until we get back," Julie said.

"If you need to go, you'd better do it now," Joanie said. "If you make him stop on the way back, he'll have a fit."

"Sir, permission for a bathroom break?" Mary asked.

"Any more of you women need to *squat*?!" Hoffman asked. He really emphasized the word squat.

"Sir, I'll escort her," Julie said, avoiding having to request to pee.

"Go ahead, you other two better not make me stop on the way back!"

"Ass," Joanie whispered as Julie and Mary headed out.

◆ ◆ ◆

"How did you two manage that whole march without having to pee?" Mary asked Catie and Joanie when they got back.

"Yeah," Julie said. "And you didn't go after the rifle drill either."

"Didn't they issue your armor yet?" Catie asked.

"Yes, but how would that help?" Julie asked.

"You do know your shipsuit wicks all the moisture away from your body?" Catie asked.

"Yeah!"

"And you know where it goes?"

"Eww, you don't mean you pee in your suit, then squeeze that pad out?"

"No! but your armor has a little bottle that you can swap for the pad," Catie said. "It fits in the same place inside your left thigh. It collects most of the moisture and all of the moisture from below your waist. Whenever you get a chance, you can just pour it out. Should take care of your needs for a few hours."

"That still sounds gross," Mary said.

"What do you think fighter pilots do when they're up for five or six hours?" Catie asked. "That's why the suits are designed that way. At least it wicks it into a bottle instead of acting like Pampers."

"Hey, if I can avoid Hoffman and his squat comments, I'm good with anything," Julie said.

"He sure seems to have a problem with women," Catie said.

"Yeah, but it looks like Baker is over his," Joanie said.

"He just lost his temper because he couldn't make Alex squirm," Julie said, giving Catie a smile.

# 10 Board Meeting – August 2nd

When Catie made it to her room on Monday, she saw a message that said that the board meeting had been moved to 3:00 p.m. That meant she would be able to attend. She set her Comm up to use her Avatar and lay down in her bunk. It was just after chow, so things should be quiet for at least an hour.

"Good afternoon, sorry about the sudden schedule change, but I had some issues I needed to take care of," Marc said as he entered the boardroom. "I see everyone is set. And I see that Catie is calling in."

"Hi," Catie said. Of course, she typed that in her Comm, and her Avatar spoke for her. "The schedule change moved the meeting into an empty slot for me."

"Glad to have you," Marc said. "Now, Blake, what's the status of a commander for Delphi Station?"

"Captain Clark has agreed to take the slot," Blake said. "He's just getting settled in, so I thought I'd cover for him this month."

"Okay, then *cover*," Marc said.

"We've made some changes to encourage people to set up permanent residence on Delphi Station. You can have a private cabin if you pay the extra rent, but you can no longer have both a condo in Delphi City and a cabin on Delphi Station unless you pay the exorbitant rent."

"Boo," Liz said. "I saw my new bill."

"I just sent that to you to wake you up," Blake said. "Catie's covering you."

"Good!"

"I'm covering you and the rent for a cabin for my bodyguards. The bodyguards that Kal makes me have!" Catie whined.

"You can afford it," Kal said. "Besides, it gives them a treat to have a nice cabin on Delphi Station."

"Moving on," Blake said. "We now have twelve hundred permanent residents on the Station, and we also have eighteen hundred potential colonists camping out up there. I'll send that bill to Sam."

"In your dreams," Samantha said.

"On a more serious note, we also have two hundred Paraxeans now living on the Station. They're the ones Liz brought back from her trip out to their asteroid. They'll be prepping for the Paraxeans' eventual move to Mangkatar."

"How are they going to get there?" Admiral Michaels asked.

"This group will go out on the Roebuck and the Sakira," Blake said. "If you haven't heard, we have renamed the Paraxean space carriers the DSS Galileo and the DSS Isaac Newton. They're converting three of the Galileo's flight bays to hold cargo and colonists."

"They're not going to transport them in stasis pods, are they?" Samantha asked.

"They will be waking them up to transport them. In the beginning, they'll want to provide extra training here where we have the facilities to accommodate them. The loss of their cargo vessel changes a lot for them."

"How many will it be able to carry?" Samantha asked.

"If you're asking how many will the Victory be able to carry, then the answer is twenty thousand, give or take," Blake said. "The Galileo will handle a similar number, but they'll probably need more cargo space."

"Thank you."

"That brings up another issue," Marc said. "We need space for at least six thousand colonists. Can we accommodate that many on Delphi Station?"

"If they're willing to camp," Fred said. "We have the room, but we don't have that many finished cabins."

"I think camping will be fine. We need to set up a cafeteria to feed them. That's what we'll be doing on Artemis, so getting them used to it will be good. But eventually, we'll need to be able to handle twenty or thirty thousand," Marc said.

"Then we're going to need to light a fire under the construction team. You can get about two thousand in a condo building, so if they finish up the eight we have going up in the new city section, that's sixteen thousand. They're going to have to camp out there too. No way we can finish out the individual units that fast. Between that and Delphi Station, we have just enough room," Fred said. "Once ring six on Delphi Station is ready, you can put all you want up there. But we're months away from having the infrastructure put in, much less cabins."

"Okay, you have my permission to light the fire," Marc said. "Anything we can do to accelerate the infrastructure on ring six, do it."

"I'm on it," Fred said, rubbing his hands together like he was really going to enjoy lighting the fires.

"And finally, we have two hundred Russians that need vetting for Delphi Station. I'm sure they'll sneak a few spies in the mix, but we'd like to avoid any commandos and such," Blake said. "Kal, Sasha's not on the list, but I can make a special request."

"Please don't help me," Kal said. "I get into enough trouble on my own." A chuckle went around the room as everyone else was glad that Blake wasn't trying to help them.

"Sam?" Marc prompted.

"I think I've found us a VP of Marketing. Sharon Bodiker from GE is looking to move up, and the person holding the VP position at GE doesn't look like they'll be retiring anytime soon."

"Do you know her?" Fred asked.

"I've been in negotiations across from her. She's smart, professional, and a tough negotiator. I have some contacts who know her personally; they say she's a good fit for us."

"Is she interested?" Marc asked.

"Yes. But she is a bit pricey."

"How much?" Fred asked.

"Two million and a twenty million dollar signing bonus."

"I'm okay with the salary, I'm not happy about a signing bonus," Marc said. "Work with Jonas to come up with a bonus package that will reward solid performance. If she stands firm on the signing bonus, we'll look for someone else."

"It does cost to move," Samantha said. "She loses her stock options, has to sell her house."

"Five million to move, factor the stock options into the bonus," Marc said.

"I can work with that. So, moving on. Margaret says that our new ambassador to the U.N. is still getting signals from countries that they'd like to form a bloc."

"That sounds like good news," Admiral Michaels said.

"I agree," Marc said. "Let's see what happens when it's big enough to sway the results." He nodded at Samantha, asking her to continue.

"And on the Russians, they will start delivering converted ships next month, new ships after the first of the year. Converted locomotives are already being delivered with new ones scheduled for October." The Russian president had negotiated a deal to get small fusion reactors to install in ships and locomotives. It was Marc's way of moving them from a colonial-like power back into the mainstream of the world economy.

"How are they doing it so fast?"

Samantha looked at Fred for some help. "The difference between the designs isn't that big, so they were able to modify their production lines and slip the change into the production process. So, they just had a few weeks of downtime for the changeover," Fred said.

"Good for them," Marc said. "Kal?"

"The Academy cadets are finishing up in Guatemala this week. They'll start coming home on Saturday, Last group shows up on Tuesday. Commandant Lewis says they've done pretty well. So far, none of them who made it to Guatemala has dropped out," Kal said.

"Too easy?" Blake asked.

*"No way!"* Catie messaged Blake and her father. *"These guys are sadists!"*

"I was there last week; they're not going easy on them," Kal said. "And as usual, when the cadets are in charge, it's actually tougher."

"That's always bothered me," Blake said. "I worry that immature cadets are risking the safety of the others as they try to prove how tough a leader they are."

"Don't worry, they're always under supervision, and we have ANDI tracking all surveillance," Kal said.

"ANDI?" Nickola asked.

"Yes, he's the new DI we made for the Sakira. He does a good job of data management. He's not as good as ADI, but we can't have her do everything," Kal said.

"Why, thank you, Cer Kal," ADI said.

"But maybe ADI isn't busy *enough*," Kal said.

ADI gave out a laugh.

"That's the first time I've heard her laugh," Samantha said.

"Oh, she's laughed before," Catie messaged. "But usually it sounds wicked; that was a nice laugh."

"Moving on," Marc prompted.

"Liz and I have worked out that we should allocate two hundred Marines for Artemis; that'll let you move them between the Victory and the ground as needed. Some of them will want to bring families along and make it a semi-permanent station, others will do a six-month deployment. We'll give you the numbers when we've identified them. For the Paraxeans, we'll allocate fifty Marines for the Galileo. We can adjust that number as we learn. Since you'll be starting out in the Sakira, we want to ship thirty Foxes in flight bay one. You'll have to use the Roebuck flight bay for operations, but we think four Lynxes and two Foxes should cover you until you reach Artemis," Kal said.

"How many pilots?" Marc asked.

"We recommend three per spaceplane, round it up to one hundred thirty."

"Okay, I assume they can do other things?"

Liz laughed, "They can eat, drink, party, . . . Oh, you mean, can they do other work? Give us a list of skills, and we'll try to match them."

"Thank you," Marc said, trying to avoid smiling at her joke. He didn't want to encourage her.

"We'll give you numbers for the space carriers once you've been on Artemis for a month or so. That will give us enough data to make some projections," Kal said. He folded his hands, indicating he was done.

"Fred," Marc prompted.

"Our new Academy and new University are slated to start holding regular classes in late August; things are on track. You can check out Jonas' report for status of production and sales, nothing new to report there. On our new airline, we were tracking for an October certification, but based on last month's discussion, we've pushed it to after the first of the year, and surprise, surprise, a lot of the politics went away," Fred said.

Marc chuckled at that, then said, "Nikola has something she wants us to see."

Masina showed Governor Paratar and an older man into the room, after receiving a signal from Nikola that she was ready.

"I've brought Dr. Feinberg to present his findings," Nikola said. "He's the quality engineer we've had examine the Paraxean Foxes and some of the other material we've removed from their ships. I think you'll be very interested in what he's learned. And since this will impact our planning for the colony missions, Marc asked me to invite Governor Paratar to sit in. Dr. Feinberg, you have the floor."

"Thank you for having me here," Dr. Feinberg said as he took his seat. "As most of you know, I started this investigation following the after-action review of the Paraxean war that exposed a few anomalies.

"The review showed that the Paraxean FX4s were not as resilient as the FX4s from Delphi. Initially, it was put down to superior pilots and some weapons improvements we had made, but Admiral McCormack asked me to dig deeper." Dr. Feinberg nodded at Blake.

"My analysis found some astounding differences. The hulls of Paraxean FX4s had over three defects per square centimeter, while the Delphinean FX4s only show one defect per ten square centimeters. It is the density of the defects that undermined the Paraxean FX4s' ability to transfer heat when they were hit with a laser or a plasma cannon. Simply put, they could only absorb eighty percent of the energy that the Delphinean FX4s could."

"I assume you've discovered why that is true," Marc said.

"I have. It comes back to the fact that the Paraxeans print their FX4s. In fact, they print just about everything," Dr. Feinberg said. "I had samples produced for me, made using both techniques, by printing and by your plasma deposition process. What I found was that the printed samples showed the same defect density."

"Is there something wrong with the printers?" Marc asked.

"Not really. The problem is inherent in the printing process," Dr. Feinberg said. "The process relies on what one would essentially call vacuum deposition, the process we use for most of our integrated circuit development. When that vacuum is not perfect, you get defects; now, when you're using the process for integrated circuits, those defects are not particularly harmful, a small variation in impedance along the circuit traces. But when you're expecting to carry the type of energy in the superconductors you deposit that are necessary to survive a plasma cannon shot, they're catastrophic."

"What do you mean by the vacuum not being perfect?" Fred asked.

"A few molecules of air here and there," Dr. Feinberg said. "Even in space, it's hard to create a perfect void. There are hydrogen ions from the solar wind and outgassing from your tools and structures. Down here on Earth, it is even worse. Things that are printed on the surface show even higher defect densities. Again, generally, they're not important, but they do reduce the strength of whatever you're making."

"By how much?" Blake asked.

"For a polysteel beam, when it is made with your extrusion process, it is fifteen percent stronger than one that is printed with a particle printer in space. If the beam is printed here on the planet, the difference is twenty-four percent."

"So, what does this mean for us?" Marc asked.

"A lot of things won't change," Nikola said. "We don't print that many things where the defect density is critical. But it does put more pressure on us to come up with a better way to make the gravity drives. And we should look at our fusion reactors and see if we can break them down into smaller components so we can avoid printing more of the structural components."

"What about the Paraxeans?" Marc asked. He looked over at Dr. Metra who shrugged and looked at Nikola.

"We need to break them of their reliance on the printers," Nikola said.

"That shouldn't be too hard," Catie said. "To them, the plasma process will just look like another printer. The hardest thing will be to get them used to assembling the final product. But they have to do that anyway when there are big defects in the print job. They go in, and pull out components, and replace them."

"But this will be at a finer level of detail," Dr. Metra said. "We're going to have to get used to replacing a gear instead of an entire engine."

"The Paraxeans from the Sakira should be able to help. They had to do that kind of stuff on the Enterprise and the Victory," Catie said. "Chief O'Donnell and Chief Hopkins would be a great resource. They were the ones getting the Paraxean team to focus on parts instead of systems."

"Good idea," Marc said. "Governor Paratar, you'll probably want to start training for some of your engineers before they head out to your new colony."

"Yes I will," the governor said. "Thank you for bringing this to our attention. We're happy to accept any help you can provide."

"Thank you, Dr. Feinberg," Marc said. "Your presentation has been very enlightening."

"You're welcome," Dr. Feinberg said as he got up and accompanied Masina out of the room.

"Now, I'd like to discuss where we are with our colony missions," Marc said. "Governor, do you have anything to add or questions before we begin the discussion?"

"I am shocked to hear Dr. Feinberg's finding. I believe you're suggesting the necessary changes, but until our scientists have time to review the data and analyze its impact on our plans, I will withhold any comments."

"Very well. You're scheduled to start out in three weeks; will you be ready?" Marc asked the governor.

"I believe so. We'll have to see if anything significant changes, but I think we can keep the timeline and make adjustments in the parameters of the mission to account for this new information."

"Good. For everyone, the plan is to have the Sakira stay in the system for two weeks, and then head back to Earth. The Roebuck will stay for four weeks, and then it will go directly to Artemis. The Sakira will carry four extra Lynxes so that the Paraxeans will have them plus the thirty Foxes to provide security once the Sakira and the scout ship leave."

"Do you think it's wise to leave them without a starship?" Dr. Metra asked.

"We'll have drones at the edge of the system watching for any approaching starships. Given our jumpdrive, we think we can respond in plenty of time relative to the arrival of one. The Galileo should be ready for deployment in December, so it should be a short gap," Marc explained.

"That does assume that we get the jumpdrives to work on such a large ship," Dr. Metra pointed out.

"It does. Both of these missions are not without risk. Do you have an alternate proposal?"

"Why not leave the Roebuck at Mangkatar until the Galileo is able to replace it?"

"That would dramatically reduce the amount of cargo we can carry to Artemis."

"How? You were never going to ship cargo for Artemis in the Roebuck?"

"Because now the Sakira will need to carry the extra six Lynxes," Marc explained.

"But if things go reasonably well, you'll have Catie's new freighter to carry more cargo out by the first of the year. That's not too long a period of time."

"I concede your point. Governor, do you agree?"

"It would make me feel more comfortable."

"Catie, the status of your freighter?" Marc asked.

"I did a walkthrough three weeks ago. It looks good. And since it is mostly empty space or cargo pods, there's not much to build out," Catie said. "Ajda says January at the latest. They're already building the hull."

"What about the jumpdrive?" Admiral Michaels asked. "Won't we have the same issue with it as with the space carriers and the asteroid?"

"No, it's designed with the drives in mind," Catie said. "Its cross-section is only a little bigger than the Sakira; its length is where we get the cargo space, and that conforms to the parameters that Dr. McDowell has already verified."

"Okay, then the Roebuck will stay at Mangkatar until the Galileo arrives to replace her," Marc said. "Governor, is there anything else you need to get ready?"

"We're well into modifying our plans," the governor said. "Our people are undergoing training, we'll need to modify that some based on Dr. Feinberg's input, but as I said, we should be able to maintain our timeline. One of our biggest issues will be access to raw material."

"Why is that?" Blake asked.

"We need iron and petroleum to produce polysteel and polyglass, as well as the solar collectors. It will take time to find them and set up mining operations."

"You should do what we did here on Earth," Catie said. "Bring a couple of asteroids into orbit. You could even bring an extra iron asteroid in and set it down on the planet right next to your colony. That would get rid of a lot of complexities."

"That would work," Marc said. "We should do the same on Artemis. It would allow you to make polysteel quickly. I'm assuming your site will also be next to a petroleum reserve."

"Natural gas. Having an iron asteroid delivered would simplify a lot of things," the governor said. "That makes the biggest issue food, and we can manage around that. We already know we can eat the local plants, and you left several greenhouses running."

"How are you going to farm?" Fred asked.

"You should have seen the orders for the electric tractors," Marc said. "We're buying the rest of the implements from Australian suppliers."

"Are they taking plow horses?" Nikola asked. "You know horses usually don't run out of parts."

"We're considering including those in the Galileo's shipment, although we might want to consider having them delivered in the new cargo ship."

"That would work. They take up too much cargo space to be able to ship them in the Sakira," Marc said. "But we could make a special cargo pod for them."

"How will they handle the microgravity?" Samantha asked.

"We would sedate them for the trip," Dr. Metra said. "But if you want to do that, you should start finding them now. I don't expect that you use very many draft animals on this planet."

"Hey, there's always the Amish," Kal said. "They have some nice horses for sale. I looked into it when we were buying horses for the horse park."

"You were going to buy a draft horse for the horse park?" Catie asked.

"No, cart ponies," Kal said. "They have horses and ponies trained to pull a buggy. The draft horses were just listed in the same place."

"You should consider some of those too," Dr. Metra said. "That was one of the biggest complaints from our early colonies, the lack of reliable animals to take the place of vehicles. Vehicles are going to be expensive and scarce for the first few years, and the horses will reproduce themselves."

"Okay, we'll stop here. I think the governor and I have enough to keep us busy for a while. I want to thank everyone for their time."

"Sam, how are you doing with the influx of new colonists?" Marc asked.

"Surviving?"

"Not having fun?"

"Not as much as with the enthusiasts. These people don't want to cross-train, and they don't think they need to get into shape."

"Interesting."

"They have one goal, to get their land or their business started. They're not really that interested in the rest of the colony."

"Sounds short-sighted."

"It is. I finally had to use the hammer."

"You're *hitting* them with a hammer?" Marc teased.

"No, but maybe I should. I had to tell them that anyone who doesn't pass the physical test will be left behind."

"Did that get their attention?"

"Once they figured out I meant it."

"Which test are you using?"

"Same as the Academy," Samantha said. "Everyone on this mission has to be able to step into another role."

"I agree. But it seems a bit harsh on the tiny tots."

Samantha slapped Marc on the back of the head.

"Blake, we've been invited to a summit of world leaders," Marc messaged Blake.

Blake immediately opened a Comm channel. "What do you mean, we?"

"They've invited the president, and since you're going to be standing in for me, I think it would be nice for you to attend," Marc said.

"You're still here, why don't you go by yourself?"

"Hey, you have to get involved sometime; why not now?"

"What's it about?"

"Earth security."

"Oh, Lord. When?"

"Two weeks."

"Just the two of us?"

"Plus, a security detail, plus you can bring Jackie if you want. I'll ask Sam if she wants to go."

"Where is it going to be?"

"Brussels."

"Jackie might want to go to that."

"I'll let you know when Sam decides," Marc said.

"You owe me for doing this crap."

"Just put it on my tab."

# 11 Final Exam

"We're going to do a little hand-to-hand combat training!" Cadet Lieutenant Hoffman yelled. "Form up behind the barracks!"

"What the hell?!" Joanie hissed. "We're supposed to be done for the day."

"No good deed goes unpunished," Catie said.

"Who the hell did a good deed?"

"Not me."

Flight One hurried from the barracks and out the back door. They lined up and they stood at attention, waiting to see what Hoffman had in mind. Flight four was forming up just down the way from them.

"First rank, about-face!" Cadet Lieutenant Hoffman yelled. "Now, start your hand-to-hand drills!"

Catie turned to face Cadet Akio Watanabe. As she recalled, he was a judo expert. They started going through the drills. Catie was doing just enough to counter what Watanabe was throwing at her.

After ten minutes, Hoffman singled them out. "Cadet MacGregor, Cadet Watanabe, up front!" he ordered. "The rest of you gather around; we're going to have a real match here. You two seem to know what you're doing, let's see what you've got! Fight!"

Catie was stunned, *"What does he mean fight?!"* she thought.

Apparently, Watanabe wasn't confused because he charged Catie right away. Catie automatically sidestepped him and deflected his arm before he could grab her uniform.

Watanabe circled back and took a stance a few feet away from Catie. Catie backed up and kept circling him, keeping her distance.

"MacGregor, I said fight, not dance!" Hoffman yelled.

Catie ignored him as she continued to watch Watanabe for his next move. He came in low, going for her legs. Catie threw her legs out behind her as she brought an elbow down hard on Watanabe's back. She rolled off him and jumped up, again circling.

Watanabe rolled over and came up, rolling the shoulder that Catie had just nailed. He feinted a few times, trying to get Catie to commit.

*"I'm not grappling with you!"* Catie thought. Although Watanabe was her height, he outweighed her by at least ten kilos.

Again, Watanabe came in low, reaching for Catie's jacket. This time Catie grabbed his hand as she stepped to the side. She wrenched his arm, driving Watanabe to the ground. Still holding onto the hand, she pressed on a pressure point on the wrist and twisted at the same time. Watanabe grunted in pain. Catie tapped Watanabe on the head with her left foot, then looked at Hoffman. "He's done!"

"Alright, now that's what I call a fight!" Hoffman yelled. "We've got our champion; Boutros, do you have yours?"

"Yep, he's warmed up and ready to go!" Cadet Lieutenant Boutros hollered back.

The two flights from Foxtrot created a new circle around Catie and Cadet Sanchez, Flight Four's champion. Catie was still breathing hard, and she couldn't believe that Hoffman was going to make her fight again without a rest. *"Gawd, that man really hates me!"*

"Okay, MacGregor, don't let us down," Hoffman yelled. "Fight!"

Sanchez rushed in and threw a three-punch combo. Catie blocked them as she backed up circling to the left. Sanchez smiled at her as he moved to follow. He lashed out with a sidekick which Catie knocked down as she moved to the right.

"Come on Chica!" Sanchez hissed, "show me what you've got!"

Catie did nothing but continue to circle and stare at him. She was studying him for any tells that would telegraph his next move. He feinted a few times as he kept trying to get closer. Catie continued to back away and circle. Sanchez rushed in and threw a combo at Catie. As she danced to the left, he threw a sidekick at her. Catie caught it and pushed hard. Sanchez fell to the ground, but the effort knocked Catie off balance, and she fell as well.

"Break!" Hoffman yelled. He was next to Sanchez and helped him up. "Sanchez, break her arm!" Hoffman whispered.

"What?!"

"You heard me. Consider that an order!" Hoffman whispered. "Now, Fight!"

Catie could immediately tell that Sanchez was being more aggressive. His moves were meant to really hurt, not just make contact. She continued to back away and circle as she fended off his attacks.

Sanchez started a combo against Catie, on his second punch, he switched up and grabbed her wrist, twisting her arm. Catie knew he would break it if she didn't do something. She bent her elbow, twisting her body and getting closer to Sanchez, then she flipped around his hold, kicking him in the head as she did. She landed back on her feet as Sanchez let go and fell to the ground. Catie immediately moved in and stomped on his leg, tearing the ligaments in his knee, then she kicked him in the ribs when he reached for his knee.

"I think he's done!" Catie yelled as she backed away.

Cadet Major Baker came running up. "What's going on here?!" he demanded.

"We were just doing some hand-to-hand training," Cadet Lieutenant Hoffman replied.

"Who authorized this?!" Baker demanded.

"We were using our initiative, sir!" Hoffman barked.

Baker turned on Sanchez, "What were you trying to do?!"

"He told me to break her arm!" Sanchez said, nodding at Hoffman.

"That was an illegal order! Why did you follow it?!"

"I knew I wouldn't be able to," Sanchez said. "She was holding back the whole time. I knew if I got aggressive, she would take me out."

"MacGregor, what do you have to say?!"

"He got aggressive," Catie said. "I think I busted his knee."

"Yeah, and cracked a couple of ribs," Sanchez gasped. He was grimacing from the pain.

"MacGregor, help him to the hospital, you broke him, now go get him fixed!" Baker hollered. "Lieutenant Hoffman, Lieutenant Boutros, you're relieved. Report to headquarters at 0600 tomorrow. Sergeant

Chambers, Sergeant Favre, you just got promoted. Take command of your flights and get them to bed, we have our final test tomorrow!"

◆ ◆ ◆

"Our mission is to capture the main house," Baker said. "Now there are several possible objectives we could have been assigned, so they don't know which one we're after. We will approach from the east after being dropped off by an Oryx. The rest of the squadron will follow an hour later. The house is on a hill here. We will set up observations and do recon around the house. We need to identify the positions of their sentries and lookouts, determine their routine. We'll plant explosives on the bunkhouse, and around the perimeter. Once we're ready, I'll signal Flights Three and Four to attack from the north. That will draw their attention, and allow us to take out the sentries and infiltrate the house. Once we have control of the house, we'll have Flights five and six join the attack from the south. We should be able to take up sniper positions on the roof of the house. We'll blow the charges we planted to distract the enemy and cover the rest of the squadron as they advance.

"The Oryx will drop us off at 0200. I want to be in place at the hill by 0330. We'll time our entry for 0400 when they will be at their deepest sleep, and the sentries will be at their most tired point.

"Any questions?"

"What types of sensors do they have?" Cadet Lieutenant Worth Lambert asked.

"They will have infrared, heat detectors, motion detectors, and night vision goggles," Baker replied.

"Then how are we supposed to sneak up on them?"

"Their sensors will only reach out for two hundred meters," Baker said. "Our battle armor will absorb energy, which will help with the motion detectors. We have to avoid any tripwires or other booby traps."

"What about the heat sensors?"

"I think the energy absorption of the battle armor will help with that."

"Sir," Catie said.

"Yes, Cadet MacGregor."

"Our battle armor has energy storage. If we discharge them before we enter their sensor range, then our body heat will go into the storage, and we'll maintain the same temperature as the ground," Catie explained.

"How do you know this?" Baker asked.

"Read it in the manual," Catie said.

"How do we discharge the storage?"

"Lie on the ground; there's a setting to route the heat to your back and radiate it into the ground."

"Excellent. Good job reading the whole manual," Baker said. "We board the Oryx in two hours. I want everyone here in their battle armor in one hour. We'll inspect our weapons and armor before we board."

"The house is four hundred meters ahead. I want scouts on the wings at one hundred meters. We'll set up base camp at two hundred meters and start scouting the enemy positions," Baker ordered.

"There is a second ravine over there," Cadet Howard said, pointing at the map projection he was sharing with Cadet Major Baker. "It looks like it's an easier approach from it to the house, now that we've got a better sense of the terrain."

"I agree," Baker said. He sent the coordinates out to the rest of the team. "We'll set up there in twenty minutes. Move out in units of two, fifty meters between each unit, discharge the heat from your armor before you go."

"Major Baker, I just took out an enemy scout," Cadet Boucher announced over his Comm.

"What!" Baker hissed.

"I took out an enemy scout."

"Where are you?"

"Northeast of the house."

"Everyone, fallback to Rendezvous Alfa!" Baker hissed into his Comm. "You too, Boucher."

Everyone quickly and quietly moved back toward their first rally point on the ranch. Catie checked the surveillance drone's feed; she could see that the Delta Squadron was already moving around the house, preparing for the assault that they were now aborting.

It took twenty minutes before they were all gathered back at Rendezvous Alfa.

"What's the problem?" Boucher asked Baker as they halted their retreat and prepared to take stock of the situation.

"You idiot. Your mission was to scout the house and identify where the sentries were."

"But this guy was way out beyond the house; he was walking right toward our camp."

"Doesn't matter, you should have reported it and waited for orders."

"What about initiative?"

"Initiative is supposed to be used to accomplish your orders, not to step outside their parameters!" Baker barked. "Now, they know that our objective is the house, they will all be awake in a few minutes, and they'll be on alert and calling for reinforcements."

"But we should have time before the sentries report in."

"No, their Comms will have reported them out of commission as soon as you took them out."

"Oh!"

*"Oh shit!"* Catie thought, She was feeling sorry for Boucher, wondering if there was any way to save the mission.

"Sir," Howard said.

"Yes?"

"We could have another part of the squadron make a feint against one of the other targets. That might keep them from sending reinforcements," Howard suggested.

"Good idea," Baker said. He got on his Comm and issued orders for Flight 6 to make a feint at the landing strip at the edge of the ranch. "They're coming from that direction anyway."

"The tunnels!" Catie thought. "Maybe we can pull this out after all."

Catie walked over to Baker. "Sir, may I have a moment in private with you?" Catie asked in a whisper.

Baker looked at her as if she had two heads, then nodded and motioned her to follow him. They walked twenty meters to the back of the group before he stopped. "Okay, MacGregor, what's up?"

"Sir. I have some intel on the ranch house that might help us to take it."

"So, what's the problem; spit it out."

"Sir, I'm not supposed to have this intel, and if anyone knew I did, it could compromise me."

"So you have it, but you can't tell me?"

"No, sir. I have it, and if I tell you, I need you to promise not to reveal its source."

"There are only twenty of us, won't they figure it out?"

"Not if you say we just stumbled across it when we were trying to figure out how to take the house."

"Did you do something illegal to gather this intel?"

"No, sir."

"Then how do you have it when you're not supposed to?"

"I overheard a conversation," Catie said, not wanting to tell him it was after Kal and his team took the ranch house from the cartel boss. She had been the pilot of the Oryx they had used for the incursion. And the conversation she had overheard was one of the Marines telling his friends about what they had found in the house.

"So, what's wrong with that?"

"Nothing specifically," Catie said. "But if someone knew that I had this intel, they would learn certain things about me that I need to keep private."

"But, it's not something illegal?"

"No, sir."

"Okay, I'm good with that," Baker said. "What do you know?"

"That bunkhouse that's about fifty meters from the house, there's a tunnel between it and the house."

"How's that going to help? They're guarding the bunkhouse too."

"Yes, sir. But there is also another tunnel into the bunkhouse from the side of the hill. We walked by it, and I didn't see a guard."

"You think they don't know about the tunnels?"

"I think the people who run the show do, but that doesn't mean they would have told Delta Squadron."

"Flight Six just finished their hit and run on the landing strip," Baker reported to his team. "I want scouts out here and here," he said, pointing to the map he was displaying on the ground. "Howard, you're with me, we'll check out this area. MacGregor, McCoy, you two hold here with flight two."

"Why are we getting left here?" Joanie asked Catie once Baker was out of earshot.

"Don't know, but I'm fine with taking a break. Let's use the time to review the footage from our drone; maybe we'll see something that can help."

Baker led Howard on a circuitous route to the coordinates that Catie had given him. They leapfrogged along the way, one covering the other as he pushed ahead, then regrouping before leapfrogging ahead once more.

"Sir, are we looking for anything in particular?" Howard asked.

"Something that the surveillance drone couldn't see or that we missed on our way here," Baker replied. "We need another way to get close to the house, or maybe that bunkhouse."

"I'm sure they'll be guarding both of them."

"Which is why we're looking for a better approach. Maybe they dump their trash out here somewhere, and we'll be able to use that. We just have to keep looking."

"Yes, sir."

As they were moving by a small cut in the hill, Howard signaled a halt. "That bush there sure seems healthy compared to the other plants out here," he said.

"It does. Do you think there's a water source there?"

"Maybe, but why aren't the other plants getting the benefit?"

"Check it out," Baker ordered.

"On it, sir."

"What luck," Baker thought. "Having Howard find the tunnel entrance would put even more distance between MacGregor and the discovery."

"Sir, there's an entrance here of some kind. Maybe to a tunnel."

"Any movement inside?" Baker asked as he reached the entrance and Howard.

"No, sir. There's a door here, it's locked, but I don't hear anything on the other side."

"Hold fast. I want to bring Flight One up to cover us; then we'll see if we can get inside and find where it leads." He messaged Fight One to head for their coordinates. They only took two minutes to get there since they could take a direct route.

When they arrived, Baker called out, "MacGregor, have you read how to pick an electronic lock?"

Catie walked up to the door, "No, sir, but I have heard that they are susceptible to lasers," she said as she aimed her armored fist with its built-in laser at the lock.

"That's not going to do anything on the restricted power setting," Baker said.

"Maybe not," Catie said as she fired the laser.

The lock clicked open. "It seems the instructors didn't want us to mess up their nice lock," Catie said, giving Baker a smile.

"Okay, you and Howard go in and scout the tunnel, keep your cameras running; we'll stay here until you give us the okay."

"Yes, sir," Catie said as she headed into the tunnel with Howard right on her heels.

"Where do you think this goes?" Howard asked.

"Somewhere up by the house would be my guess," Catie said. "It was owned by the leader of one of the cartels, so he probably had an escape tunnel in case the Federales stormed his ranch."

"That would be sweet," Howard said. "We could get in behind Delta and nail them."

"We'll see," Catie said as she kept moving forward down the tunnel. They were using the infrared camera on their helmets since there was no light in the tunnel.

*"Sir, MacGregor here,"* Catie messaged on her Comm when they reached the end of the tunnel.

"Baker here."

*"Tunnel is clear; we've reached a hatch in the ceiling; no ladder is visible. I would suggest some backup before we head up."*

"Wilco!" Baker said. He posted four cadets to guard the tunnel entrance, then led the other eight into the tunnel.

"Where do you think it goes?" Baker asked when he and the rest of the squad reached Catie and Howard.

"I counted two hundred fifty meters," Catie said. "I think that would put us under the bunkhouse."

"Cadet Delacroix front and center," Baker ordered.

"Yes, sir," Julie said as she rushed over.

"Howard, MacGregor and I are going to lift her onto your shoulders. Delacroix, squat down before he stands up, so you don't hit your head on the ceiling, then after he stands up go ahead and stand and see if you can lift the trapdoor."

"Yes, sir."

Howard knelt down on one knee so that Catie and Baker could help Julie onto his shoulders.

"Are your lasers armed?" Catie texted Julie.

Julie nodded as she turned on her lasers via her HUD.

"Delacroix, we'll hold your legs to keep you steady," Baker said. "Stand up, Howard."

Julie was essentially sitting on Howard's helmet as he stood up.

"Okay, Delacroix, stand up and see if you can open the trapdoor," Baker ordered.

Julie stood up; her helmet almost touched the ceiling once she was standing. "It won't move."

"Julie, use your legs," Catie said.

"Okay." Julie squatted back down, extending her arms above her head, locking her elbows. "Ready!" she hissed as she tried to stand up. "It moved."

"Can you open it?" Baker asked.

"It's too heavy."

"Howard, squat down, Delacroix lock your legs. . . . Now, Howard, stand up!" Baker ordered.

"Wait!" Julie hissed.

"Okay, what's up?"

"There's something on top of the door," Julie said. "It's starting to slide off, but we might tip it over or something. That's likely to be noisy."

"Okay, one second. MacGregor, you and I will help by pushing up on Delacroix's butt when Howard tries to stand. I'll trigger one of our remote explosives to cover any noise. On three. One . . . Two . . . Three, push."

The sound of the explosion could be heard. It muffled the sound of something falling above them as Julie pushed the trapdoor open.

"It's open! . . . the room is clear. Looks like a closet," Julie reported.

"Okay, do you need help getting up?"

"No," Julie said as she put her hands on both sides of the opening and lifted herself up and onto the floor above. "It's a utility closet; there were some boxes stacked on the hatch." She stood up and moved to the door. "It's quiet outside."

"Okay, let's get some backup up there with you, here's your rifle," Baker said as he handed Julie her rifle. "MacGregor, McCoy, you're next. Give me your rifles."

"You okay being a step ladder?" Catie asked Howard.

"I'm good."

Joannie and Catie quickly joined Julie in the utility closet. Once their rifles were handed up to them, they took a position on each side of the door.

"Ready?" Catie asked.

Julie nodded her head, and Catie opened the door a crack.

"Clear so far," Julie said. Catie opened the door enough that Julie could get her head out into the hallway. "Clear."

The three women moved into the hallway and cleared the two rooms, the kitchen, and an office. "Okay, next is the main bunkroom," Catie said.

They edged down the hallway until they could make out the room. It was quiet, and they quickly assessed that it was empty.

"Joanie, go guard the back door; Julie, go get the rest of the team up here," Catie ordered.

When Julie got back to the utility closet, she turned on the light. It didn't take her long to find the ladder that was in an inset in the wall. She pulled it out and lowered it down the hatch. "You guys ready to come up?"

"On our way. Go ahead and help cover us," Baker said.

"I'll make us some snacks, be back in a minute," the Delta team cadet said as he opened the door to the bunkhouse.

Catie stepped behind the door to hide; she waited until he closed the door, then she placed her armored hand against the seam where his helmet met the body armor. She grabbed the same seam with her other hand and yanked the cadet to the floor. Straddling him, she put her fist at his throat. "One move and you die!"

The Delta team cadet recovered from his shock. He stared at Catie for a minute, then tried to knock her off. Catie fired her laser into the seam. His suit immediately registered that he was dead and locked up.

"Easy to be a hero when it's not real," Catie said as she stood up.

"Won't his Comm announce that he's dead?" Julie asked.

"No, I disabled it with an EMP when I took him to the floor," Catie said. "It will miss the next roll call, but that's not going to be that unusual for the next few minutes. We need to dump his body back into the tunnel."

"I've got him," Howard announced as he grabbed the guy under his armpits and started dragging him back toward the tunnel.

"How much time do we have?" Baker asked.

"A few minutes," Catie said.

"Then we need to figure out if there's a tunnel to the main house, or if we have to assault from here."

"On it!" Catie remembered the Marine saying that the second entrance was in the kitchen pantry, so she headed there first. It only took a minute to find the hatch to the tunnel under some boxes of soup. She and Julie moved the boxes, turned the light out, lifted the hatch, and checked the tunnel. It was dark and unoccupied, but this one had a nice set of stairs leading down to it.

"We've got it," Catie announced.

"Good, I'm calling in the rest of our team," Baker said. "Everyone, converge on the tunnel. Meet Howard in the bunkhouse."

"Yes, sir."

"Howard, we're going to go through the tunnel. You hold the bunkhouse. Once we know the situation in the house, we'll decide if you follow us or hold here during the assault."

"Wilco!"

"Assault Group Alfa, begin moving in. Assault Group Bravo, give them five minutes, then start your assault."

"On the move," Cadet Lieutenant Harper, the leader of Assault Group Alfa, announced.

"Watanabe, Delacroix, MacGregor, you're with me. MacGregor, lead on," Baker ordered.

Catie led the way down into the tunnel. The tunnel was dark, so everyone used the night-vision in their helmets.

*"Fifty meters is a lot farther when you're being sneaky,"* Catie thought. The tunnel was well maintained, the floor was flat and even. It looked like it was made of pavers, although without light, it was hard to tell.

"We're at the end," Catie texted to the team.

*"How can she get messages off so fast?"* Baker wondered as he inched his way forward until he was next to Catie. "Okay, Delacroix, you're on."

"Why her?" Catie asked.

"Lighter, less noise, smaller target," Baker said.

Julie smacked Catie on the butt as she walked by and started up the stairs. After a bit, she signaled that all was quiet.

"You're next," Baker said as he tapped Catie on the shoulder.

Catie climbed the stairs and joined Julie at the door; she was a bit surprised that it was a door instead of a hatch in the ceiling.

"No hatch?"

Julie pointed to the open trap door that was against the wall. Looking around, Catie realized that they were in a coat closet.

"Anything?"

"No."

Catie armed her lasers and readied her rifle, then gave Julie the nod to go ahead and crack the door open. All was quiet. Catie tapped Julie on the shoulder, then reached into the ammo pouch on her thigh and pulled out a surveillance puck. *"Slide this against the wall and then close the door,"* she texted Julie.

Julie hesitated a moment. *"It'll stick to the wall,"* Catie texted.

Julie nodded and slid the puck into place, pulling the door closed right after. Catie tapped into the feed, sharing it with the rest of the team. It showed a short hallway with what one would guess was the great room to the left, the main door to the house was to the right. There appeared to be a stairway just to the right of the closet.

Baker and Watanabe joined Catie and Julie in the closet and prepared to clear the house.

"Go!"

Catie and Julie exited the closet and turned toward the left. Her guess had been correct, it was the great room. It was empty with a set of French doors leading to the outside. As they moved farther into the room, they could see another doorway leading to the left behind the dining room. *"Probably the kitchen,"* Catie thought.

They used the puck from Julie's ammo pouch and slid it into the kitchen. The video showed clear, so they entered. Just when they made it inside the kitchen, someone came out of the pantry. Catie wheeled, leveling her rifle at the person, who dropped the bag of flour she was carrying and raised her arms.

*"Solamente soy la cocinera,"* she said. "I'm just the cook," their Comms translated.

Catie motioned for her to take a seat on the floor, which the cook was happy to do since it didn't look like she was going to be standing much longer anyway.

Julie checked the pantry, then moved the surveillance puck so that it covered the delivery door to the kitchen. *"Quédate aquí, no te muevas* . . . Stay here, don't move," Catie ordered the cook. She and Julie then went back and joined up with Baker and Watanabe.

"Cook in the kitchen; we put the surveillance puck on the wall so it can watch the delivery door. I think that's an office down that way," Catie reported, pointing to the small hall that went to the left of the main door.

"You and Watanabe clear it," Baker ordered.

"Yes, sir!" Catie motioned to Watanabe to follow her. They set up next to the hallway and used the puck to verify that it was clear. Turning down it, they eased their way to the door. There was a large one to the left and a small one to the right. "Bathroom, we'll do it first," Catie texted Watanabe, pointing at the small door.

Watanabe nodded and took up position. When Catie was ready, he reached over and tried the knob. The door was unlocked. *"All the way at once,"* Catie texted.

Watanabe pushed the door open and dropped to one knee, his rifle level, Catie came in high. She could hear water when the door opened, so Catie fired as soon as her rifle was inside, sweeping right to left with the laser pulse.

"You've got to be kidding me!" the man standing at the toilet cried out.

"You're dead, so you cannot talk!" Catie snapped. "Now, clean up, then sit on the floor!"

Watanabe grabbed the towel and wiped the moisture off of his armor, Catie smiled and tried hard not to laugh, but a little snicker came out.

"What happened?" Baker asked.

"We took one tango down," Catie said. "We still need to clear the office."

She and Watanabe set up next to the big doors into the office. Watanabe tried the knob; again, the door was not locked. Catie held the puck up for him to see, telling him to open it only enough to roll the puck through the gap.

There were three tangos sitting around the room at various stations that had been set up. None of them were in armor, nor did any of them have a rifle handy. Since their armor could handle anything a handgun could deliver, Catie texted Watanabe to go in low on three.

"One . . . two . . . three!"

They pushed the door open.

"Jack, you're finally done, took you long enou . . ."

Catie and Watanabe fired three bursts each, taking down all three.

"Do not touch that keyboard!" Catie ordered. "You're dead! Office is clear," she reported to Baker.

"Good, I'm bringing the rest of the team in. Wait until we get some help here before you clear the top floor," Baker ordered. He moved to the office with Julie and started checking the displays. "Nice setup you have here," he said.

"Why don't they have surveillance in the house?" Catie asked.

Julie smacked Catie on the shoulder. "Are you complaining?"

"They did," Baker said. "It's on this monitor over here, but the window is minimized."

"Smart, real smart."

"Alfa team here!" Malory said. "We're in position."

"Give us five minutes," Baker said, "then start the assault. Bravo team, how are you doing?"

"We got tangos on our six. They're coming from the landing strip. We're going to divert to the northeast and try to lose them."

"Copy, once you have a good position, start your assault," Baker ordered.

"Wilco!"

Howard and Lambert were the first to make it into the house. "The others are just two minutes behind," Howard reported.

"Good, you two go with Watanabe and MacGregor and clear the top floor. Delacroix and McCoy, take charge of these monitors and start feeding us intel," Baker ordered.

Catie motioned the others to follow her and headed up the stairs. The monitors in the office had shown clear hallways, but they didn't have coverage in the rooms. It didn't take long to clear all of the rooms; they were as empty as the hallway.

"The roof is next," Catie said, pointing at the stairway that led up.

"You first," Howard said. "Watanabe, follow her."

"Howard, fire a full load through the door, it might not take him out, but it should knock him off of the roof. Same thing for you, Lambert, through the wall here. You can see where he is on the probe's video feed. It's not perfect, but you should be able to hit him. Then we'll all burst through and take the other three out as fast as we can. On three," Catie ordered.

"One . . . two . . . three!"

Crack! Crack! Crack! The big rifles that Howard and Lambert were carrying retorted with an unexpected third shot.

Catie and Watanabe burst through the door, rolling on the floor then came up firing. Catie nailed the tango on the right and immediately rolled to get a shot at the other one. She took a hit to her armor, but it didn't register any impairment, so she kept moving, firing as she went. Watanabe went left and got off two rounds before his suit locked up, indicating he was wounded. But he'd nailed his target.

"We're clear up here," Catie announced. "Watanabe is down!"

"Lambert is down!" Howard barked. "He's out of it!" Which meant he was registered as dead.

"Watanabe is just wounded. Howard, can you come and take him downstairs so we can administer first aid? He's just showing a leg wound."

"On it."

"What happened to Lambert?" Catie asked as she helped Howard get Watanabe to the stairs.

"As soon as I fired, one of the tangos nailed him through the wall, lucky shot," Howard said. "He took one of those big rounds to the head. I'm sure glad this is a simulation."

They made it downstairs to find the rest of their team had arrived. Baker was talking to his command staff. "Chambers, I want four snipers on the roof. Favre, prepare defenses around the house. The assault teams are heading this way; they'll drive the enemy back to the house. Have the snipers, take out as many as they can from long range; you need to be ready for any tangos that get through."

"MacGregor, Howard, back on the roof, grab two sniper rifles," Chambers barked. "Favre, who are your best snipers?"

"Chen, Rosenbach, grab your sniper rifles," Favre ordered. Then she proceeded to dispatch the rest of her Flight to positions by the windows where they would have a view of any attacking force.

Catie grabbed the sniper rifle that someone had carried in for her and headed to the roof with Howard on her heels.

◆ ◆ ◆

"Here they come!"

Catie moved to the south side and found a spot where she could set up. The drone would let them know if the enemy started coming from another direction, but for now, all four of them would line up here.

"Find your shots and take 'em!" Sergeant Rosenbach ordered.

Catie adjusted her scope; she could see about twenty-five tangos making their way toward the house. They were still over one hundred meters away. She lined up her first shot. CRACK!

"Good shot, now do it again!" Rosenbach yelled as she finally fired.

CRACK! CRACK! The shots kept ringing out. Catie had taken out three before the enemy dropped down and covered up.

"We've taken out nine!" Rosenbach reported.

"Keep them pinned down," Baker ordered. "Flight Six is coming up behind them."

"Yes, sir!"

"We've got incoming from the east!" Julie yelled from her station in the command center.

"MacGregor, Howard, shift over, we'll hold here and keep these pinned down!" Rosenbach yelled.

"Yes, sir!"

Catie and Howard scooted along the deck to the left, getting into position to fire on the new wave of attack. Catie lined up another shot, CRACK! She nailed one. But it was clear that the attackers knew there were snipers covering them as they were approaching cautiously, leapfrogging between cover.

Catie adjusted her position to line up her next shot. CRACK! "Damnit," she gasped as her armor shocked her in the left shoulder, partially paralyzing it.

"MacGregor's hit!" Howard yelled. "We need another sniper up here!"

"No! I'm okay," Catie yelled. "It's just my shoulder!"

She shifted around, grunting through the pain her battle armor was applying to her shoulder. *"Where are those simulated painkillers?"* She shifted the rifle to her right shoulder and pushed her left hand out to steady the aim. The armor was allowing her to move her hand without much pain, but any big movement hurt. CRACK! She got off her next shot.

Baker was watching on the video feed; he shook his head as he realized that Catie could fire the rifle from either side. *"Where did they find her?"* he wondered.

Catie and Howard kept the new attack pinned down as Flight Four came up behind them. Slowly the Foxtrots whittled down the enemy. An hour later, they finally surrendered.

Foxtrot Three had been caught from behind and decimated. Foxtrot Four had only lost three, mainly due to the cover fire provided by Catie and Howard. It had kept the enemy pinned down so they could maneuver around them and take them out with grenades and crossfire. Foxtrot Five had suffered heavy casualties as it had engaged the enemy before they were in range of the snipers.

"Alright, people. The Oryx will be here in five minutes to pick us up and haul us back to the compound. Be thankful they're not making us march!" Baker shouted.

"Foxtrot Squadron, form up!" Baker ordered once everyone had disembarked from the Oryx that that brought them back to the main base. There were a few groans as everyone realized that they weren't going to be able to go to their rooms to shower and rest up.

Baker was chatting with Sergeant Major Jefferies while Foxtrot Squadron formed up into Flights. "Ready for inspection!" Cadet Lieutenant Favre barked as she snapped to attention in front of Baker and the sergeant major.

"Everyone who was wounded or killed during the action, front and center!" Baker ordered.

Now there were real groans as the cadets made way for the casualties. *"What kind of hell is Baker thinking of putting us through,"* Catie wondered.

Finally, the twenty-six cadets formed up into ranks and awaited whatever punishment or retribution that Baker had in mind.

"I want everyone to look at these cadets. They are the real cost of war. They are your comrades, your mates. This is over one-third of our number. That's why you train so hard, to avoid this. To protect your own. Every mistake you make adds to that number. Every time you hesitate and the enemy gets by and then returns to attack, you add to that number. Every time you succeed in taking that enemy down, you subtract from that number. When we avoid a war, we keep all of them safe; when we make a mistake and start a war, or force a battle that could have been avoided, we add to that number.

"They are the true cost we pay. All those slogans like Honor, 'For Home and Country,' 'Truth, Justice, and the Delphinean Way' are why you join the force. They're what drives your training, what gets you to the battle. But in the end, your mates are why you fight, why you dig deep and keep moving. In the heat of battle, it's your mates who keep you alive, drive you forward. Remember that! You don't want to have to stand here looking at a row of graves in the future. So, train hard, and learn from your mistakes when the cost of them is cheap; when you can talk with the casualties and review what happened. Because in a real war, there are no second chances."

"Wow, he actually understands what it's like," Catie thought. "I wish he'd been around during the Paraxean war."

"Now, the sergeant major tells me we get to go home tomorrow. We've all passed our final test for this training. Go get cleaned up and meet me in mess hall four; beer is on me. Dismissed!"

There were cheers as everyone raced to the barracks to get cleaned up.

"He did say beer?!" Joanie asked as she and Catie finally got to their room.

"That's what I heard," Catie said.

"He's not as big an ass as I thought," Joanie said.

"Maybe not," Catie said. "He seems to have a sense of what war is like."

"Or he memorized a good speech."

"I don't know, it felt like he really understood," Catie said.

"How would you know?"

"I just felt it."

# 12 Artemis Mission Prep

"Hey, aren't you coming to bed?" Samantha asked Marc. It was already past midnight, and she was tired of reading.

"I need to finish reviewing this," Marc said.

"What are you reviewing?"

"The summary from Dr. Pramar on the plants from Artemis," Marc replied.

"What does it say?"

"It catalogs all the plants and shows the results from the monitors in the greenhouses that they left. They have the bots maintaining them and reporting results."

"So, what does it say about the plants?"

"It says that our plants grow well there, that they don't cross-pollinate with the local plants. The local plants as a whole are not harmful if we eat them, and most of them are nutritious," Marc said.

"What about the grasses?" Samantha asked. "If we take livestock, it would be nice if they could eat the local grass."

"Most of it's fine. But there this one grain that dominates most of the area where we want to start the colony. It's like wheat, but we can't digest it."

"That's too bad. Why can't we digest it?"

"Well, I might have overstated that. We can digest it, but it takes a lot of energy and time, so it mostly just passes through our systems."

"Don't the bacteria in our gut break it down, so we at least get the minerals from it?"

"They have the same problem. It takes a long time and a lot of energy, so they don't do that well on it," Marc explained.

"Do we have any of it here?" Samantha asked.

"I think Dr. Pramar has about fifty kilos of it. Why?"

"Oh, just thinking. Don't stay up too long, and don't wake me up when you finally come to bed."

"I wouldn't think about it."

"That's the problem, you don't think about it," Samantha said, giving Marc a slap on the back of his head.

"Sorry."

"What time did you come to bed last night?" Samantha asked Marc when they sat down to breakfast.

"Two o'clock."

"And you got up at six?"

"Sure. I'm usually up a lot earlier."

"I thought those youth treatments would help me keep up with you," Samantha said.

"You're doing just fine; everyone needs a different amount of sleep. I've never needed much."

"It's not fair," Samantha complained. "Anyway, what are you working on now?"

"I'm sorting through the list of applicants for the colony mission."

"Anyone interesting?"

"I've got two artists who want to come along."

"Artists?"

"Yes, they say they'll do whatever clerical work we want them to do until they get established. They think people will be wanting art for their walls, a few portraits, things like that."

"Are they together?"

"No, unrelated, but their applications are almost identical."

"Well, as governor, you should commission a few paintings," Samantha said.

"I guess so," Marc said. "That reminds me. I should try to get a few professional painters."

"Aren't they professional?"

"No, building painters and car painters," Marc said. "Blake and I painted our parents' house once. Thought we did a nice job. Then

Linda and I had our house painted by a professional; we were too busy by then. They did a much better job, less time, and a lot less paint."

"How many job types are you planning on?"

"I have over fifty job classifications that need to be filled right away."

"Fifty?! Like what?"

"Doctors, nurses, and teachers just to start. Then you have to have farmers and fishermen, machinists, mechanics, electricians, plumbers, and the list goes on. Some of them will have multiple skills, but it is daunting."

"How did they do it in the old days?"

"Back then, people were more versatile, and you didn't have to worry about electricity and electronic equipment, much less spaceplane mechanics and pilots."

"But they had wagon masters, drovers, and such."

"And they lived a lot rougher at the start than we hope to."

"You'd better not be hoping about that," Samantha threatened.

"Liz, I want you to command the Sakira when it goes to Mangkatar with the Paraxeans," Marc told Liz when she joined him in his office.

"I guess I could. Isn't that going to be a six-week mission?" Liz asked.

"On that order," Marc said. "The exact timing will be subject to the exigencies of the situation."

"Of course," Liz said. "Who will command the Roebuck?"

"I want your input on that. What do you think of Lieutenant Payne?"

"He's a pain in the ass," Liz said. "But, joking aside, Catie thought he did an excellent job as her XO, and Captain Desjardins was pleased with his performance as well. What does Blake think?"

"He suggested him," Marc said. "It's a long mission. It could be six months to a year before the Galileo actually makes it out there."

"He's a big boy. Have you talked to him?"

"Not yet, I didn't want to get his hopes up. But if you'll command the Sakira, that puts you in command of the mission until you bring the Sakira home. It's your decision, and you should tell him."

"I'll take care of it. Who's going to command the Galileo when you send her out?"

"Desjardins or Fitzgerald?"

"Good choices," Liz said. "Jodi was the XO of the Victory, so she's ready to handle a detached mission like that, Desjardins has the experience of commanding the Sakira for the end of the asteroid mission as well."

"It'll be Blake's call. You should let him know what you think," Marc said.

"I will; what do I need to do now?"

"Work with Governor Paratar and get the ship ready to leave. I assume she's completed her test jumps."

"About three weeks ago," Liz said. "They've been loading cargo into her and installing the last of the passenger cabins for the past two weeks. Am I going to command her when she goes to Artemis?"

"Not unless you want to. I'd rather you were here for Catie," Marc said. "We can have Commander Desjardins command her, assuming Blake picks Jodi for the Galileo."

"I'm good with that," Liz said.

"Okay, I'll let Blake know, and he'll handle the change of command," Marc said.

"Anything else?"

"No. But I do want to say how much your being there for Catie has meant to her mother and me," Marc said. "You've been instrumental in her life. That's why I want you here on Earth while I'm on Artemis, that way you'll be more available for her."

"And she has been there for me," Liz said. "It's surprising what you can learn from a teenager."

◆ ◆ ◆

"Thanks for having us over," Blake said as Samantha met Jackie and him at the door.

"My pleasure," Samantha said. "And I see you brought the wine."

"Yes, someone told me I should," Blake said while giving Jackie a smile.

"Come on in and sit down," Samantha said. "Marc is just finishing up a call, and after that, he's on the do not disturb list, right ADI?!" The three of them sat on the two sofas in the conversational group in the condo's common room.

"Of course, Cer Sam," ADI said.

"You mean you can do that?" Jackie asked.

"Oh, you haven't met ADI?" Samantha asked.

"I don't think so."

"Hello, Cer Jackie," ADI said.

"There you go, now you've met her. From now on, she'll always be listening on your Comm. You can ask her for help, or sometimes just for info."

"She's always listening?"

"I'm very discreet," ADI said. "I compartmentalize all information to ensure your privacy."

Jackie looked at Samantha, totally confused.

"ADI is the Digital Intelligence that Marc found on the Sakira," Samantha said. "She's very useful and completely reliable."

"Why, thank you, Cer Sam," ADI said.

"And she also has a mild sense of humor."

"I'll keep that in mind," Jackie said.

"Hello, Jackie," Marc said as he entered the room. He walked over and stood behind Samantha, giving her a kiss. "I see you're having a positive influence on Blake." Marc pointed to the bottle of wine to emphasize his point.

"I think it's similar to the positive influence Sam is having on you," Blake said.

"Well, if there's one thing we McCormack boys need, it's a positive influence."

"I'll let Mom know you think so," Blake said.

"That sword will cut both ways," Marc said as he sat down on the sofa next to Samantha. "Jackie, how are you adjusting to life in Delphi City?"

"I was adjusting just fine, but now I hear I'm going to have some more adjustments to make," Jackie said, referring to the fact that Blake would be taking over the public duties of the president.

"Oh, you'll love it," Samantha said, waving her hand at Jackie. "Just a few parties a year. And you'll have to get used to having security around all the time, but you'll hardly notice them, and they are handy for carrying things."

"You're not supposed to give them things to carry," Marc said.

"Hey, my gal always offers to carry stuff for me," Samantha said. "I think she's afraid I might drop it and cause confusion." Samantha winked at Jackie.

"I guess I'll get used to it," Jackie said.

"Sure, did you even notice the two guards that shadowed you here?"

"There were two guards?"

"Yes, there were," Blake said. "We'll start having one actually with us soon, as well as the two shadows. I've been able to avoid that until now."

"I'll give you the contact info for the clothier I use," Samantha said. "She'll either make you a gown or get one for you. Takes the hassle out of a lot of things. I'll also leave you a bunch of the jewelry I've got. I don't think I'll be wearing much on Artemis."

"You don't have to do that."

"They belong to the state," Samantha said.

"Oh, nice."

"Now, would anyone like an aperitif?" Samantha asked.

"I would," Jackie said.

"We have a full bar, but I have some champagne on ice if you would like to try it."

"I'd love to."

"Blake?"

"I'll have some champagne, too."

Marc went to the kitchen and popped the champagne, returning a minute later with four flutes.

"Dinner will be ready in ten minutes or whenever we're ready," Samantha said. "I just want the sauce to simmer some more. The pasta is in the warming drawer, waiting for us."

"Sam is an amazing cook," Marc said.

"But how do you find the time?" Jackie asked.

"It's my hobby, so I usually manage to budget some time. If I get behind, I have someone come in and be my sous chef."

"How does that work?"

"This is Delphi City, there's a service for everything," Samantha said. "Even when we're on Delphi Station, there's always someone available. There's a directory of services on your Comm. You can get anything from someone to wash the vegetables and clean up, to a nice chef to do everything. There are even some gourmet chefs who are amazing. Whatever you need, there's someone at a price willing to come and work. Ask ADI, and she'll be able to get you started."

"That might be nice. I'm always too rushed to cook lately. But it's been busy finishing up the new airliner, and we're starting to bring staff in for training," Jackie said.

"I thought we weren't going to start the airline until next year," Samantha said.

"We're not. But you have to bring in certain staff early enough to get things set up," Jackie said.

"Before I head back to the kitchen to finish up, I wanted to know if you're going to Brussels?" Samantha asked.

"If you're going, it might be fun. We can leave these two behind and do some shopping. And maybe we can squeeze in a side trip to Paris."

"If you want to do that, you have to let the security people know right away," Marc said. "Things like that are more complicated when you're the state representative."

"Hey, you said this would be fun," Jackie whined.

"It will be, you just have to put up with a few inconveniences."

"Dinner's ready; everyone, have a seat," Samantha said. She and Marc each carried two plates filled with pasta covered with a Bolognese sauce. There was a small serving of broccoli on each plate.

"Marc, please pour the wine," Samantha said as she went back to the kitchen. She returned with a basket of bread and set it on the table before sitting down.

"Pasta and bread," Marc said. "That's an unusual treat."

"Why, you don't look like you need to lose weight?" Jackie asked.

"Someone wants me to watch my triglycerides," Marc said. "I need to see if Dr. Metra has a treatment for that. I miss my bread."

"Well, you might not have to miss it much longer," Samantha said.

"Why not, are you giving up on your health campaign?"

"No, we'll talk about it after dinner."

"This is really good," Blake said as Jackie discreetly pushed some of her pasta off onto his plate.

"Did you really like it?" Samantha asked.

"Yes, this pasta is delicious."

"What about the bread?"

"The same. Did you make it?" Blake asked.

"Yes, I did, and I think we've found one of Artemis's first exports."

"What?" Marc asked.

"The pasta and bread are made from that grain you were complaining about," Samantha said. "You know the one that yields zero calories."

"Zero calories?" Jackie asked as she scooped some of her pasta back onto her plate.

"Actually, negative calories; can you imagine how it would improve the diet of the average American if they could have bread that is non-fattening? It fills you up, tastes good, and yields no calories, and the little microbes in your intestines have just as much trouble digesting it as you do, so there won't be any stomach distress."

"I'm not sure the American wheat farmers are going to like that," Blake said.

"There are still plenty of places that need wheat for calories," Samantha said. "This just creates another option."

"Won't they just start growing it themselves?" Jackie asked.

"We'll get a patent on the grain," Samantha said, "so we'll be able to control it. But Dr. Paratar says that we should be able to come up with a sterile form of the wheat so that the plants wouldn't reproduce. His initial research says that you wouldn't be able to cross-pollinate with an Earth variety anyway."

"Why wouldn't you just grind it up before you shipped it?" Blake asked.

"Shipping flour is a lot messier than shipping the grain. And there are all kinds of problems with flour, such as moisture, heat, things like that. Grain is just easier to ship."

"We should have Marcie make some inquiries for us. Oh, damn, she doesn't work for us anymore."

"I'm sure she'll be willing to help us out. Catie can't be keeping her that busy yet," Samantha said. "I'll let Sharon know, and ask Marcie to make some inquiries."

"When will the next presidential ball be?" Jackie asked Samantha as dessert was served.

"I think it'll be the bon voyage party for the Artemis mission," Samantha replied, looking at Marc for confirmation.

"That's right, we're targeting the first of October to head out, so the ball will probably be in late September."

"I think you're crazy to go to Artemis; it's going to be like roughing it," Jackie said.

"And we all know how much Sam likes to rough it," Blake said.

"Oh, it won't be that bad," Samantha said. "We'll be able to stay on the Sakira until we have adequate accommodations on the planet. But just think, every day we'll be doing something that really makes a difference to the colony."

"Is everything going to be ready?" Jackie asked.

"The Sakira just got back from testing its jumpdrives," Blake said. "The Paraxeans are already loading her up for their trip to Mangkatar."

"So, they're going to go first?" Jackie asked.

"Only seems fair. They've been waiting a long time," Marc said. "And they're a bit more prepared than we are."

"Really?" Blake asked.

"They don't need to recruit," Marc said.

"Oh, yeah. They just need to wake them up."

# 13 First Week of Classes

"Hi, I'm Yvette LeClair," the tall brunette introduced herself to Catie. She had a French accent to go along with the French-sounding name. "I believe I am your roommate."

"I'm Alex MacGregor," Catie introduced herself. "And welcome." The Academy required roommates to be in the same class. Since Catie was a second-class cadet and Joanie was a third-class cadet, they had had to change roommates after Basic.

"Thank you."

"I don't think we've met before."

"No, I was in Alfa Squadron," Yvette said. "I've seen you around, but we've never been in the same class or training exercise."

"Oh, so you have previous academy experience," Catie said.

"Yes, I was at the French Naval Academy," Yvette said. "I got sick my junior year and had to withdraw. I came to Delphi City to get treated, and when they opened the Academy, I applied."

"Did you take time off after Guatemala?"

"No, I just got here; we were the last squadron to go through that final exam. I can still smell that mud. I wanted to burn my uniforms and everything else from Guatemala."

"I know how you feel. Well, you've got the right side of the room. Do you need any help getting settled in?"

"No, though I appreciate the offer. What's your major?"

"Aerospace engineering," Catie said.

"Nice, I'm doing computer science. Math is not my best subject, but I do great with set theory and pattern recognition."

"You must have had to take a few core classes that required math at the French Academy."

"Sure, but I really had to work at them. I have a more artistic bent, so those classes weren't as fun," Yvette said.

"How long have you been in Delphi City?" Catie asked.

"Eight months," Yvette said. "I was diagnosed in December and came out here in February, then stuck around after I was cured."

"What did you do?"

"I worked for Vancouver Integrated while I was waiting for the University to open. The Academy was a nice surprise."

"Vancouver Integrated, they're the ones that make our Comms," Catie said.

"Not anymore, they spun that division off."

"Oh," Catie said, although, of course, she knew all that.

"Are you new to Delphi City?"

"I spent a summer here with my parents. My father was working in one of the construction crews. But I'm from San Diego, California."

"I see. I'm from Nice, PACA," Yvette said.

"PACA?"

"Provence-Alpes-Côte d'Azur, what you would think of as the French Riviera."

"Sounds nice."

"You've never been?"

"No, but it's on my list."

◆ ◆ ◆

"I have to go see the commandant," Catie said. Yvette was still arranging her things in the various drawers and the closet.

"I hope you're not in trouble."

"So do I. I'll see you when I get back, maybe we can go have dinner together."

"Bien sûr, au revoir."

Catie made her way to the commandant's office, wondering why she was being summoned again. Hopefully, the commandant was just checking in, but Catie was afraid it would be about Hoffman.

"I'm here to see the commandant," Catie said to the aide who was seated behind the reception desk in the outer office.

"One moment, please," the petty officer said as she signaled the commandant.

"Have a seat, the commandant will be ready for you shortly."

"Oh, great, she's going to make me sweat," Catie thought as she sat down to wait.

Five minutes later, the aide announced that the commandant was ready for her, and Catie went in.

"Cadet MacGregor, reporting as ordered." Catie snapped to attention in front of the commandant's desk and saluted.

"At ease, Cadet. Please have a seat."

"Yes, Ma'am," Catie said as she sat down.

"I just have a few questions following up on our earlier meeting," Commandant Lewis said. "How are you and Cadet Major Baker getting along?"

"Just fine, Ma'am."

"He gave you a glowing report on your training in Guatemala."

"He did?" Catie said. She wasn't surprised since their squadron had been one of the few that had made a successful attack against a defending force during the exercise.

"Yes, he did, and several of the squadron's Flight leaders submitted separate reports, several recommending you for commendations."

"I think everyone in the squadron performed exemplary during the final exam," Catie said.

"What about Cadet Lieutenant Hoffman and Cadet Lieutenant Boutros?"

"They didn't participate in the exercise."

"No, they didn't. I see they were dismissed by Cadet Major Baker for holding an unauthorized martial arts exhibition where a Cadet Sanchez was injured."

Catie stared ahead, *"Here it comes,"* she thought.

"Cadet Hoffman has been asked to leave the Academy, Cadet Boutros was demoted and allowed to stay. What do you think of that?"

"I think that's probably the right call," Catie said.

"Why?"

"Cadet Lieutenant Hoffman was the instigator. I doubt that Cadet Lieutenant Boutros knew what he was planning."

"And what of Sanchez?"

"He didn't do anything but follow orders," Catie said.

"Even the order to break your arm?"

"He said that he knew he wouldn't be able to do it," Catie said. "I give him the benefit of the doubt."

"You do? Do you think we should have him repeat the training in Guatemala next summer since he was unable to participate in the final exam, . . . due to a busted knee?"

"No, Ma'am. As I recall, he did very well in the earlier part of the training. I think he would be better served having a different experience next summer."

"And the cadet who busted his knee?"

"She didn't feel she had a choice," Catie said. "Sanchez outweighed her by twenty-five kilos and she wouldn't have been able to keep up with him if the fight had kept going on much longer at that level of intensity."

"And the cracked ribs?"

"Possibly the cadet lost her temper," Catie said. "Some disciplinary action might be in order."

Commandant Lewis smiled. "Cadet Sanchez indicated that he deserved the kick in the ribs. He said he was getting tired and wanted you to end the fight, so he was more aggressive than needed."

"I see," Catie said.

"Moving on. When I asked Cadet Major Baker why he hadn't made you a Flight leader once you were back, he said that you had asked him not to. Care to explain?"

*"Oh, so that's where she's going. I guess he had to rat me out,"* Catie thought. "Ma'am, I've been told by people I trust that I need to learn to follow more than I need to learn to lead," Catie said.

"Interesting, but that is true no matter what rank you hold."

"Yes, Ma'am. But if I'm not in a leadership position, it'll be easier for me to focus on the following part."

"Ah, I see. There are twelve reviews from your time in Guatemala that say you're a natural leader," Commandant Lewis said. "Half of them are from the Marine instructors. It's quite unusual for them to make such strong comments about a cadet."

Catie just looked straight ahead. She didn't know how one should respond to such a statement, and since it wasn't a question, she decided on silence.

"I see. Very well, I'll respect your wishes and reevaluate after the semester," Commandant Lewis said. "You're dismissed."

Catie stood to attention, saluted, did an about-face, and left. She breathed a sigh of relief once she was out of the office, then made a beeline for the dorms.

"What did she want?" Yvette asked once Catie made it back to their room.

"Just checking in," Catie said.

"About Baker?" Yvette asked.

"Oh, I guess everyone knows about that," Catie said, "and, yes."

"*Mon Dieu,* it was the talk of the leadership team," Yvette said. "Poor Baker couldn't move without someone asking for his help in deciding who they should date. It was a good thing they sent him to Guatemala early. Even then, I heard the instructors there gave him a hard time about it."

"I didn't realize that," Catie said.

"Then Cadet Baker must be a good officer," Yvette said.

"I thought he did a good job in Guatemala."

"And Cadet Hoffman?"

"He was an ass. I guess he's been asked to leave the Academy."

"That's good. That story also made the rounds. Most of the leadership team were happy to see him go."

"Glad to hear that. Are you ready for dinner?"

"*Oui.*"

◆ ◆ ◆

"You know, I find this city amazing," Yvette said.

"Why, besides the fact that it is floating in the middle of the ocean?" Catie asked.

"Because people come from everywhere, but everyone speaks English. In France, there are protests about the fact that we have to provide services in so many languages."

"Oh!" Catie said. "Well, Delphi City requires everyone to learn English as soon as they arrive."

"Requiring people to learn a language is one thing, but how do they get them to learn it?" Yvette asked. "I learned English in school as a little girl, and still, mine is not so good."

"Oh, they teach them using their Comms and specs," Catie said, pointing to the specs they were both wearing.

"We too have computer programs to teach French, how can this one be so much better?"

"First, everyone wears specs all the time, and they always have their Comm with them. When you first start learning a new language, they tell you to wear your earwig when you sleep. Then when your Comm detects that you're sleeping, it starts to play recordings in the language while you sleep."

"Hah, learning while you sleep, that doesn't work!"

"It only helps. They say that when a baby is born, it already understands the grammatical syntax of the language its mother speaks. Just by hearing it all during the pregnancy, its brain has already started to parse it. So this does the same, helping your brain learn to hear the language. It's especially important for the sounds that are not in your native language; some people cannot even distinguish certain sounds from similar ones in their language."

"Okay, so maybe that helps. But how do they teach you?"

"From day one, your Comm points out objects you encounter by highlighting them in your specs, while it says the word for them. It saves all those in a database, then it replays them for you later, showing you the image you saw and resaying the word. Eventually, it starts to test you on them. After you have a vocabulary of objects, it starts to point out actions or activities. Most people develop a rudimentary understanding within a couple of weeks."

"Within a couple of weeks?"

"The program is relentless," Catie said. "And everything around you is in English, so there's plenty of reinforcement."

"They don't allow you to speak your native tongue?" Yvette asked, not sounding happy about it.

"Oh, sure they do. You hear other languages all the time," Catie said. "But your Comm tells everyone that you're learning, so they know to only speak English around you."

"How do they learn to speak?"

"Mimicry, at first. After three weeks, it has you repeat all the phonics that you've heard until you get them right. I've heard that it's pretty miserable for a couple of days, but then it gets easier."

"Sounds like torture."

"Pavlov's principle. You get a nice tune when you get the phonic right, an awful buzzing sound when you don't."

"And it works?"

"Yes, you could use the program to improve your English if you want. You could even train yourself to lose your accent. That is, if you want to lose it."

"I might try it. It would be nice not to have an accent, except when I want one," Yvette said.

"Do the guys think your accent is sexy?"

"Some of them," Yvette said. "How long does it take?"

"Within two months, everyone is functional enough that they can get a job."

"What do they do for money before they can get a job?"

"The city pays them to do things like clean the streets and stuff like that; unless they have children, then they are paid just to take care of their children while they all learn."

"But how much can they make sweeping the streets?"

"Oh, the job doesn't really matter; you get your condo rent-free and an open account to use to buy food and essentials; after two months you get a job and have to start paying for your own shopping, but your condo is still rent-free for the first six months."

"That is generous," Yvette said.

"I guess, but then everyone has to work. They say the taxes pay back the money within a year, and the city doesn't have anyone on long-term welfare."

"No people who just want to live on the, what is the word, dole?"

"That's the word the British use. Last I checked nobody was living on the dole," Catie said.

"I should get my brother to come here. Maybe they could get him to get a job," Yvette said.

"What does he do?"

"He lives with my parents and goes to school."

"So, he just needs to graduate."

"He is five years older than I am. School is his job; he keeps changing what he studies so that he will never graduate. My parents just keep paying for him."

"I guess there's always someone who will take advantage of any system. I'll have to check and see if Delphi City has anyone doing it now. It's been a year since I was here before."

"Hey, Alex!" two cadets called out as they walked by their table.

"Hi, Charles, hi Ricardo," Catie replied.

"Isn't Ricardo the one you had the fight with?" Yvette asked.

"Yes, but he's cool."

"You know that it is not always too good to be well known at the Academy?"

"Yeah, I've heard that. I keep trying to keep a low profile, but I guess I'm not very good at it."

"Maybe I can help you with that."

"You can try."

The next morning, Catie was reviewing the report from Ajda on the StarMerchant when Yvette's alarm went off.

"What the . . ." Catie jumped as the blaring music started up. She caught her breath and looked over to see when Yvette would turn the thing off. She saw a hand come out from under the covers and paw at the Comm sitting on the table. After a few attempts, it finally found the Comm and silenced the alarm. Catie checked the time in her HUD, *"0545, plenty of time to keep reviewing the specs."*

"What the . . ." Catie jumped again as the same music started blaring. She looked over and saw Yvette's hand reaching toward her Comm again. "Oh, no you don't!" Catie walked over and pulled the blanket off Yvette.

"Rise and shine!" she yelled.

Yvette rolled over and pulled the pillow over her head. "Not a chance!" Catie hissed as she grabbed the pillow. Then she took the glass of water from the bedside table and sprinkled a little on Yvette's face.

"What!" Yvette squealed.

"Your alarm is going off!" Catie said as she thrust the Comm at Yvette.

"It's only the second alarm," Yvette said. She grabbed her Comm and silenced it.

"Well, it's the last one I want to hear," Catie said. "Now get up and get ready. PT starts in twenty minutes."

Yvette sat up, gave Catie a dirty look, then stumbled into the bathroom, taking her Comm with her. Fifteen minutes later, Yvette came out and got dressed. "I could have slept for another five minutes," she grumbled.

"You could have lived another five minutes," Catie said. "One more blast of that music and I would have killed you."

"What were you doing up?"

"I woke up at 0430 and was doing some work," Catie said.

"What would possess you to get up that early, are you still on Guatemala time?"

"No, I always get up early. That way, I can take care of my morning routine in peace, get some work done, and not be rudely awakened by anyone."

"Oh, they don't do that to us second-classers," Yvette said. "I don't even think they do it to the fourth-classers anymore."

"Well, I always get up at 0430," Catie said. "If nobody's pounding on me, I do just fine with five hours of sleep."

"Wow! And sorry about the alarm. I should have warned you."

"That would have been nice," Catie said as she pulled on her running shoes. "You need to get ready."

Yvette quickly pulled on a shipsuit and shoes, ran a brush through her hair, and slapped her face a couple of times. "I'm ready."

"You know I can wake you up if you like."

"I don't like your wake-up method," Yvette said. "It's too harsh."

"And loud music isn't?"

"Not to me."

"Why don't you leave your earwig in and have your Comm start playing the music. It can keep raising the volume until you finally decide to get up."

"Oh, I'll try that. I'm sure it will be more pleasant than water in my face."

"I wasn't trying to be pleasant when I chose the water," Catie threatened.

When Catie walked into her first class of the morning, she was shocked to see the other cadets spread out and chatting with each other while they waited for the instructor to arrive. It was a small classroom, which was what she'd expected for an advanced class. As she recalled, it was similar to her eighth-grade classrooms, the last formal classes she'd attended. The lack of discipline was still discomforting. She shook her head and took a seat, waiting for one of the cadet officers to come in and start yelling at everyone.

The professor arrived just before the top of the hour. "Please take your seats," he called out in a strong voice. "This is advanced aerodynamics; if that's not the class you were expecting, please exit."

He waited to see if anyone left, before continuing. "During class time, I expect everyone to pay attention, there will be no use of phones or other electronic devices."

"Sir, our Comms are disabled during class hours," one of the cadets informed him.

"Excellent, then we shouldn't have any problems," the professor said. "I'm Dr. Carl Madison. Now let's talk about wing deflection when an aircraft is at supersonic speeds."

Catie's last class of the day was Military Space Strategy, and the instructor was Admiral Michaels. This time everyone was in their seat, sitting at attention. Catie followed suit and waited. She wondered if Admiral Michaels might recognize her. She was pretty sure that her father had kept her attendance at the Academy secret from him.

Admiral Michaels entered the room wearing civilian clothes. He was after all the minister of defense for Delphi Nation.

"At ease," he said to stanch everyone's rise to attention. "This class will be taught by a collection of men and women who served in the war. We are still developing the concept of how to fight in space, so you can consider yourselves guinea pigs. As part of the course, you will be presented with various scenarios. You will develop battle plans to deal with them, and then we will conduct simulations to test those plans.

"These simulations will be conducted by some of our most valuable assets, so do not take the work lightly. This is an elective class, but if you do not take it seriously, I will not hesitate to dismiss you so you don't waste our resources," Admiral Michaels said as he gave everyone in the class a hard stare.

"We have records from previous encounters that the Paraxeans have had with other civilizations as well as our experience during the war. We will break down each of those encounters into minute detail, examining what worked, what didn't work, and what opportunities were missed by both sides."

Catie leaned forward, *"This is going to be a lot of fun,"* she whispered to herself.

"Yes it is, Cer Catie," ADI said. "And since I'll be the *asset* running the simulations, I'll be able to make sure you have extra fun."

"No fair picking on me!" Catie messaged.

"I won't be picking on you, just making sure you're suitably challenged."

"How were your classes?" Yvette asked when she joined Catie in their room.

"Interesting," Catie said. "A lot more relaxed than I expected."

"This is a college, so unless you're in one of the military electives, it's just the same. You'll have to watch for when you're taking a normal class from an active-duty officer, they can be a bit of a pain. But most of your instructors should be normal college professors."

"How's your homework load?"

"I've got two chapters to read in the theory of logistics management," Yvette said. "Plus, I have to read the first three chapters of Brave New World. How about you?"

"I have to read the after-action reports from the first battle of the Paraxean war. I'm also supposed to read the first chapter of Advanced Aerodynamics, but I've already read the book."

"You've already read the book?!"

"Hey, I'm studying to be an aerospace engineer, I read it last year. It was part of a project I was working on," Catie said. She'd read the book when she was trying to figure out the sonic-suppressors on their spaceplanes that allowed the planes to fly at supersonic speeds without creating a sonic boom. Eventually, Dr. McDowell had been able to decipher the math and close the gaps that allowed them to design the supersonic airliner that they were now building.

"So you're one of those."

"What do you mean by one of those?"

"A brainiac," Yvette said. "I think you call them nerds."

"I guess I am, but that doesn't mean I'm not fun, or *dangerous*."

"Well, Cadets Watanabe and Sanchez can testify to how dangerous you are; I'll let you know if you're any fun after a few weeks," Yvette said with a laugh.

On Saturday morning after PT, Catie headed over to Dr. Sharmila's house. The Cadets were allowed to spend the weekend with their Academy family or their real family, but only from 1000 Saturday to 2200 Sunday unless they requested official leave. Catie waved goodbye to Yvette, who was also going to spend the weekend with her Academy family.

When she arrived at Dr. Sharmila's house, Catie was swamped by the twins. After hugs and kisses, they wanted to know everything that had happened in Guatemala as well as her first week of classes.

"Hey, hey, I need to have some time to do work," Catie said.

"Why?!" the twins demanded. "This is the weekend; you're supposed to be on break!"

"Cadet MacGregor is on break, but Catie McCormack has projects she has to review," Catie explained.

"Later, we've been waiting for a whole month."

"Girls," Dr. Sharmila scolded.

"Tell you what. You give me two hours while people I need to talk to are still available, and then you can have the rest of the day," Catie said.

"Girls, you could finish your homework," Dr. Sharmila said. "Then you'll be free to spend the rest of the afternoon with Catie. Catie, we're going out to dinner tonight; 7:00, and dress nice."

"Anything special?" Catie asked.

"Just your visit," Dr. Sharmila said.

Dr. Sharmila shamed Catie into wearing a dress for dinner since they were going to Deogene's. When they arrived, Kenyon met them at the door and escorted them to the back room.

"Surprise!" Marc said meeting her at the door to the room.

"Oh my gosh, Daddy, how, why?" Catie asked as she rushed to hug her father.

"We thought we would take advantage of this room so we could all get a chance to see you after your big summer, and do it without the risk of blowing your cover," Marc said. "Here I brought you a set of contact lenses, it'll make it easier to explain your appearance to the others."

"Thanks, Daddy. Oh, this is so nice; I've missed everyone!"

"Now go put in your contacts then say hello to your mother; after that, you can start hugging all your friends," Samantha whispered to Catie.

Catie rushed to the restroom and put in the contacts, then she returned and made her entrance into the room. "Hey, everyone, what a surprise!"

Several of her friends waved at her, but left her alone as it was obvious that she was heading toward her mother.

"Hi, Mommy," Catie said as she wrapped her arms around Linda.

"Hi, Sweetie. How are you surviving?"

"It's been rough, but now that we've started classes, I think the hard part is over."

"That's what your Uncle Blake says."

"Hey, Zane," Catie said as he came over and handed Linda a drink.

"Hi, Catie, come by and chat when you're free," he said before he headed to the other side of the room.

"You don't mind that he's here, do you?" Linda asked.

"Hey, he's your boyfriend, why would I?" Catie asked.

"It's just . . ."

"Don't worry about it, Mommy. Daddy and I are both glad to see you happy."

"Good, now go ahead and visit with your friends."

"Hi, Uncle Blake." Catie walked over to Blake and Liz. "Hi, Liz."

"Hey, Squirt. Break any knees lately?" Blake asked.

"Oh, so you heard about that?"

"It came across my desk," Blake said. "Just part of the weekly update from Commandant Lewis."

"You broke someone's knee?!" Liz asked.

"Just tore the ligaments," Catie said. "He's fine."

"What was going on?"

"Martial arts demonstration," Catie said. "It got out of hand."

"I'll say. Did you get in trouble?"

"Not much!"

"There's more to this than you're saying, I want the real skinny," Liz said.

"Maybe later," Catie said as she saw Sophia heading her way. "Hi, Sophia."

"I owe you one!" Sophia snarled.

"For *what?*" Catie asked, all innocent-like.

"You know what!"

"I have no idea what you're talking about," Catie said.

"Dad had the police look into it, but they couldn't find anything," Sophia said. "But I know you did it."

"Did what?"

"Green, did you have to choose green?!"

"I still don't know what you're talking about," Catie said. "Are you here to get some dirt for your next book?"

"You know someone was going to write it sooner or later; at least I was a friend," Sophia said.

"I know, but it was still a shock," Catie said. "But, I forgive you."

"Arr," Sophia shook her head. "Okay, I forgive you too!"

"For what, oh, you mean being mad at you. Well, thanks," Catie said.

"By the way, what's with your hair?" Sophia asked.

"Just trying out a new look," Catie said. "What do you think?"

"I like your normal look. This look doesn't look as fun."

"What was that all about?" Liz whispered to Blake.

"Apparently Sophia's shower had some green food coloring in the water one morning. Dr. Metra cleaned most of it off for her, but she still had a light green tinge for a few days," Blake said.

Liz started giggling. "I could have told her she was going to get nailed. Catie always gets even," Liz said. Catie must have heard Liz giggle and looked their way, so Liz gave her a little wave.

"They couldn't prove anything; they don't even know how she pulled it off," Blake said.

"Was Admiral Michaels pissed?"

"No, his attitude was no harm, no foul, and Sophia should have known better."

"What about Pam?"

"Same thing. They both had a hard time not laughing, Sophia was being so histrionic about the whole thing."

"I'm sorry I missed it."

"I have several videos of her throwing a fit," ADI said. "Two of the best are when she was still very green."

"Oh, please send them to me," Liz said.

"I will, but don't share them with Catie."

"Why not?"

"She and I are having a little disagreement," ADI said.

"Oh, she didn't tell you?"

"Something like that," ADI replied

# 14 What About Earth?

"Have they told you any more about what this is all about?" Blake asked Marc as the two men and their ladies boarded the Lynx for their flight to Brussels.

"No, I think they're planning to ambush us with the details. They don't want us to be able to have a prepared response," Marc said.

"Like that's going to work," Samantha said. "ADI will be able to analyze and provide options on anything they come up with."

"Well, they don't know about ADI," Marc said. "She and I have been going through probable issues all week."

"What about Blake?" Samantha asked.

"I've been getting helpful summaries," Blake said. "And I do appreciate being left out of the nitty-gritty."

"I assumed you would. Now let's enjoy our flight," Marc said. "We've timed it so we can have a nice dinner while en route. We'll arrive right after their breakfast."

"So, after a nice big dinner, we'll arrive, check-in, and have a nap," Jackie said. "Then we'll be ready for the day. It's exactly twelve hours difference between Delphi City and Brussels."

"What's the final guest list?" Blake asked as he and Marc prepared to leave for the conference.

"The G20 plus us."

"Who's attending, their ambassadors, or the political leaders?"

"Brazil and Mexico are sending their ambassadors. Mainly, I think, to express disapproval at the late invite. I think the rest are sending the head of state."

"Politics is so much fun," Blake said. "Are you prepared for the roasting?"

"We'll see."

"We expected just you, Mr. President," the President of China said when Marc and Blake entered the conference room. Apparently, he had been elected as chairperson of the conference.

"Since you said this was about Earth's defense, I thought bringing the commander of our space fleet would be appropriate," Marc replied.

"You didn't tell them I was coming?" Blake whispered.

"I like to provide a few surprises as well," Marc whispered back.

"Very well, if you will give us a moment, we'll rearrange the table to make room."

"Thank you. I would also like to offer the use of our translation service," Marc said. He held up the briefcase he was carrying. "It will do simultaneous translations for each of us and allow us to minimize the number of people in the room."

"I am quite happy with my translator," the Chinese president said.

"Suit yourself," Marc said as he placed the receiver in the center of the table and started to hand out earwigs to any of the other representatives who asked for them. The Russian president was the first to request one, followed quickly by most of the other representatives. Only China, Brazil, and South Africa refused.

The Chinese president turned and whispered to his aide, "Bring a hard chair for Admiral Blake, we should express our displeasure at his late addition." Everyone with an earwig turned to look at them. It was obvious that they had heard the comment, and that most of them were not happy about it.

"I apologize," the Chinese president said. "Please bring Admiral Blake a comfortable chair. And I would like one of your earwigs as well."

The Brazilian Ambassador and the South African president both followed suit.

"We represent the major economies of Earth, and like in the earlier war with the Paraxeans, we also represent the major resources of the planet, and should have been informed that you intend to send two of the space carriers out to these new planets you have discovered," the Chinese president said.

"Your sources are correct. We are planning to send the Victory to Artemis and the newly renamed Galileo to the Paraxean colony on Mangkatar," Marc replied. He noticed the Russian president winked at him. He had a smile on his face as he seemed to appreciate Marc's tactics.

The Chinese president didn't seem to appreciate them; he was obviously expecting more of a reply. "And you did not think you should inform us?!" he asked.

"No," Marc replied, which further frustrated the Chinese president. But if the man was going to scold him, Marc was firmly decided to be as brief and uninformative with his answers as possible.

"And why not?!"

"The carriers belong to Delphi Nation."

"But what about the defense of Earth?!"

"You just pointed out that you and the leaders who have joined you here were the true defenders of Earth," Marc said.

"How do you expect us to defend Earth without space capabilities?!"

"I was wondering that myself," Marc said. "Maybe you can explain it to me."

The Chinese president let out a series of expletives that the Comm device dutifully translated for everyone, leading to quite a few laughs.

"Can we please quit playing games," the Chinese president said.

"I would be happy to, as you say, quit playing games. I came here for a discussion and to provide information, not to be scolded like a schoolboy."

"Again, I apologize. Please explain to us how the loss of two of the space carriers will not affect the planet's security."

"We only had two space carriers during the war," Marc said. "We will still have two carriers when the Victory and Galileo redeploy. We are bringing the battleship that we captured to Galileo, where it will be broken apart, and its components used to build more starships to defend Earth."

"I see."

"What about the crews and spaceplanes?" the French president asked.

"We have been replacing the Foxes and Hyraxes we lost during the war. The Victory and Galileo will only carry two squadrons each, so the remaining space carriers will both have a full complement of the appropriate spaceplanes. As for pilots, we are continuing to recruit and train pilots to replace those that your countries recalled. But I'm sure that if the need arises, the pilots and ground crews will be made available."

"But what if someone attacks us with more force than the Paraxeans did?" the German Chancellor asked.

Blake leaned forward, indicating he would answer this question. "Madam Chancellor, we won the war against the Paraxeans, not by superior numbers but by superior innovations and tactics. It is impossible to prepare for the unknown, but if we were to commit our resources to defend against what we encountered in the last war, we would very likely be creating obsolete arms and ships. We need to make sure we have resources available to respond when we understand the threat. We're mining the key elements we need from the asteroid belt. Delphi Nation is building a strategic reserve of the resources necessary to build new weapons, but we don't know what they should be. We're better served to build adequate defense capabilities and make sure we have the capacity in place to quickly add to or change them."

"And you are confident that you have done so?" the chancellor asked.

"As confident as we can be with the information we have."

"And the command of these forces?" President Novak of the U.S. asked.

"I assume we would follow the same model as during the last war," Blake said.

"And if we are not comfortable with that model?" President Novak asked.

"As already mentioned, you would need to do something about your lack of space capabilities," Marc said, "or come up with a better option."

"What would you consider a better option?" President Novak asked.

"I'm not sure. None of you is willing to give control over the space forces to anyone except your own countries, so that leaves us with a null set. The U.N. is ineffective because of the veto capability that each of the five permanent members of the Security Council has, plus the main assembly is composed of too many small nations with competing agendas."

"That is why we have the veto!" the Chinese president seemed to be getting a bit testy.

"I understand that, but it still results in an ineffectual governing body."

President Novak leaned forward, "We'd like to create a more formalized structure for the alliance." She obviously thought Marc would respond better to her, given their past relationship.

"Such as?"

"Something more on the lines of NATO," President Novak said.

"I'm not sure I'm all that fond of the NATO structure," Marc said. "But what would it look like?"

"More officers and personnel from the allied nations serving."

"There were some problems with that the last time," Marc said, referring to the time that the previous president had tried to engineer a coup using the U.S. officers assigned to the alliance.

"We believe we're beyond such childish behavior," President Novak said. "Everyone on Earth understands the importance of the alliance, and I don't think anyone will be so easily swayed."

"What else?"

"A rotating command?"

"That's not going to happen, at least not in the near future," Marc said.

"Then at least a military committee with key members present. We would like to have a way to be involved with decisions and to influence them."

Blake put a hand on Marc's arm to quiet him. "That's not unreasonable," Blake said. "But the Delphinean commander will have the final say."

"Yes, of course. We understand you cannot run a military based on a majority vote, but we would like to be confident that the commander will listen to our people."

"I haven't noticed your people having trouble being heard in the past," Blake said. "But I'm sure we can work things out."

They spent over two hours working on a basic outline of the changes in the alliance. Marc allowed Blake to deal with most of it since he was familiar with the structure of NATO and the armed services in general. Finally, they made enough progress to hand the effort off to the yet-to-be appointed military committee.

"I thought they were going to make us stay there and write the whole damn thing," Marc complained as they made their way to their limousine.

"When did you become so impatient?" Blake asked.

"When I'm forced to deal with petty politics and crap like seating arrangements."

"That was a bit much," Blake said. "Who's going to be our chairman?"

"Admiral Michaels."

"Are you sure? He seems to like Delphi City, and he is the Minister of Defense. Who would replace him?"

"I'm sure; the man loves politics. And I think Captain Clark will be able to handle the defense ministry."

"You just made him the commander of Delphi Station."

"You have to roll with the times."

"You two need to get ready for dinner," Samantha said. "And we do not want to hear you talking about your day. We have far more interesting things to discuss."

Blake laughed at his brother and followed Jackie into their room. They had a suite at the Steigenberger Wiltcher's Hotel and shared the sitting room. Blake wondered if that was such a good idea as he watched Samantha take over.

"Did you have a tough day?" Jackie asked.

"Not really, just frustrating politics. Can you believe I had to restrain Marc?"

"That is hard to believe," Jackie said, agreeing a little quicker than Blake would have liked. "Did you accomplish anything?"

"Yes and no. They got most of what they wanted, but it really doesn't change anything. It just adds a lot more bureaucracy to the alliance coordination, but if it makes them happy . . ."

"It has to do more than that."

"Probably over the long term," Blake said. "It sets things up for a more coordinated effort in the future. And who knows what will happen when we have three or four colonies we're responsible for."

"You are ambitious. Now zip me up," Jackie said as she turned around so Blake could zip up her evening gown. "What's on the agenda for tomorrow?"

"Economics."

"That sounds interesting," Jackie said as she turned around and started to tie Blake's bowtie.

"Sound's boring to me. It's going to be a bunch more whining, although I'm sure Marc will provide some entertainment as he puts them in their place."

"Puts them in their place?"

"Get Sam to allow him to describe the first five minutes," Blake said. "It was quite entertaining."

They exited the room and met Marc and Samantha in the sitting room as they prepared to leave the suite. The four bodyguards standing around the room were so discreet that it was easy to forget they were there.

"We're giving you guys a break and eating downstairs today," Samantha said.

"And why are you being so nice to us?" Blake asked.

"Because tomorrow we're dining at the royal palace," Samantha said.

"Oh no," Blake groaned.

"Be nice. I think it was nice of Queen Mathilde to invite us. Princess Elizabeth remembers Catie from the birthday party," Samantha said.

"Oh, and has Catie ever forgiven you for that stunt?"

"We've reached a truce," Samantha said, as she thought about Catie spreading the rumor that she and Marc were getting married so that Samantha would have a taste of her own publicity medicine. Samantha had called her out on it, and they had agreed to call their differences even.

"I'd love to hear the inside story on that," Blake said. "I assume that at least you didn't come out of the shower green."

"Thankfully," Samantha said. "Did you guys ever figure out how she pulled that off?"

"I think she had help," Marc said.

"I did not assist her in any way," ADI said.

"Oh, but now you're acknowledging that she was behind it," Marc said.

"I did not, but like you, I assume she did it," ADI said.

"Do you believe her?" Samantha asked.

"Mostly," Marc said. "She can't lie, but I still think she was in on it."

"A true friend never tells," ADI said.

"Your table is right this way," the Maître D' said. He obviously recognized someone in their party.

Jackie did get Samantha to allow Blake to tell about how Marc had checked the Chinese president's scolding, but then they spent the rest of the dinner talking about the ladies' visit to the Saint-Michel Cathedral, the Grand Palace, and the Royal Museum.

The next morning Marc and Blake made their way back to the conference room to see what the G20 members had in mind.

"Welcome back," the Chinese president greeted them. "We hope we can have as fruitful a discussion today as we had yesterday."

Marc thought he was piling it on since he didn't think anyone considered yesterday that fruitful, but he ignored it.

"One of the things we members of the G20 do is oversee the global economy. We continually look for opportunities to enhance the economic wellbeing of our countries through cooperation," the Chinese president said.

"I'm aware of your agenda," Marc said without voicing the fact that they tended to do only things that enhanced their country's economies at the expense of all the other countries of the world.

"We know that you are carefully introducing the technology you've garnered from the Paraxeans into the world economy. We would like to help in that process."

"I'm not sure we need any help there," Marc said. "We've been tracking our plan pretty well. In fact, I'm sure all of you know that last year was the first time in recent history that carbon emissions actually fell. And last month appears to be the first time the CO2 levels in the atmosphere also fell."

"We are aware of that and are grateful for your efforts that have made that possible."

"Thank you."

"What we would like to see is a more equitable distribution of that technology," the Chinese president said.

"Such as?"

"A more equitable distribution of the small fusion reactors for one."

The Russian president smiled at Marc; he obviously wasn't interested in a more equitable distribution of the reactors since Russia was the main consumer. They were re-exporting them as the powerplants of ships and locomotives.

"I don't recall you having that concern when you were getting the majority of the large fusion reactors," Marc said.

"We were simply taking advantage of what was offered. At that time, you were offering the fusion reactor to anyone who met your terms," the Chinese president said.

"We were. However, at this time, we are at capacity on the small fusion reactors. We feel that the agreement we have with Russia will result in their equitable distribution throughout the world."

"But this is hurting the economies of many of our countries."

"Only by a small amount," Marc replied. "I'm sure that the Russian economy will start to purchase more from your countries as the money starts to flow into it."

"Of course we will," the Russian president said.

"But it is disruptive changes such as that which we would like to manage," the Chinese president said.

"I understand," Marc said. "I know you would prefer to fight among yourselves for the economic opportunities and leave the rest of the world to pick up the crumbs. Our stated goal is to balance that out, and I see no reason to change that."

President Novak stepped in to calm the discussion. "But you must see that we have to avoid too severe a change. If our economies fail, then they will bring the rest of the world economies down with them."

"I am aware of that, and we are taking careful measures to ensure that doesn't happen," Marc said. "Our goal is for the world economy to improve."

The French president jumped in. "The concession for polysteel that you've given to Algeria has had an adverse impact on French steel production. We would like to avoid things like that."

"Unfortunately, that is impossible," Marc said. "You were happy enough when the price of oil dropped. The price of steel dropping will benefit other parts of the economy, both in France and the rest of the world."

"But you can see why we would be concerned," President Novak said. "The U.S. steel industry is very worried about the impact of Algeria's polysteel coming onto the market."

"And they're worried about us reaching a similar agreement with someone in the Americas," Marc suggested. "Well, you can tell them that we are considering a similar license with Brazil."

Everyone looked at the Brazilian ambassador. "I was only made aware that such discussions were in the works just before I came to this conference," he said. "I'm told that Delphi has set a precondition of stopping all deforestation and the institution of a plan to regenerate parts of our rainforest."

"It is just such a shock that we would like to avoid. If we are notified in advance, then our industries can start to shift their jobs and capacity around to lessen the impact," President Novak said.

"If I believed that you would do that instead of trying to block the agreement, I would be more inclined to provide such notice," Marc said.

"How can we assure you?"

"You have five minutes to tell us how your meeting went," Samantha said as Marc and Blake walked into their suite. "Then we have to get dressed."

Jackie was just tipping the two hairdressers who had just finished putting the finishing touches on the women's hair for their dinner at the royal palace.

"It wasn't nearly as fun as yesterday," Blake said. "I think they won most of the arguments."

"I wouldn't say that," Marc said.

"Well, you agreed to timeline the introduction of technology with them."

"Sure, but I was always planning to do that. I was waiting until I could force concessions on helping out the third world countries as well as more focus on reducing environmental impacts."

# 15 A Home at Last

"Governor Paratar, I'm Commander Farmer. I'll be the Captain of the Sakira and in charge of the Delphinean forces for your colony mission. This is Lieutenant Beaulieu, my XO, and this is Lieutenant Payne, who will be the Captain of the Roebuck."

"Thank you for meeting with me," the governor said. "I am very excited to see the final preparations for our colony mission to Mangkatar. Please let me know if there is anything I can do to make your job easier."

"Since the Roebuck will be staying with you until the Galileo arrives to replace her, you'll have use of her two Lynxes until that time. You need to decide how many total Lynxes you want so we can finalize the cargo space on the Sakira," Liz said.

"I've noted that on my datapad. You'll have an answer by tomorrow," the governor said. "More cargo space would definitely be welcomed. However, what we could really use would be an antimatter reactor."

"I'm sorry, but the president is steadfast on that point," Liz said. "We cannot afford to give one up, and he also is of the opinion that you would be better served to learn to manage on less power."

"He has made that point abundantly clear," the governor said. His scowl told Liz how much he thought about Marc's opinion on the Paraxeans' over-reliance on power. "So how many fusion reactors are we allocated?"

"Four," Liz said. "I would be willing to plead your case to raise that to six, but I expect you'll quickly exceed their limit as well. You would do well to look at the designs for Artemis's power needs. You should be able to adopt them without too much trouble."

"Our engineers are already studying them."

"The Sakira will be in orbit for two weeks. During that time, you'll be able to make use of printers in her to produce solar arrays and whatever else you need to produce in microgravity. You will need to furnish the materials."

"I understand," the governor said. "What about livestock?"

"We are not willing to carry any large animals on the Sakira or the Roebuck. You have to plan to survive without them until the StarMerchant is complete and can make a delivery," Liz said. "Of course, we don't have any problem carrying the fertilized eggs you're asking for as long as their incubation period doesn't end until after we arrive."

"You can be assured that Dr. Teltar is fully capable of calculating the incubation period of a chicken or a duck."

"I'm sure he is. We have also agreed to carry four baby goats," Liz said. "That's as much livestock as we feel we can manage." Liz was obviously not happy about carrying any livestock on the Sakira.

"Thank you for that. Dr. Teltar asks that they be at least ten weeks old. That will allow us to start milking them a month after we arrive. We will need the milk as a food source right away."

"How are you going to start milking a baby goat at sixteen weeks?" Lieutenant Payne asked.

"Goats are sexually mature at sixteen weeks. We'll trick their systems into believing they've been pregnant. Once they start producing milk, we'll also put three embryos into each goat so that we can create a viable herd as soon as possible," the governor explained.

"I see, do you guys really like goat's milk that much?" Lieutenant Payne asked.

"Not particularly. But we'll use it to make yogurt, and then the rest will be fed into our meat vats as part of the nutrients needed to produce meat. We have to maximize the production of the proteins we need."

"Oh, I see. I guess we'll be doing the same on Artemis," Lieutenant Payne said.

"Please coordinate the rest of the loading with Lieutenant Beaulieu and Lieutenant Payne. Once he's selected his XO, he'll bring them by to meet you," Liz said. "Now, if you'll excuse me, I'll see about some additional fusion reactors for you."

◆ ◆ ◆

"Marc, how's it going?" Liz asked as she met Marc for her four o'clock appointment.

"Crazy; I'm still trying to finalize the list for our first group of colonists."

"Are you getting enough volunteers?"

"Plenty."

"What will you do with the extras?"

"Some will come to Delphi City to do training, and work to prepare for the next group. Others will stay where they are until we have the Victory ready, or yours and Catie's cargo ship can bring them."

"You don't sound like you like that last option," Liz said.

"Gives the various governments more time to try to turn them into spies or whatnot," Marc said. "I like it better when they're immediately in our protection here in Delphi City."

"Then, why not make that a requirement?"

"We don't have enough space, and some of them would go nuts. We don't have the right kind of work available to keep them interested."

"Then don't accept them; leave them and their government hanging," Liz said. "The governments will have to waste resources to cover all the applicants, so they'll either not bother or not be able to do as good a job. Besides, won't ADI be able to detect the spies with her test?"

"Of course I will," ADI said.

"Right. But there will be some who will have a weakened resolve. They might change their mind once they're on Artemis, and things get tough."

"Could happen, but you'll deal with it."

"I'm sure I will," Marc said. "Now, you wanted to talk about the Paraxean mission."

"Yes, Governor Paratar would like to get more fusion reactors. He would like an antimatter reactor, but I told him no way."

"He's stubborn."

"Yes, but if we free up a few fusion reactors, he'll quit bellyaching and focus on the mission. And it would be a sign of goodwill on your part."

"After letting them keep the Roebuck! . . . Whatever, talk to Fred. He can pull a few from the shipment for the Russians. See if he can swing four."

"Thanks."

"Are you going to be ready to leave next week?"

"We're heading out on Saturday, with or *without* the governor," Liz said.

"Good. Oh, I wanted to talk to you about Fred," Marc said.

"Okay, he's alright, isn't he?"

"Yes. I'm planning on making him President of MacKenzies."

"About time! You work that guy to death. We all dump work on him," Liz said. "I really feel sorry for him, with the workload he carries."

"You do, but not enough to stop dumping work on him?"

"Well, he never complains."

"He does have a staff of over fifty helping him."

"Fifty?!"

"Yeah, I always bite my tongue whenever he hires another one. They're always busy, and like you said, he accomplishes an amazing amount of work."

"He was a logistics officer in the Air Force," Liz said. "He's used to organizing a big staff and big missions. I'm really happy for him. When will it be official?"

"Should be in the next six weeks. He wants time to finish romancing one of the pilots before we announce," Marc said. "He wants to know they've got something real before he asks her to put up with all that goes with being president."

"What goes with being president?" Liz asked. "All I ever see is you issuing orders and working insane hours. Fred seems to have that part handled already."

"Well, it will be a more public position when he's in it. MacKenzies has a lot more visibility now."

"Is it okay if I congratulate him?"

"Just do it privately."

"Does Catie know?"

"Of course, she congratulated him at the dinner the other night."

"How can I help you, Dr. Teltar?" Marc asked. Dr. Teltar had asked for an urgent appointment, and Marc was very curious as to what could be so urgent.

"I'm here on behalf of myself and the other Paraxeans who accompanied Captain Blake on the exploration mission," Dr. Teltar said. "We would all like to accompany you on your mission to Artemis."

"What about Governor Paratar's mission?"

"He has other specialists available to cover what we do," Dr. Teltar said.

"Interesting, but I still don't understand?"

"We all find Artemis more interesting. You'll be doing more serious terraforming, and also will likely introduce more plants and animals from Earth than will be done on Mangkatar. We think there will be more to learn."

"Have you talked to the governor yet?"

"No. We didn't want to antagonize him until we were sure you would take us."

"I don't have an objection as long as it doesn't jeopardize the mission to Mangkatar," Marc said. "Is there another reason?"

"Only that we enjoy interacting with you humans," Dr. Teltar said. "We find you more impulsive and exciting. We'd like to see what else we can learn from you."

◆ ◆ ◆

It had been a hectic week. Liz was reviewing her checklist on the datapad her aide had given her. She regretted for the umpteenth time not having the nanite treatment like Catie so she could handle these checklists without having to carry a pad around.

"I don't care if the Paraxeans want more space, we are not going to fly with our one flight bay packed with other crap. We have to be able to conduct operations from there, and we need room to conduct any necessary repairs. Tell them to stack their stuff tighter, triple bunk, or leave the stuff for the StarMerchant to bring later," Liz told her loadmaster.

"Yes, Ma'am," the loadmaster said with a big smile. She had obviously wanted to tell the Paraxeans the same thing.

Liz stepped off the lift and into the converted flight bay. She was here to inspect the rec space. With the pressure building on the cargo space, she wanted to make sure the Paraxeans hadn't started using this space, too. She was not interested in finding out how two thousand Paraxeans interacted with the two hundred Delphinean crew after a few weeks of forced confinement. They each needed to have their own space that they could retreat to if things got tense.

"You cannot stack that here!" Liz ordered.

"But we need this," the Paraxean loader said.

"I don't care. You have to leave this space open, so it's available during our voyage."

"But it's so much space."

"I don't think you're going to think that after having to go three weeks or so with this being the only space you can relax in."

"But the trip is only supposed to take two weeks."

"Yes, and we'll be spending the next three weeks after that unloading all the stuff from the Sakira. And during most of that time, you'll still be living up here."

"But . . ."

"I don't care, get it out of here!" Liz ordered.

"Yes, Ma'am."

"Chief, are these cabins secure?"

"Yes, Ma'am. We've inspected them and done a few tests. They'll handle up to six Gs."

"How about our spaceplanes?"

"They're all tied down, so they'll stay in place. Just don't go flipping her around willy-nilly like, and they'll be fine," the chief replied.

"I think I can manage that," Liz said as she headed back to the lift with her aide rushing to keep up.

◆ ◆ ◆

On Saturday, August $21^{st}$, at 2340, the Sakira and the Roebuck headed out on their trip to Mangkatar. It would take two weeks to reach the planet, and most of the time, the crew and passengers would be under restrictions due to the high acceleration they would be experiencing. Liz felt the time pressure; they needed to complete this mission on time so that they could get the mission to Artemis underway. Everyone wanted to make sure that the colony was well established before the aliens showed up in the spring.

"Hey, Catie. How are things at the Academy?" Liz asked. She and Catie were trying to talk at least twice a week, which usually ended up being during one of Catie's two self-study sessions. The study sessions were really time set aside when Catie could freely use her Comm to catch up with her projects; one of them had been set so it coincided with the board meetings.

"It's going fine. I like my new roommate. We're going to visit her family in France during the fall break."

"That's over your birthday, right?"

"Yes."

"Are you keeping up with the coursework?"

"Sure, it's not that hard."

"How are you and Baker getting along?"

"He's fine. After Guatemala, we seem to be on the same page a lot more."

"Good. Is Morgan looking after you?"

"She is. For someone who's supposed to be the volleyball coach, she sure manages to be in the same place as me a lot. And I'm not even on the volleyball team."

"She was always clever," Liz said. "How are you doing with the leadership training?"

"It's okay. I am getting tired of rifle drills, though."

"That stuff should start slacking off now."

"I hope," Catie said. "How's your mission going, *Captain*?"

Liz laughed a bit. "It's going fine. We're making the jumps now, so we're under reduced acceleration for a while. Everyone's enjoying the ability to get up and around. We should make the last jump tomorrow, then we have six days of high deceleration before we make orbit."

"Sounds good. Are you dropping a Lynx off on the way?"

"*No,* why would we do that?"

"It would save a week getting the asteroids you need for the colony. The crew can do a really hard decel in the Lynx and then grab the asteroids while you're still heading to the planet."

"I'll check with Chief Hopkins and see if he can set that up," Liz said. "Anything to keep this schedule."

"How are you guys doing syncing up the jumps between the Sakira and the Roebuck?"

"That's gone smoothly. We hit the jump point right behind each other. Timing was a bit off on the first one, but we fixed that."

"So, Lieutenant Payne isn't living up to his name?"

"Not so far. He's been real solid. You trained him well."

"I think he trained me more than I trained him."

"That's not the way he tells it."

"I think he's just being nice."

"Or he really *likes* you," Liz said.

Catie laughed. "Yeah right."

◆ ◆ ◆

"Chief, is our Lynx ready?" Liz asked. They had just finished their last jump and were entering the Mangkatar system.

"Yes, Ma'am. Four fusion reactors, twelve grav-drives, and assorted cables, just like you ordered."

"It all fit?"

"Of course, Ma'am. They'll need to go into the lower hold to get the last set, and we had to use up part of the passenger space, but they'll manage."

"Good. Lieutenant Girard, your carriage awaits, good luck."

"Thank you, Ma'am," the lieutenant said. He immediately got up from his station on the bridge and headed to the lift. He was excited to be given an independent command, even if it was just to grab a few asteroids.

"What did I ever do to you?" Kasper complained as he waited for the EVA team to connect the cargo pod to his Fox.

"Quit complaining, or I'll transfer you to the Roebuck, and you can stay here for a year," Liz threatened. "It's tricky flying with that ostrich egg, and you're the only one with experience."

"That's because you never assign anyone else to ferry it down."

"Next time, you can take a co-pilot with you to train."

"Thanks!"

The Paraxeans were eager to get started; they'd already used the four Lynxes to ferry crews down to the compound. They were waiting on the cargo pod so they could assemble the excavator and start pulling up the material necessary to start building the new housing they would need. The plan called for all six thousand colonists to be living on the planet by the end of the week.

"Marc, the Paraxeans are demanding to have us remove the cabins in the Sakira's flight bay and ship them down. They want to use the material for their planetside housing," Liz said.

"Oh, that's clever of them, but I wasn't planning on replacing all the cabins," Marc said.

"What do you want me to do?"

"Just a sec," Marc said before he put Liz on hold. "ADI, get me Chief O'Donnell."

"Yes, sir?" Chief O'Donnell said as he answered his Comm.

"How long would it take to build and install new cabins in the Sakira's flight bay?"

"Those buggers want to keep the cabins?"

"Yes they do. I wish I'd have thought of it."

"We can build the cabins while we wait for the Sakira to get back here. It'll slow down the work on the Victory, but we can make that up. Then we can install them in about four days. I think we should be able to work around all the other loading."

"Okay, then start making the cabins," Marc said. "Liz, I assume you heard?"

"Yes," Liz said. "I'll let them know they can take them. Thanks, it'll make my life easier; they can be very persistent."

"You don't have to tell me about it."

# 16 Board Meeting – September 6th

"Good morning, everyone," Marc said as he entered the boardroom. "Catie, are you good?"
"Yes, I'm in a study room in the library," Catie said.
"Okay, I'd like to start the meeting by making an announcement. As of today, Fred is now President of MacKenzie Discoveries."
Everyone started applauding. Blake immediately brought out the scotch and poured drinks so they could toast.
"To our favorite President, Fred Litton!"
"To Fred!"
"Thank you for that," Fred said. "I'm glad to hear I'm starting out as your favorite because, when I put your lazy asses to work, you'll probably start to resent me."
"We'll just offload that work on our favorite guy," Liz said. "Oh, wait, that's you. I guess that won't work anymore." Liz laughed while giving Fred a questioning look. She was one of the worst offenders at moving her work to Fred.
"Don't worry, I'll have plenty of staff that you can try that on. But just be careful; I only hire the smartest people, and they'll probably figure out all your tricks in no time."
Fred sat down and motioned to Marc that he was ready to get out of the spotlight and that Marc should continue.
"One of the things Fred is going to do is break MacKenzies into several subsidiary companies. He's essentially already done that by the way he has organized his staff, but it will be formalized over time. There will be a real-estate concern, a trading company, the electronics, solar power. We'll see how many he comes up with. They'll all be wholly-owned subsidiaries, but it should make things easier. And it might make Herr Hausmann and Herr Pfeifer happier."
"Won't that make some of our projects more complex?" Catie asked.

"I don't think so," Fred said. "You always have ignored the organizational structure on your projects, so I don't think this will be much different. Everyone will know we ultimately work for MacKenzie Discoveries."

"Another thing it does is simplify this meeting. Fred will only bring things here that require us to act. Otherwise, we'll assume that all is well. I'm sure Herr Pfeifer will let us know if our numbers start to sag."

Jonas gave a stern nod to that.

"So our top-of-mind agenda item is the status of the Paraxean colony mission. Liz?"

"We just got here, but things are moving fast," Liz said. "We've unloaded the Roebuck so we could put it in position above the ecliptic. That allows it to keep track of anything that might be approaching the system without the planets getting in the way. We have a probe below the ecliptic to cover any blind spots."

"Isn't the Roebuck an expensive probe?" Blake asked.

Liz gave a little laugh. "Yes it is, but the astronomers and communication guys on it are tuning the sensors. When they're happy, they'll modify two probes and launch them. Then the Roebuck will be free to return to orbit around the planet."

"Is that the best position for them?" Samantha asked.

"Yes, with our high acceleration profile, they're better positioned to reach any area of the solar system from here deep in the gravity well. If the Roebuck were out on the rim, they wouldn't have the ability to accelerate to a new location as fast if something is detected. Although, we assume we'll actually have months if not years to respond to anything we detect."

"I can never get used to how huge the distances are," Samantha said.

"Anyway, we've assembled a barracks down on the planet and offloaded our livestock, so things are moving along."

"Thank you," Marc said. "Catie, anything new on the jump ships?"
"I have just now gotten the privacy I need to be able to start checking on things, but they're tuning the drive size and the capacitors and reactors. They're going to need an antimatter reactor, but we want to scale it down. We have Dr. Nakahara working on that."
"Yes, and he's making significant progress," Nikola said. "I think he'll have what you want by your October date."
"Great," Catie said.
"Now for Artemis, I'm sorting through all the applications from would-be colonists," Marc said. "We're not having any problem attracting them. We'll need to figure out what to do with the ones we bring in to Delphi City that won't be going out until Catie's and Liz's new cargo ship can ferry them out."
"What about the Victory?" Kal asked.
"It won't be ready until after the first of the year, especially now that we're going to have to replace the cabins in the Sakira."
"What?!" Fred asked.
"Oh, those clever Paraxeans figured out that the cabins represented quite a bit of cargo and supplies that they could use. They're going to pull them all out. We'll do the same on Artemis," Marc explained.
"And you just gave in?"
"It's a great idea. I couldn't very well say no to them, then turn around and do it myself."
"Exactly!" Dr. Metra said, giving Fred the evil eye. Her ears were forward and raised in what they had all learned was a state they struck before the Paraxean pounced on its prey.
"Yes, of course," Fred conceded. He definitely didn't want to find out what happened when a Paraxean pounced.
"Sam, how's training going?"

"Still working the new people in. The teachers are doing a great job of keeping the kids busy. I'm using the ones who've been here from the start to help coordinate with the new people."
"That hammer still working?"
"Yes."
"Hammer?" Blake asked.
"She had to threaten to leave people behind if they didn't measure up on fitness and cross-training," Marc said.
"Woo, who knew Sam could be so tough?"
Samantha stared Blake down until he coughed, encouraging Marc to move on.
"Back to Artemis: The aliens who are approaching Artemis have not made any changes in course or speed since we exchanged messages; of course, they're assuming we haven't received their answer yet. They are still on target to arrive in system late May to early June," Marc continued.
"Admiral Michaels, update on our surface fleet?" Marc prompted.
"We've deployed three as of today. One in the Mediterranean Sea, one in the Atlantic Ocean, and one in the North Pacific. Each has two frigates accompanying it. We have minimal crew aboard each carrier; we'll send crew and aircraft to them as needed. Hopefully, we'll not need them," Admiral Michaels said. "How are we feeling about the G20 group?"
"First, have you decided if you're going to take the position as Military Chairman?" Marc asked.
"I think so. Pam is still trying to decide if she wants to move to Brussels."
"We could force the issue and have them pick another city to host the alliance," Marc said.
"I think you'd play hell trying to get them to change to a city like Nice," Admiral Michaels said. "And given a choice, we'd prefer a European location."

"It's only one thousand kilometers," Blake said. "With a hover Lynx, you could commute. At Mach four, it's only fifteen minutes from Nice."
"But I have to get to the airport," Admiral Michaels said.
"I said hover Lynx," Blake said. "It can pick you up at your country estate just outside the city and drop you off at the office. We could require that they provide a helipad."
"That would probably swing the deal with Pam," Admiral Michaels said.
"What about Sophia?" Catie asked.
"She'll come with us, at least for most of the year. She and Pam can split their time between there and here in Delphi City," Admiral Michaels said. "So, you two will be able to continue to torment each other."
"Dr. Metra, is there an update on our new enterprise?" Marc asked, ignoring the little drama about Sophia and Catie.
"We've registered with the IRODaT, which stands for International Registry of Organ Donation and Transplantation. They say they're excited to work with us, and we've received twenty requests for organs that we are currently growing. Once we have success with those, I'm sure we'll get many more requests."
"Excellent. Again, let me know if you need anything. We'll close here. Everyone, have a good day."

◆ ◆ ◆

"Hey, Brainiac, do you have some time to help me with this problem?" Yvette asked Catie.

"You don't sound like you want help," Catie said.

"Why? . . . Oh, I meant it as a term of affection. I'm frustrated with the math on this heat dispersion problem. And you know how I love math."

"Okay, link to my Comm, and I'll look it over with you."

Yvette linked her Comm and put the problem up on their HUDs.

"You did the integration wrong," Catie said.

"That's it?"

"Yes. If you fix it, your answer will be correct."

"How can you know that? It took me longer than that to read the problem, much less figure out what they were asking for."

"I've had to solve problems like that before," Catie said.

"You have? Is that why you're not in this class? All first- and second-class cadets are required to take Basic Structure of Starships. There are three of these classes running, and you're not in any of them."

"Yeah, I had a class like it at UCSD, they accepted it as credit here," Catie said. The truth was that Blake had worked it out so that she had credit for the class. He and Marc figured it would be easier to explain away the credit than it would be to explain away Catie schooling the professor in a class that she'd almost written the book on.

"Are you willing to tutor Miranda and me on it? We both hate this class and are having a hard time keeping up."

"Miranda?"

"Cordova, the Cadet Wing Commander."

"I'm not sure about that," Catie said.

"Come on, she's nice, she just has a tough job. I'm a second-class cadet, and she treats me just fine when we're in class or studying together."

"I'm pretty busy."

"Come on, just a couple of hours a week," Yvette pleaded.

"Okay, I'll try."

"Don't you have some classes you need help with?"

"I could use a way to get out of my comparative literature class," Catie said. "I can't believe they wouldn't transfer credits from UCSD for that one."

"Oh, Professor Oliver is a tough one," Yvette said. "Oxford man. He wouldn't accept credit from anywhere but one of the Ivy League schools, and then he'd probably make you take his test to prove you knew the material."

"Well, he's driving me nuts," Catie said.

# 17 Freeloaders

Judge Marianna Muñoz looked at her calendar for the day. Her court clerk had circled one case, noting that it would be interesting. It was Starman's Bar vs. four tourists. Although it wasn't unusual for tourists to get into fights at a bar, it was unusual for those cases to make it to court. They were usually taken care of in arbitration, with the tourists paying damages, apologizing, and leaving Delphi City. In this case, The Cook Islands had made it abundantly clear that they did not want the tourists back in their territory, the tourists had refused to pay damages, claiming poverty, and were even refusing to make an apology.

"Interesting," Judge Muñoz thought. "We shall see."

After she had dispensed with the first four cases on her docket with her usual efficiency, her clerk called the Starman case. Under Delphinean law, minor crimes were adjudicated with the judge acting as the inquisitor. The prosecution or plaintiff could only ask questions after the judge was satisfied that the facts of the case were clear.

"Mr. Maguro, you own the Starman Bar?"

"Yes, Your Honor."

"Please give me a brief summary of the events of the night of August 20th."

"Yes, Your Honor. These four men," he pointed at the defendants, "came into the bar at six o'clock that evening. They took a table in the corner and started drinking and watching the game. They ran up a three-hundred-dollar tab. Then, around ten o'clock, they started arguing with each other. They got very loud, so I asked them to pay their tab and leave. They said they didn't have any money and that they weren't going anywhere."

"Did they cause any problems before that?" Judge Muñoz asked.

"No, Your Honor."

"Did they interact with any of your other patrons before that?"

"Yes, Your Honor. Sydney came by and did some card tricks for them."

"Who is Sydney?"

"He's a local guy, he comes in most nights and cadges drinks. He does card tricks and stuff for the patrons."

"Okay. What did you do after they refused to pay?"

"I told them I would call the constable, and they'd get put in the slammer until they paid."

"And what did they do then?"

"They pushed me, and then they started fighting with each other. They broke up the place pretty bad, broke my mirrors, lots of glasses. They chased most of my customers away."

"And?"

"The constable came, they started pushing her around, so she stunned them and had them hauled off."

"Is the constable here?" Judge Muñoz asked the prosecutor.

"She is, Your Honor."

"Do you or Mr. Maguro have anything else to add?"

"Not at this time, Your Honor."

Judge Muñoz turned to the defense. "Would you like to refute or clarify anything?"

"We would, Your Honor."

"Then proceed."

"My clients were at Mr. Maguro's establishment for two hours, minding their own business when Sydney came along."

"This is the same Sydney that Mr. Maguro referred to?"

"We so stipulate," the prosecution said.

"Very well, go on," Judge Muñoz said.

"Anyway, Sydney tricked my clients out of their money," the defense said.

"And how did he do that?"

"He showed them some card tricks, and then bet them that he could tell them which card they had. He had other tricks he used; do you want me to explain them?"

"Are they pertinent to your defense?"

"Your Honor, the prosecution will stipulate that Sydney conned them out of their money."

"Very well," Judge Muñoz said. She nodded to the defense attorney, telling him to continue.

"So, by the time Mr. Maguro asked them to leave, they were pretty mad. They blame him for allowing Sydney to come in the bar and cheat them."

"I see. And is that why they started fighting with each other?"

"Well, by the time Mr. Maguro asked them to leave, they were pretty drunk and pretty mad. So, they just lost control. Fighting was their way of relieving their frustration."

"Let me summarize," Judge Muñoz said. "Your clients came in the bar at six p.m. with money, had some drinks, fully intending to pay. Sydney comes along at around eight p.m. and cheats them out of their money. Am I correct so far?"

Both the prosecutor and the defense nodded.

"Then, after being cheated out of their money, and no longer being able to pay, your clients continued to drink for another hour?" She looked at the defense, expecting an answer.

"That is correct," the defense attorney said after conferring with his clients for a minute.

"Then, at that time, they were loud enough that Mr. Maguro asked them to leave. They pushed him, then started fighting."

"That's correct, Your Honor."

"Can they explain why they pushed Mr. Maguro?"

"They say he was rude to them when he asked them to leave."

"How was he rude?"

"He called them a bunch of useless wankers and told them to piss off."

"I see," Judge Muñoz said. "It says here that Mr. Maguro is asking for the payment of three hundred for the tab and eight hundred for the damages to the bar."

"That's correct," the prosecutor said.

"Is the prosecution preferring any charges related to their pushing the constable?"

"Not at this time, Your Honor. The constable feels that stunning them, and a night in jail was sufficient punishment."

"I see, very commendable of her," Judge Muñoz said. "And the defense is claiming that since Mr. Maguro allowed Sydney into the bar, they should be held blameless."

"That's correct, Your Honor. Without Sydney cheating my clients, we wouldn't be here."

"Okay, give me a moment," Judge Muñoz said. She spent a few minutes conferring with her notes and looking some things up before she turned back to the court.

"Okay, I agree with the defense that Mr. Maguro is culpable due to his allowing Sydney to work his bar. Therefore, I'm absolving the defendants of the three hundred for the tab. I am also absolving them of half the damages. They will pay Mr. Maguro four hundred dollars."

"Your Honor, my clients do not have any money," the defense attorney said.

"They have no money and no assets?"

"They were on a fishing boat and were let go," the defense attorney said. "They've spent everything they had."

"Then I suggest that they find a job. Take them to one of the starter barracks and get them signed up."

"Yes, Ma'am," the defense attorney said. He didn't look too excited to have to continue dealing with his clients. Now he had to take them to the clinic to get a physical, then to the barracks. At least there, he could just hand them off.

◆ ◆ ◆

"I am not happy to see your clients back here," Judge Muñoz said as she looked at the four tourists and their defense attorney. It was three days later and she couldn't imagine what the problem could be now.

"I'm sorry, Your Honor, they refuse to work."

"Ms. Ungerer, can you explain?"

"I've never had nobody like them at the barracks. They eat like pigs, act like pigs, and refuse to go to the jobs we got for them."

"And why are your clients refusing to work?"

"They say they're not slaves," the defense attorney said.

"I see. Have you explained that if they refuse to work or pay off their debt, I will be forced to throw them in jail?"

"I have, Your Honor."

"Alright, I impose a one-hundred-dollar fine for the two days they spent in the barracks without working, to be added to their current debt. I also sentence them to ten days in jail. Constable, please take them to the jail. Tell Constable Maryanski that she is to use the Seneca protocol."

"Yes, Ma'am."

"I told you she'd throw us in jail," tourist A said.

"Who cares, that jail is nicer than that barracks they put us in. We need a vacation," tourist B replied.

◆ ◆ ◆

"Hey, are you going to feed us?!" yelled tourist A.

"Ms. Ungerer said she already fed you this morning," the jailer replied.

"That was this morning!"

"Well, this is a jail, and you're on the Seneca protocol. We only feed you once a day."

"This isn't looking so good," tourist C said.

"We'll get used to it," tourist A said.

◆ ◆ ◆

The next morning after their shower, the four tourists were led back to separate cells.

"Hey, how come we're being separated?!" tourist A demanded.

"That's part of the Seneca protocol. If you don't like it, you can go back to the barracks and take a job," the jailer replied.

"Whatever, I was tired of those guys anyway," tourist A said. "Hey, where's my bed?"

"It's daytime," the jailer replied. "You don't need a bed."

"What am I supposed to do all day?"

"There's a chair when you want to sit, just flip it down from the wall," the jailer said, pointing to a fold-up chair.

"This cell is too small!"

"It's one meter by three meters. What more do you need?"

"Where's a blanket?!"

"You don't need a blanket."

"But it's cold in here!"

"It is exactly twenty degrees Celsius, sixty-eight Fahrenheit. If you're cold, walk around a bit, that'll warm you up."

Tourist A ran in place for a bit to warm up, then sat in the chair. It wasn't very comfortable, just barely big enough to sit in. If he tried to slouch, he would slide off the chair. *"Ha, they think they can break me! I've suffered worse."*

◆ ◆ ◆

"Lunch is served," the jailer announced. A tray flipped down from the wall, and the jailer slid a plate with a large round biscuit on it through the slot.

"What is this?!" tourist A demanded.

"Your meal."

"This is not acceptable. You cannot put me on bread and water, that's inhumane."

"That is three thousand calories and the prescribed amount of fiber that the doctor says you need. It has all the minerals, protein, and vitamins your body needs."

Tourist A broke off a piece and ate it. "This tastes like sawdust."

"If you want fine dining, I suggest you get a job."

After tourist A finished eating, a bot slid into his cell and swept the floor. It even wiped down the walls before it left.

At nine o'clock, a bed slid out from the wall with a pillow and blanket.

*"Well, at least this is comfortable,"* tourist A thought as he crawled in and went to sleep.

◆ ◆ ◆

At six a.m., the lights came on, and an alarm went off. Tourist A woke up, trying to remember where he was. "Damn, jail. Well, I'm not getting out of this bed," he said.

Ten minutes later, the bed started to slide back into the wall. He grabbed the blanket, trying to keep it, but it was attached to the bed, and nothing he could do would detach it. It took a full minute before the bed, the pillow, and the blanket disappeared.

"Son of a bitch, this is inhumane!"

"Get a job!" shouted the jailer.

◆ ◆ ◆

"Lunch is served."

"The same thing!"

"If you want fine dining . . ."

"I know, get a job. Is there any entertainment available here?"

"You can read a book. Over there is a panel; a shelf will slide out for you to lean on, and you can select a book from the library to read."

"I have to stand up to read?!"

"Like I said. If you want the comforts of home, . . ."

"Get a job," tourist A muttered.

After finishing his biscuit, he went to the panel and looked up what books were available from the library. Most of them were teaching manuals about how to do various jobs. Then there was a selection of books that he'd been told he should read but never had. The Grapes of Wrath, by Steinbeck. The Great Gatsby, by F. Scott Fitzgerald, To Kill a

Mockingbird, by Harper Lee, 1984 and Animal Farm by George Orwell; the list went on.

"Bah, what a waste of time," tourist A said.

◆ ◆ ◆

"Hey, do I get a shower?!"

"What, you've worked up a sweat?" the jailer asked.

"No, but don't I at least get a shower?"

"You get one every other day. If you want one every day, you should . . ."

"Get a job," tourist A muttered as he started to jog in place to warm himself up. He tried lying on the floor, but it was too cold. Without a blanket, his bones started to ache.

"What do you people do if someone can't work?!"

"Everybody can work."

"What if they're crippled?"

"We fix them up. The doctors here can fix anything."

"What if they're retarded?"

"There's always something they can do! Most people like being useful, even the mentally handicapped."

"Bah!"

◆ ◆ ◆

"Time for your shower!" the jailer announced.

"Finally," tourist A said. He was looking forward to seeing how his friends were doing.

The jailer led him down the hall to the shower. "There you go. You have thirty minutes."

"Where are my buddies?"

"They decided they wanted a job. Left right after lunch yesterday," the jailer said.

"Wimps!"

"Marc, how's it going?" Kal asked as he met Marc for lunch.

"I'm okay, worried about Catie, but ADI says she's doing fine."

"That's good. Where have you been?"

"On the Mea Huli with Sam."

"I hope you had a nice time."

"Of course we did."

"Hey, can you believe this; they used the Seneca protocol at the jail this week."

"No way!"

"Yep, four idiots refused to work after they tore up a bar."

Marc laughed. "Really, how long did they last?"

"Three of them lasted a day and a half," Kal said. "The other one lasted four days."

"That's insane. We came up with that as a joke—a mental exercise. I can't believe anyone would ever go that far. Which judge assigned it?"

"Judge Muñoz."

"Well, she's certainly fair. If she assigned them to it, they must have deserved it."

"Constable Maryanski made a hundred bucks on the pool."

"What pool?"

"The one betting how long they would hold out."

"What did she bet?"

"She bet that one would hold out for three days."

"And the rest of the bets?"

"Nobody had over thirty-six hours."

"I'm not surprised. So how are our miscreants doing now?"

"The hold-out is barely meeting the standards, but he is meeting them. The other three are doing just fine."

"I guess there's always at least one to defy all logic."

"I'm sure he's going to get tired of living in the barracks and having no money."

"Are we kicking him off the city once they've paid their debt?"

"Nobody will take them," Kal said.

"You mean, we're stuck with them?"

"Looks that way."

"Maybe we should assign them to your team as combat dummies."

"I like that idea, too bad it's against that constitution you wrote."

"Damn, what was I thinking?"

# 18 Board Meeting – October 4th

"Are we all here?" Marc asked. After receiving positive confirmation from Admiral Michaels, Liz, and Catie, he continued. "I'm canceling next month's meeting. I'll just be arriving at Artemis around that time, and I suspect I'll be too busy with other issues to attend."

"Yay!" Catie exclaimed.

"I'm with you, Girl," Liz added.

"You two are just asking to be uninvited," Marc threatened.

"Oh, sorry," Catie said. Before, she would have been happy to not have to attend the meetings, but she'd come to like the quick updates and sharing that occurred at them. And besides, they were one of her few opportunities to connect with all of her friends, given the Comm blackout rules at the Academy.

"Liz, where are you?" Marc asked.

"We just finished our last jump, and we're heading toward Earth. Our deceleration profile has us arriving by Saturday."

"Any issues?"

"No, things went well; you'll see the report. Lieutenant Payne is now in command of the colony defenses," Liz reported.

"Do you think he's up to the task?" Blake asked.

"Of course," Liz said. "He's a squared-away sailor."

"Good for him," Catie said.

"Okay, Admiral Michaels, how are you settling in?"

"We're just getting moved in," Admiral Michaels replied. "I report for my first day tomorrow."

"How is Sophia liking Nice?" Catie asked.

"She seems to be enjoying herself. Her French is still a little weak, but she's working on it. You should give her a call."

"I'll try to fit one in," Catie said.

"Has the prime minister named my replacement?" Admiral Michaels asked.

"She's selected her, but hasn't named her," Kal said.

"Her! I thought we were suggesting Captain Clark for the position," Marc said.

"We were, but the prime minister likes Cecily Lawrence."

"That woman hasn't seen a day of combat!" Liz said.

"Well, we're talking about the minister of defense, not the head of the defense forces," Blake said. "And Cer Lawrence did a pretty good job of managing the buildup for the war with the Paraxeans."

"Yeah, I guess that's right. The defense minister really should be able to figure stuff like that out."

"I'm glad you agree," Blake said. "And it means we don't need to find another base commander for Delphi station."

"Okay, I'll message her that I approve her choice," Marc said. "Next agenda item, the status of our mission to Artemis. We've selected all the colonists for the mission and they are in isolation on Delphi Station. Our cargo is also on Delphi Station, ready to load as soon as Liz arrives with the Sakira. The passenger cabins are sitting next to the station, ready to be installed. And I'm sure we're forgetting something and will remember it right after we launch."

"You're such an optimist," Samantha said. "We'll do just fine."

"Who is going to be in command of security?" Catie asked.

"Major Kobayashi," Blake answered.

"He's good," Kal added. "I'm also sending Mariana Ramsey with them."

"Nice," Catie said. She really liked Mariana after the time she spent with her in Guatemala, the time before, not the one during Basic.

"These meetings are going to get a bit more complex when we have to sync them up between our various locations," Marc said. "It's eleven hours between Nice and Delphi City, and who knows what it is between Delphi City and Artemis."

"Artemis has a 26.5-hour day," ADI piped in. "The colony site is currently three hours ahead of Delphi City. It also has a 330-day year, using Artemis days."

"Oh, this is going to get complex," Blake moaned.

"That's only because we have the quantum relays," Catie said. "Otherwise, we'd just have to do a simple reference, it's real-time syncing that makes it so hard."

"Are you going to stick with a seven-day week?" Catie asked.

"Yes, that and twelve months. I haven't decided how to name the months," Marc said. "Should we keep the names used here on Earth or make up new ones?"

"You don't just want to number them?" Catie asked.

"People like names better than numbers," Samantha said. "If we don't name them, someone will."

"Hmm, I'll try to think up some names," Catie mused.

"Moving on, Fred, how has your first month as President of MacKenzies been?" Marc asked.

"Pretty sweet," Fred said. "I've been invited to join three other boards. I'm making a trip to Hawaii to attend a conference next week; Latoya is really liking that."

"I'm glad to hear that it's livening up your personal life, but I was asking about the business," Marc said.

Fred gave a big laugh. "Business is good. I held my first board meeting on Friday. No problems."

"Was anyone surprised?" Liz asked.

"Besides Latoya, not really," Fred said. "I just changed the name of my staff meeting to board meeting and continued as usual."

"Good. You're going to pick up some more appearance stuff once I'm out of here," Marc said. "Sounds like you'll fit right in with all those other presidents and CEOs."

"You think?"

"Just tell them about your first trip to Morocco," Blake said. "If that doesn't work, ask them if they want to go out on a fishing boat." Blake was referring to the incident where they'd rescued Catie from the kidnappers, then taken over the crime lord's compound so they could hand him over to his biggest enemy.

"That might work. Or I could just invite them out drinking with you and Kal. That will show them that I can put up with anything."

"Okay, back to business. Catie, where are you with your new cargo ship?"

"We're going to call them StarMerchants," Catie said, "and the first one should be ready to go out for a test flight next week. I'm taking a break over the weekend, so I can do a walkthrough and fly her."

"When will you do the first test jump?"

"After we do the test flight, we'll have ADI fly her out and make a few jumps. Then we'll bring her back and finish building out the bays. She'll be ready to make a cargo delivery in January."

"Okay, I'll inform Governor Paratar to get his shopping list ready," Marc said.

"And his exports prepared," Catie said.

"Do we know what he intends to export?" Liz asked.

"Goats, according to Lieutenant Payne," Blake said.

After a week of tutoring Miranda and Yvette, the group had grown by six. They had to move the session into one of the classrooms to accommodate everyone. Catie had wanted to just do it virtually, but Yvette had convinced her that it was much better if they were in the same room.

Catie was now looking at sixteen cadets in her tutoring session as she started to review the material that Professor Gossmann had introduced earlier in the week.

"Instead of making the hull thicker when it's formed, adding a second layer to achieve that thickness increases the strength of the hull, because . . ." Catie paused as a straggler entered the room.

"Please continue," Professor Gossmann said.

"I'm sorry, we were just reviewing the material from your class," Catie said apologetically.

"I understand. Please go on, I'm interested in how you explain the material. The eight most improved grades in my class belong to the cadets in this room. I think I might learn something."

"Umm . . ."

"Please, Cadet MacGregor. I'm serious, I'm here to learn. This material is complicated, and you apparently have a way to simplify it. I'd like to understand it."

"Busted!" ADI said.

*"ADI!"* Catie messaged back.

*"He's a nice guy,"* ADI said. *"Just pretend he's not here."*

"Go on, pretend I'm not here," Professor Gossmann said.

# 19 StarMerchant One

By taking leave, Catie was able to leave the Academy on Friday afternoon, a day early. She wasn't due back until Monday at 0600. "Whew, it feels good to be out of there," she told Liz, who was picking her up in a minicar.

"I thought you were enjoying the Academy," Liz said.

"I am, but it's still nice to be out from under all that discipline and structure. I can let my hair down."

"Just not too far. We don't need to get arrested," Liz said.

Catie snorted a laugh. "Don't worry. Are we flying up tonight?"

"Of course. Now remember, not a word to the twins, or we'll both be in trouble for not taking them," Liz said.

"I still think we still could have taken them," Catie said.

"Sure, but then it'll take twice as long to get anything done."

"Are we taking off from the city airpad, or from the airport?"

"The airpad."

Liz handed the car over to the bodyguard who had been shadowing them and grabbed her bag out of the trunk. Catie grabbed hers, and they both headed over to the Lynx that was sitting on the pad waiting for them.

"Hi!"

"What!" Catie almost jumped out of her skin.

"Did you think you were going to leave us behind?" the twins asked.

"ADI!"

"I was only following orders. If you didn't want them to know where you were, you should have blocked them," ADI replied.

"Busted!" the twins said. "Let's go!" They each had an overnight bag with them.

"Does your mother know?" Liz asked.

"Sure, she just dropped us off ten minutes ago. She wanted to thank you for taking us off her hands for the weekend."

"*Alright*," Liz said, giving in to the inevitable. "But we don't have time for games, this is a working weekend."

"Fine by us."

The four of them boarded the Lynx and prepared to fly up to Delphi Station.

"I can't believe you were spying on me," Catie said.

"We knew you were getting ready to test fly her," the twins said. "We think we deserve to be on her maiden flight."

"And what possible reason did you come up with for deserving to be on the flight?"

"We helped launch the probes that found the planets. It's because you found the planets that you came up with the idea for the StarMerchant. Ergo, we deserve to be part of the next step."

"I think they've got you there," Liz said. "Now, get seated, we're cleared for takeoff in one minute."

"It looks weird," the twins said as they approached the ship. They were watching the feed from the forward camera as Liz flew the Lynx toward the cargo ship.

"That's not a very nice thing to say about our new ship," Catie said.

"It looks like something ate its middle. Why are there two big gaps?"

"That's where the cargo pods go," Catie explained. "The big bulb on that end is the front. It has the bridge, crew quarters, the flight bay we're going to land in, and four cargo bays; that disc in the middle is the gravity drives and power plants; they have to be extra big to work as jumpdrives." Catie didn't mention the missile bay, figuring she'd keep that secret.

"If the power and drives are in the middle, what's in the back?"

"We have a big flight bay, engineering, and another two cargo bays back there," Catie said.

"If you have cargo bays, why do you need cargo pods?"

"Because we want to carry lots of cargo. The pods are supposed to carry cargo for one customer, or one kind of cargo. That way, you can just drop the whole pod off, and they can empty it on their own time. Hopefully, they'll fill it with cargo they want to ship back, and we'll pick it up on the next trip."

"What about the first trip?"

"We send the design of the pods ahead; they have to make a pod so we can exchange with them. After that, we just keep exchanging pods."

"So then why do you need cargo bays?"

"For last-minute cargo, for extra cargo, or for things that have to be under environmental control while they're shipped."

"Hey, we're going into the ship sideways?" the twins exclaimed.

"Yeah, because we have to be accelerating all the time and want to jump while moving, we have to align gravity along the long axis. We don't want to try to rotate that ship before we go through a wormhole."

"We're here," Liz announced. "Thank you for flying with us, even if you ignored your pilot for the entire trip."

"Sorry, we were distracted," Catie said.

"Oh, I heard them distracting you."

"Let's go!"

"No, we have to wait for the bay to pressurize," Catie said. "Think of it like a big airlock."

"Oh, we forgot."

It took five minutes to pressurize the flight bay. During that time, the twins pestered Catie with question after question, all while donning their exosuits.

"ADI, why don't you answer these questions? You're the one that leaked my location, so it's your fault that they're here."

"They aren't asking me," ADI replied. "Besides, I'm busy."

The light above the hatch finally turned green, indicating that the pressure was equalized.

Catie opened the hatch and pushed both twins out. They both flapped their arms to help them drift toward the deck, where the magnetic coupling in their boots connected and held them down.

"Hi, Ajda, sorry for throwing a couple of bodies at you," Catie said.

"Don't worry about it. I know the Khanna twins, and I also know how adept they are in microgravity," Ajda said. "Are you ready for your walkthrough?"

"Yes, we are," Liz said as she pushed Catie out the hatch. She immediately jumped down after her.

"You're in flight bay one, which is forty-five meters deep and fifty meters wide. You have over eighteen meters of height, so since this is a space only craft, you can fit four Foxes or three Lynxes in here," Ajda said. "You just have to use thrusters to get them above the other spaceplanes so you can rotate them and fly out. The rear bay will hold twelve Foxes and Five Lynxes. You have to maneuver around some support beams, but it shouldn't be too bad."

"That shouldn't be a problem. A little trickier if we're under acceleration, but a good pilot can handle it," Liz said.

"Through here is the lift; cargo bays one and two are just above us," Ajda said as she led them into the lift. "These bays are forty-nine meters high at the peak then follow the hull curve down to sixteen meters. They're forty-eight meters deep by seventy-five meters in width, again, they follow the hull curve. The two are side by side with separate airlocks and separate cargo doors."

"Wow, it's big," the twins said.

"Yes, you can certainly carry a lot of cargo in here," Liz said.

"We'll put racks in here eventually to hold the containers. That way, they'll be secured in place, and you'll be able to get to the ones you want."

"Doesn't that make half the space aisles?" Liz asked.

"Twenty-five percent," Ajda said. "You have racks on both sides of the aisle. You can put stuff in the aisles if you're confident about your load and unload order."

"Good," Catie said.

"And cargo bays three and four?"

"The same except they start at sixty-four meters in height and follow the hull curve down to thirty-five meters tall," Ajda said.

"And cargo bays five and six?" Catie asked.

"They're the same as three and four, except they start at fifty meters, then follow the hull curve down to twenty, and of course they're upside down."

The twins giggled, and both of them flipped over, so they were floating upside down, looking at the three women.

"I know upside down is not a great term to use in microgravity, but relative to where I'm standing," Ajda said. She smacked the twin closest to her on the back of the head.

"What about the iris?" Catie asked.

"Amazingly, it works," Ajda said.

"What's the iris?" the twins asked.

"You remember how long we had to wait for the flight bay to pressurize?" Catie asked.

"Yes!"

"Well, this space is way bigger and would take even longer to pressurize. So we designed the iris so we could bring in cargo without having to depressurize the bay."

"How's that work?"

"Like the shutter on a camera, you turn it, and the hole in the middle gets bigger."

"But how does that keep the pressure in?"

"Each blade in the iris has a bunch of small polysteel plates attached to it. They're magnetized and connect to the metal cargo container and seal the air in."

The twins frowned as they tried to imagine that. "But that means the container has to be round."

"Right, actually, it has to be shaped like an egg," Catie said. "Or like this ship, egg-shaped on the ends and round in the middle."

"That seems weird," Aalia said.

"It sounds impractical," Prisha added.

"You only use it for last-minute deliveries," Catie said. "We'll keep some containers like that just in case."

"I've also designed a portable eggshell," Ajda said. "You can have a bunch of them of various sizes. They unfold like an accordion around the crate, so you can just open it up, slide the crate in and then close it and push the crate through the iris."

"Way cool!"

"This way, and I'll show you the bridge and crew quarters and accommodations," Ajda said.

"Were you able to fit in enough capacitors to manage the hull if we get hit by a plasma cannon?" Catie asked as they boarded the lift.

"Yes, these ellipsoid hulls have an amazing amount of unusable space, or at least only useful for sticking things like capacitors in."

"Good," Catie said.

"Seems like a big expense to go through for a cargo carrier. And the second flight bay seems excessive too," Ajda said.

"We can always put cargo in the second bay," Catie said. "And since we don't know what we're going to run into out there, I'd rather be over-prepared."

"You're paying for it," Ajda said, "so no skin off my nose."

"Alright, you have sixty crew cabins, and they all have double bunks. Captain's cabin is twice as big and also has the day cabin. Same for the owner's cabin. Nice big rec area here. These rooms can be configured for passenger cabins or for cargo storage. You have a galley big enough to handle five hundred people or more, although why I don't know."

"We can carry one hundred passengers with the extra cabins, and we're going to build passenger pods," Catie said. "They'll be right up against the front, so they'll match the shape of the forward section. They'll replace one of the cargo pods, and have an airlock to access the crew area and galley. Each pod should have about five hundred fifty cabins. We'll need to feed them."

"So, with four pods, we could carry one thousand?" Liz asked.

"Two thousand if they double up," Catie said. "But I'm estimating about seven hundred fifty per pod."

"How many pods are you thinking about?"

"I think we could do two deep, so eight," Catie said. "And remember, the Paraxeans have decided to keep the cabins. So, we'll sort of be exporting them. But it'll be a lot easier to send the pod down to the surface than to tear the cabins out."

"Good planning," Liz said. "I wanted to strangle Governor Paratar by the time they were done pulling the cabins out of the Sakira."

"Now you've got two elevators to traverse the spine; they operate in opposition, one goes up the other down," Ajda said.

"Why do you need elevators?" the twins asked.

"Remember, I told you we have to accelerate along the long axis?"

"Yes."

"So that means you have to use a ladder to get from the front of the ship to the back, which is really the top to the bottom."

"Yes, oh, that's kind of weird. But that means you have to climb down the spine to get to the engines."

"Right, that's four hundred meters, or two if you're just going to the jumpdrive. That's a lot of climbing."

"Yeah. Let's check out the elevator."

They spent the rest of the day going through the bridge stations, engineering, and examining the jumpdrives and the power plants. The twins wandered off after the second hour. They found them in the rec area playing tag when they finished the walkthrough. Scottie Murphy, the system engineer for the airliner, and Chief Hopkins had joined them when they were reviewing the more technical aspects of the ship. They were also going to ride along on the test flight the next day.

◆ ◆ ◆

The next morning, they were ready to take the ship out for its test flight. Scottie Murphy and Chief Hopkins joined them for breakfast.

"What in the world are you going to do with that big flight bay on that ship?" Chief Hopkins asked.

"Time will tell," Catie said. "But right now, five Oryxes can fit into it. So, we'll be delivering them to the colonies. We can put cargo in them on the way back."

"Oh, I didn't think about that. I guess they couldn't fit one in the Sakira."

"Especially after they piled all those cabins in her," Liz said. "I'll bet those colonists will be happy to have a few Oryxes around."

"Yep. They're big enough that you can set a printer up in them and print some critical items. You can even make a solar array in them."

"Oh, like a mini space station," the twins said.

"Yeah. It's a huge investment to build a space station, but an Oryx can take care of most of what they would need one for," Catie said.

"What are you going to name her?" the twins asked. "Can we name her?!"

"I haven't made up my mind," Catie said. "I was thinking of the Flying Dutchman."

"The ghost ship?!" the twins asked.

"Yes, with the jumpdrive, she'll be like a ghost, showing up suddenly."

"I like it," Liz said.

"Okay, then the Flying Dutchman it is," Catie said.

"I really like that rec space you put in," Scottie said. "But it seems a bit of overkill for a two- or three-week trip."

"First, you have to remember it's a round trip," Catie said. "And second, you're assuming a high acceleration profile. When this ship is loaded, it's going to be hard to accelerate it much over one-G, so you're talking at least a six-week or even a ten-week trip."

"You can't be serious," Liz said.

"Depends on how much mass you're moving."

"Boo, hiss," Liz said, knowing she was going to be the one piloting that mission.

"Hey, you might be able to pull off a two- or three-G profile; we probably won't be shipping that much mass out."

"Easy for you to say, you're going to be stuck in Delphi City while I'm stuck flying a long mission to Artemis," Liz said.

"I wish I could trade places with you."

"Can we come?" the twins asked.

"I think that's going to be a little too long for your mom. Three weeks out and three weeks back."

"I guess that is a little long," the twins said. Clearly, they were disappointed at being excluded from the momentous event.

"Let's get this show on the road. Everyone, get to the Lynx, and we'll fly over," Liz ordered.

"How come she's in charge?" the twins asked.

"I think it might have something to do with that six-week trip to Artemis," Catie said. "And that's after a five-week trip to Mangkatar, plus unloading and loading."

"Yuck!"

"Shh!"

The test flight went as planned. The Flying Dutchman, with its oversized jumpdrives, didn't have any trouble maintaining a six-G profile. The thrusters, with the aid of the gravity drives, allowed them to spin her around on her axis.

"She's good," Liz said. "Not that an eight-hundred-meter ship can be very agile, but she'll squeeze in where we need her. We can even manage to fit her up to the docking ring, as you'll see in about thirty minutes."

Liz carefully maneuvered The Flying Dutchman up to the docking ring. "See, smooth as silk," she bragged.

"But we didn't make a jump!" the twins complained.

"That would be a minimum of three weeks," Catie said. "We have to decelerate to zero at the fringe if we're running a test. Besides, we're not putting people on her for the first jump. ADI's going to fly her."

"ADI gets to do everything!"

"Except do flips in microgravity," ADI said.

◆ ◆ ◆

On Sunday night, when Catie arrived back at the Academy, she had a message on her Comm. The Academy message center only worked for cadets while they were on the Academy grounds. Checking her messages, she saw that her English Professor had finished grading their essays on For Whom the Bell Tolls.

*"A B!"* Catie yelled to herself. How could she possibly have gotten a B on the paper? She'd read the book, detailed everything. *"A B?!"*

She immediately set up an appointment to talk to the instructor. On Monday at 1500, she reported to the instructor's office to ask what she had done wrong. She'd suffered the entire day wondering what was wrong.

"Cadet MacGregor, what can I do for you?" her English instructor asked.

"Sir, I would like to understand my grade better," Catie said.

"Oh yes, your paper on Ernest Hemmingway's For Whom the Bell Tolls. What do you need to know? And I'm just an English professor, you don't have to call me sir."

"Your only comment is, 'What did you think of the book?,' Professor," Catie said. "I don't understand."

"You did an excellent job highlighting Hemmingway's use of metaphors, his language style, and his historical accuracy. But . . . let me ask you this, what was your favorite passage in the book?"

Catie was shocked by the question, "My favorite passage?"

"Yes, what was your favorite passage in the book?"

Catie starting flipping through the book and her paper in her head, trying to identify a significant passage.

"Don't bother. The fact that it was not in the forefront of your mind makes my point. You read the book; by the look of it, you memorized it. But you didn't really read it. Did you even enjoy it?"

"It was a good book."

"That doesn't answer my question. Did you enjoy it?"

"I just read it," Catie said.

"If you want a better grade, you have to do more than just read the assignments. You need to let them affect you; impact you emotionally. You need to open yourself up to what it's trying to say. This book is not some pulp fiction that you just consume. It is a work of art, you have to let it into your soul; otherwise, you might as well just read the CliffsNotes on the book."

"I see," Catie said. "Thank you, Professor."

Catie left his office still wondering what she had done wrong. She decided she would reread the book like it was a play and she was going to be one of the actors in it. Maybe that would help her understand what the professor wanted.

# 20 Artemis

Marc took a page from Liz's book and released a Lynx and crew as they passed the asteroid belt. They were ordered to send three asteroids under grav-drive to Artemis, a methane one, and two iron asteroids. They were then to start lobbing ice asteroids toward the planet, as many as they could in two weeks. Then they could join the team on the planet. Another team would be positioned to catch the ice asteroids and drop them into the planet's atmosphere or put them into orbit for later use.

The first thing they had done on reaching the planet was erect some temporary barracks on the surface. Marc had stayed on the Sakira during that time, out of the way of the construction crew. They knew what they were doing and didn't need any extra supervision. But now they had space for the crews and enough material down on the surface to start the big construction jobs.

"How's the well going?" Marc asked as he stepped off the Lynx.

"We're still drilling through the shale," the drilling foreman said. "We should break into the anticline trap in a couple of days. Then we have to pump concrete down to seal the well, blast through that in a few places to let the oil in, so, two more days. On my oath, we'll be pumping oil by Monday."

"Good. Is our excavator ready?"

"Not my department. You should go ask your dig foreman."

Marc walked over to where they should have been starting to dig the main channel. The dig foreman was reviewing the plans and talking with one of the structural engineers.

"Why aren't we digging? Isn't the excavator ready?" Marc asked.

"Yes, but we've got a bit of a problem with the crew."

"What kind of problem?"

"They're arguing about doing such a big dig. They're advocating that we do less."

"Let's go talk to them."

"Yes, *sir*," the dig foreman said. He was clearly not enthusiastic about confronting the crew. "I was thinking about having them do one of the side streets first, give them some time to work out their frustrations."

"We could, but I want to know what the problem is," Marc said as he walked up to the big excavator. "What seems to be the issue? Why haven't we started digging the main channel?" Marc asked.

"What do you mean *We*?" a big Aussie asked. "We're the ones that'll be digging that trench."

"I understand, but the effort is for all of us. What's the problem?"

"*We* think you're wasting *our* labor, digging such a big trench. We won't be needing something that big for years. We want to get more done, then we'll be able to get this town up and running faster, and that means we'll be able to get our land sooner."

"That won't make a difference. We won't be assigning private land for two years. I want to stick to our original plan. We want to avoid rework, and having that main trench is the basis of the entire design."

"What you don't seem to understand is that that pretty plan of yours needs to change. No plan lasts past the first day you actually start working. And we think you need to let those of us with experience run the show now that we're digging."

"I appreciate your input," Marc said. "And if you have concerns, I'll be happy to discuss them with you. Just make an appointment, but for now, get this machine running."

"You don't understand. I said you need to let us run things," the big Aussie said as he raised himself up to his full six-foot-four height.

"No, you don't understand. I'm in charge. If that doesn't suit you, you can go back to the Sakira and ask them for some work you can do until you can go back to Earth."

"And how are you going to make that happen? You can have your security guys come over here and pound on us. But that will just make you look like a Nancy-boy," the Aussie said, puffing out his chest and clenching his fist. He moved up to within half a meter of Marc, looking very threatening. "Now, why don't you go back to your office and work on your plans and leave us in charge?"

Marc took a half-step back with his left leg, like he was going to turn around and leave. Then he slammed his left palm into the center of the big Aussie's chest. He hit him right in the solar plexus, and the big Aussie crumpled to the ground.

"Well, fancy that, he just dropped like a stone; I guess I'm still in charge," Marc said loudly. "Now get that machine working! And someone, get a medic over here to take care of him."

The rest of the crew's resolve melted away, and they moved back to the excavator and started it up.

"He's going to be pissed when he quits gasping for air," Garity said. "And I don't think a cheap shot is going to work the next time."

"That wasn't a cheap shot, it was an example."

"You sound pretty confident you can take him."

"Sure, he's big and slow."

"He's got two inches and thirty pounds on you."

"Like I said, big and slow. Where are our asteroids?"

"They're still flying them to the planet."

"Damn, it would be nice if we had some iron ore here by the time the oil starts flowing."

"Things can only go so fast. You've got to be patient."

"Patience is a virtue, and I've been told I'm irredeemable," Marc laughed as he moved on, leaving the dig foreman scratching his head.

◆ ◆ ◆

"Paul, give me an update on our mining," Marc said once he got to the office building in the compound.

"We've reached the limestone at the cement plant. We'll be extracting it by tomorrow. Dr. Pittman has finally decided which clay he likes, so we'll start digging at that location and hauling it to the plant. He also told us that using an iron asteroid for the polysteel is great, but it won't work for cement. We need iron oxide for that. Dr. Qamar told us where the iron deposits are, so we've sent a team over there to dig some up. The one we selected is only two hundred kilometers, and we don't need that much, it's only three percent of the mixture."

"What about the alumina?"

"Big bauxite field just one hundred kilometers to the south; again, we only need about five percent. Those Paraxeans sure know how to pick a good location."

"I'll let them know you think so," Marc said. "So we're set for making cement and concrete, and we can make aluminum wiring if we need to. Any word on a copper source?"

"I can't believe they didn't locate a deposit of copper," Paul said. "Nattie's out with a crew surveying for a deposit. It's looking like that mine is going to be a couple of thousand kilometers away."

"I guess you can't find everything in one place," Marc said. "What about silver and gold deposits?"

"Same thing; you'll be having to set up remote mines to take care of those. But we'll get them set up. It'll be like California in forty-nine: small town, lots of small mines, I figure."

"Hopefully, we can find a collection of mines in close proximity, so we only have to establish one town."

"You can hope. Anyway, when are you going to let the kids come down?" Paul asked.

"Next week. I'd like to wait until we've completed the main channel, but another month seems too long."

"Darn right it is. They need to get out into the fresh air."

"That's what their mothers are telling me, *and* telling me."

"Hah, they'll keep you straight."

◆ ◆ ◆

"I saw that fight," Samantha said when Marc made it back to the Sakira for the night.

"What fight?"

"Between you and that big Aussie!"

"That wasn't a fight, that was just me providing a little education to the work crew," Marc said.

"So, you've been training?"

"Where did you think I was going at five o'clock all those mornings?"

"Running."

"We ran some, but mostly Blake and I were working out with Kal."

"I guess he taught you that punch?"

"Palm strike, and yes he did. He says he learned it from Liz, it's her go-to strike."

"Then, you're not worried about him coming back?"

"The Aussie, no. He's a little bigger than Blake, but not nearly as fast."

"That's a relief. I guess I shouldn't worry about you then. You do know that was a bit Neanderthal of you."

"As I recall, when I had my DNA done, I did have some Neanderthal genes," Marc said.

"Funny, but how do you justify brute force to keep people in line? What is this, 1900 Chicago?"

"No, if it was, I'd have just shot him. I didn't want to waste time arguing about objectives. I could have stood everyone down for the day and explained it all. But he kind of pissed me off, so I took a short cut."

"I hope you don't have to take very many more of those shortcuts," Samantha said.

"I'm afraid I made that lesson too easy. I should have let him take a few shots and bloodied his nose. I'll take my time next time."

"You think there will be a next time?"

"Seventy-thirty."

Marc's Comm woke him up the next day. "Your first asteroid is here," Captain Desjardins reported.

"I assume it's the one we're putting on the surface."

"Yep, those big grav-drives didn't have any problem getting it here fast."

"Okay, I'll be up in thirty minutes."

"We'll have it waiting for you."

Marc spent the morning watching them lower the asteroid into place. It was obvious that they didn't need his help, his only contribution was selecting the site. They broke the asteroid into smaller chunks in space so they could bring one of the chunks down to the planet's surface. Finally, they landed a one-hundred-meter by fifty-meter chunk of rock next to the lot that they'd designated for the polysteel foundry. It was pretty exciting, momentous actually. They'd excavated the site so that the grav-drives would be accessible once the asteroid was down. They needed those drives to make the big freight haulers they would need to bring in the limestone and other materials they would be mining.

As soon as it landed, Paul went out to check on the quality of the iron ore. He took samples from several spots to run an assay on. "We'll let the scientists tell us how they did picking this one, but I'd say it looks like they did a good job," Paul told Marc.

"That's good; I'd hate to find out that I'd wasted my morning watching them land a useless piece of rock."

"Pretty amazing sight wasn't it," Paul said. "Something to tell the kids about when I have them."

"Yep, the second time in known history that it's been done," Marc said. "The Paraxeans landed theirs six weeks ago."

"Yeah, too bad we couldn't be first."

"There'll be plenty of firsts in the next few months," Marc said. "Your kids will be dutifully impressed."

"They'd better be."

"I'm heading back to the office to do actual work," Marc said. "I'll see you later."

◆ ◆ ◆

By the next day, they'd mined about one ton of iron ore from the asteroid. It hadn't taken much to get started, and the miners were having a good time.

"Careful you idiot!" Paul yelled when he came out to check on them. "What's your problem?"

"One of those expansion bags could explode and take your head off, or it could make the others collapse and that layer of iron ore you're trying to sheer off could slam back down and crush your foot. Just because we're not in space doesn't mean you can ignore your safety protocols!"

As if to accentuate his point, one of the bags exploded.

"See! Now get back to work and do it right, or I'll find some other miners, and you can go work in the greenhouses!"

Once they had excavated a good section of the main channel, the engineer came out and inspected the hole.

"We're digging right on top of a sandstone layer down here. I don't think we'll need to do any compaction. We'll separate out the sandstone and grind it up. We can backfill with it once we have the tube done."

"So when can we start making the tube?" Marc asked.

"If you're in a hurry, we can start making the tube behind the excavator. We can divide the channel into two-hundred-meter lengths. Make a separate ramp for each section. Once one section is done, we can start the tube. We'll just follow the excavator, four hundred meters behind it."

"I'm always in a hurry," Marc said.

"Okay."

By that afternoon, they had erected scaffolding to hold the tube up above the bottom and keep things level. They ran the system on the ground to test it out and to create a ten-meter length of the tube as a starter section. Then they moved that into the ditch and leveled it, then started it up. As the tube grew, the crew moved in behind and put scaffolding under it to keep it level and support the weight until they filled the trench with polycrete.

"How fast do you expect to go?" Marc asked the foreman.

"I'm shooting for two hundred meters a day," he replied. "You're asking for four thousand meters for this first run."

"Yep, that should cover us for the first few months. I want to get everyone focused on the building as soon as possible."

"Okay, you're the boss."

"Hey Nancy-boy, I'm ready for you now!" the big Aussie yelled. "No cheap shots will work this time."

Marc sighed and turned to face the idiot; he'd expected to see him sometime today, but he'd hoped that maybe the guy had learned his lesson.

"I'm surprised you didn't have your guys hold me up so you could hit me!"

"I didn't think you'd collapse so completely," Marc said. "Otherwise, I'd have asked them to break your fall."

"Think you're funny, don't you? Well, let's see how funny you are after I pound on you a few times."

"Sir," Marc's bodyguard said.

"Stand back, don't worry," Marc whispered as he raised his hands and took up a defensive posture.

"Now you're worried about being hit!"

Marc just circled, ignoring the taunts.

Marc ducked the left jab that shot out. He used his elbow to deflect the right cross aimed at his ribs. "Oomph." He didn't deflect it completely, and it caught the back of his ribcage.

"Not so fancy now, are ye! Not when you have to square off in a proper fight! Well, I'll tell . . ."

Marc's left jab struck like a cobra, catching the Aussie square in the nose. The Aussie backed up as he brushed his arm across his nose, smearing the blood across his face and onto his arm.

"So, you got another lucky shot in ya!" the Aussie taunted Marc.

Marc just circled and waited. When the Aussie moved in for another combo, Marc used his left forearm to push the Aussie's jab to the left, then he stepped to his right to avoid the counterpunch and delivered a hard-right hand to the Aussie's kidney.

"Oomph!"

Marc bounced back out of range and kept circling.

The Aussie stayed out of range while he got his breath back. When he did, he started talking again. Marc just rolled his eyes.

"So, you can fight, but I can take a lot of punishment, can you?"

Marc feinted with his right hand, then stepped in and did a palm strike to the Aussie's solar plexus. He dropped like a sack of potatoes, again.

"Take him to the medic! And when he wakes up, tell him that next time I'll break his arm and put him in jail while it heals!"

"You know, you're pretty good looking for a Neanderthal," Samantha said as she kissed Marc hello.

"Ah, so you heard."

"ADI keeps me informed about all your activities."

"ADI!"

"I was only following orders," ADI said.

"Daddy, you shouldn't get into fights," Catie said over their Comms.

"ADI, who else have you told?"

"Do you really want the whole list?" ADI asked.

"No, I can guess."

"Daddy!"

"Yes, Sweetie. I'll try to be more careful. How are classes going?"

"Good, we get a week off for Thanksgiving, even though it's a U.S. Holiday."

"That covers your birthday this year, doesn't it?"

"Yes, lucky huh?"

"What are you going to do?"

"I'm going to Nice with my roommate. Liz says she'll come up with a reason to give us a ride."

"That's nice of her. Now, bye."

"Bye, Daddy."

"ADI, refuse all calls from that list unless it's an emergency," Marc said.

"Yes, Captain."

"Chicken," Samantha said.

"Just tired. How are you doing?"

"I'm doing fine. I had a meeting with all the parents today. We're trying to figure out how to handle school once the colonists start dispersing to their land."

"I assumed you'd go virtual," Marc said.

"That's what most people assume. But we need to socialize the children, too. We're going to set up a daycare co-op so that the young ones will be able to play together and the moms can work, or have a day off."

"Sounds good."

"We'll do the same for school. That way one of the parents doesn't have to stay home and supervise the kids. We also want them to come into town for classes once a week or so. We'll work out the details."

"That should make everyone happy."

"You do realize that means we need cellphone coverage?" Samantha said.

"Yeah, that and satellite coverage," Marc said. "I wasn't going to worry about that until next year. Until then we're covered by the town's antennas."

"But what about your mining town?"

"We've brought one satellite that will cover them and the city. We'll launch it in a few weeks."

"But what about long trips, explorations, things like that?"

"Damn. Okay, I'll tell Fred to start making satellites for us. We'll have Liz bring them out on the first StartMerchant shipment."

"Will that cover GPS?" Samantha asked.

"For this continent, at least. We'll have to get more on the next shipment before we can cover the other continents."

"Marc, O'Brian wants to be the construction foreman for the mining town," McCovey informed as they started their meeting.

"He does? What's his experience?"

"He was on the team that built a new mining town in Australia. That's why we picked him for this mission."

"Well, let's give him a chance. We need that town up and running fast. We'll be out of copper and gold in a few weeks. We need to get the mines going out there."

"You sure you don't want him on the excavator crew?"

"Yeah," Marc laughed. "That's what I want to do, convince him that we should dig a canal to bring the river next to the town."

"That would be fun to watch," McCovey said. "But, now that you mention it, why are we doing that?"

"Mainly to keep the excavator busy. We're going to have to do it eventually. We'll be using the river to move freight as we grow, and we need to set up a fishing village on the coast, plus we'll pull our irrigation water from it. Saves having to lay all that pipe."

"A fishing village?"

"I'm assuming the fishermen won't want to have to sail all the way upriver every day. And we need the fish if we're going to be able to feed everyone."

"If we're going to have a fishing village, then why the canal?"

"Move the fish up here, and cargo down there."

"Okay, so when they finish up the four side streets, we'll start digging the canal."

"Right, we need to keep all of our equipment running as much as possible; they're going to be the limiting factor on our growth. Every day they sit idle means that eventually we'll lose that day."

"We've finished the second set of barracks," McCovey said. "So we can bring down the final group of colonists. We've had to expand the cafeteria to accommodate everyone. We'll still have to set shifts for when people eat, so we don't have lines."

"Hi, Nattie," Marc greeted Natalia as she joined the meeting.

"Hey. Busy?"

"Always. How's the treatment plant doing?"

"It's up and running. We're set up to handle half a million liters of wastewater per day. That means you can bring down the rest of your colonists, and you can move one of the portable systems we brought with us to your mining town," Natalia said.

"Perfect timing. We were just talking about starting that up. And we can put the second system down by the coast for the fishing village," Marc said.

"Does that mean I get a beachside cottage so I can go down and make sure it's running okay?"

"Sure you don't want one up by the mining town?"

"A cabin in the mountains would be nice too."

"I assume you won't mind sharing with the other engineers we have to send around to inspect things?"

"If I have to."

◆ ◆ ◆

"Marc," Commander Desjardins commed.

"Yes?"

"Your ice asteroids will start arriving tomorrow. You need to decide what you want to do with them."

"How many?"

"Those boys have been busy; we're going to be getting three or four a day."

"Great, we've identified a depression here by the city that is suitable for a lake. Just start setting them down in it. If they come in faster than you can move them down here, then drop the extras in the ocean. Don't make too big a splash."

"Got it, do you have a line on the lake to tell us when it's full?"

"There's a small hill in the center of the depression, we want it to be an island," Marc said. "We'll have the lake overflow into the canal once we finish digging it."

"Okay, we'll stop filling it up when we get the island down to a few hundred square meters. Are you putting fish in the lake?"

"We might, do you have a preference?"

"Lake trout are my favorite."

"I'm pretty sure we brought a bunch of lake trout eggs, so I'll have Dr. Teltar figure out when to release them."

"You're a good friend."

"You're going to love Nice," Yvette said as she and Catie finished packing for the fall break.

"I'd better," Catie said. "You owe me big time for getting me in trouble with Professor Gossmann."

"You didn't get in trouble. And his lectures have gotten a lot better since he started coming to your tutoring sessions."

"Yeah, like that's not going to come back and bite me."

"Well, at least he stopped coming after three weeks."

"Yeah, but is that because of midterms, or is he really going to stay away?"

"I think he figured out what he wanted. Like I said, his lectures are much easier to understand."

"Okay, we'll see."

"Hey, you said you were going to try to get us on a hop to Nice, or at least somewhere close. Right now, we have to fly to Paris, then wait three hours to catch a flight."

"Oh, I forgot, I've got us a ride," Catie said. "You can cancel your flight to Paris."

"What about coming back?"

"I've got us a ride for that one, too."

"And how did you manage that?"

"I know someone," Catie said. "You'll meet her tomorrow at the airport. She's flying us."

◆ ◆ ◆

"Yvette, this is my friend, Liz. She's the pilot I told you about."

"*Bonjour,*" Yvette said. "I can't tell you how much it means to me to get home so fast."

"Oh, don't worry about it. I have to ferry some stuff out to Admiral Michaels. He's the chairman of the Delphi Alliance, and he's living in Nice."

"In Nice? Doesn't the Delphi Alliance meet in Brussels?"

"They do, but his wife likes Nice better, so he commutes."

"He must really love his wife."

"It's a fifteen-minute commute," Liz said. "He probably gets to work faster than the rest of the council."

"Must be nice to be so important."

"Rank has its privileges," Liz said. "You'll learn that soon enough. They really wanted him to take the job, so dedicating a Lynx to him wasn't that big a deal."

"Is he the same Admiral Michaels that taught the first two weeks of Military Space Strategy?" Yvette asked.

"The one and the same."

"He seemed like a nice guy."

"He is as long as you don't get him mad," Liz said. "Now, get on board, and we'll head out."

"Are we the only passengers?"

"Yes," Liz said. "We're ferrying cargo, and nobody else needs to go that way." The truth was they didn't want anyone else to spend three hours in a Lynx with Catie and risk blowing her cover.

◆ ◆ ◆

"What are you girls going to do while here in Nice?" Liz asked as they deplaned.

"I'm going to make Alex go with me to the Musée Matisse and the Musée Chagall to give her some culture," Yvette said. "Then, we're going to shop and just hang out."

"And we're going to go to Monaco," Catie said.

"Monaco?" Liz said, giving Catie a hard stare.

"Yeah, I want to learn how to play a few card games. I'm over eighteen now, so I can gamble."

Liz just shook her head. Catie didn't gamble as all her friends knew. With her eidetic memory, she could memorize all the cards. It was as if they were marked. Variations in shape, bent corners, all gave her an edge over the competition. Plus, she could spot a player's tell within five minutes of sitting down.

"Have fun, don't lose too much money there," Liz said.

As the girls headed off to meet Yvette's father, Liz nodded to the two security guys they'd pulled from Admiral Michaels' detail to watch over Catie. Maybe they would have some fun in Monaco.

"Alex, this is my papa," Yvette introduced Catie to her father.

"Hello, Monsieur LeClair," Catie said as she allowed him to take her hand. He gave her a hand a small brush with his lips.

"Call me Leon," Monsieur LeClair said. "Now we must go quickly before *un flic de stationnement* gives me a ticket." He led them to his car that indeed had a parking cop eyeing it.

"Mama!" Yvette cried out when Monsieur LeClair pulled the car into a parking space beside the mansion.

"Wow, that's a nice house," Catie said.

"Oh, it was a nice mansion years ago," Monsieur LeClair said. "Now it is a condominium. We have the unit on the top two floors. Come, I'll show you inside, Yvette has forgotten her manners in her excitement."

"That's okay," Catie said as she followed Monsieur LeClair up the stairs and into their condo. It was compact, but certainly more spacious than Catie's condo in Delphi City. The floors were hardwood in a herringbone pattern with a few area rugs in strategic locations. A nice conversation grouping was the central focus of the room.

Yvette and a woman Catie assumed was her mother were holding hands and chatting a mile a minute in French. Both had tears on their cheeks.

"Mama, this is my friend, Alex," Yvette said. "Alex, this is my mama."

"Madame LeClair," Catie said as she grasped Madame LeClair's hands. They exchanged air kisses.

"Please call me Alma. Yvette, take your friend to your room so she can freshen up after your trip. Then we will have some wine and hors d'oeuvres," Madame LeClair said.

"Come," Yvette said as she led Catie up the stairs. Her room was at the end of the hall and overlooked the street. The room was small but very neat. An armoire sat in the corner, with a small desk in the other corner, and a bed along the opposite wall.

"Cozy," Catie said.

"*Oui*."

"I should have brought a sleeping bag."

"*Non*, we can share the bed, we are not so big."

◆ ◆ ◆

"Some nice wine, some cheese, a little bread and voilà, a nice snack for after your trip," Madame LeClair said.

"Mama, we ate on the plane," Yvette said.

"But it is such a long trip."

"Only three hours."

"Still. Now be quiet and have some wine."

"Monsieur LeClair . . ."

"Leon."

"Leon, Yvette tells me you're an architect," Catie said.

"Yes, I am the architect, and Alma is the structural engineer. We make a very good team."

"Yvette didn't tell me you were a structural engineer," Catie said.

"Only because I didn't want you to judge me for my poor math skills," Yvette said.

"Yes, Yvette only got her good looks from her mother," Leon said. "She got her sense of art from me, and of course, her *joie de vivre* from both of us."

"And Yvette says that your father is a construction engineer," Alma said.

"Yes, and my mother is a nurse," Catie said. Everyone had decided that a doctor and a math professor was too close to the truth.

"Such long hours your mother must have worked," Madame LeClair said.

"Yes. When I was little, and my mother had the late shift, I used to go to my father's office after school to do my homework. We would go out to dinner together instead of ordering takeout. Daddy has never been a very good cook."

"Well, Leon is an excellent chef," Alma said. "You will see tonight when he cooks for us."

At breakfast the next morning, Gaspard, Yvette's brother, showed up. He had been out late the night before.

"I will take you to the museums," he offered. "I can tell you all you want to know about the artists."

"But we are going shopping after," Yvette said. "And Papa said I could have the car."

"That is alright, I will take a taxi home."

Yvette rolled her eyes at Catie and sighed, "Very well, but I am driving, and you must behave yourself."

"I always behave myself!"

"I'm sorry about my brother," Yvette said after they dropped Gaspard off next to a taxi stand.

"He was okay. He sure knew a lot about the art," Catie said.

"Yes, he is quite . . . how do you say?"

"Loquacious if you want to be fancy, or talkative."

"*Non,* loquacious is the right word," Yvette said. "Or *pompeux*."

"Pompous," Catie translated. "Yes, he is certainly full of himself."

"Yes, and when you asked him what he did with all that knowledge and education, he certainly shut up for a while."

"Do you think he doesn't have a job because he doesn't want one, or because he's so offensive that he cannot get one?"

"Oh, maybe he cannot get one," Yvette said; she looked as if the idea had never occurred to her.

"He should get a job doing graphic arts, but one where he can work from home and only communicates via email. That way, he won't have an opportunity to slip in those 'I'm better than you' comments," Catie said.

"That might work, but poor Mama, she works from home," Yvette said before she and Catie broke out in giggles.

"How did your trip to Monaco work out?" Liz asked when Catie and Yvette met her at the airport for the ride back to Delphi City.

"It was fun," Yvette said. "Alex spent too much time at the card tables, but we still had fun."

"Did you win?" Liz asked.

"Yes, but it was a lot of work," Catie said.

"They asked her to leave the 21 table," Yvette said with a laugh.

"Oh, you got kicked out?"

"Just at one casino," Catie said. "I varied my bets, so they figured out I was counting cards."

"Why didn't the other casinos figure it out?"

"I didn't vary my bet so much. But then it took a lot longer to make money."

"Did you play poker?"

"Yes, that was easier."

"So how much did you make?"

"Just enough to pay for our stay and shopping trips," Catie said.

"Shopping?"

"Yvette likes to buy clothes."

"Yes, and Alex was so nice to pay with all her winnings," Yvette said.

"Yvette, what did you do while Alex was gambling?"

"Oh, I played the slots and craps," Yvette said. "They are much more exciting."

"Did you win?"

"*Non,* Alex covered my losses, so it was just fun."

"I should have come with you guys."

"Yes, you could have gotten Alex to buy you a new outfit," Yvette said.

"Oh, I should have thought about that," Liz said. "Now let's get home."

# 21 We Ain't No Communists

## Nov 29th

"Marc, I've had four requests for transfers to the mining village just this week," McCovey said as he and Marc started their meeting to review job allocations.

"Why? It's not like they get paid more for working there. Do they like the isolation?"

"I don't know, but there have been a lot of complaints about job assignments in the last two weeks."

"What kind of complaints?"

"Things like, why should I do this job, it's too much work, why can't I have one of the easy jobs. And some complaints about hours, too."

"I wonder what's behind all that. I need you to look into it," Marc said.

## Dec 1st

"Marc, there is a crowd gathering outside," McCovey said. "They're yelling something about not signing up to join a commune."

Samantha, Chief O'Donnell, Natalia, Paul, McCovey, and Major Kobayashi all looked concerned. This was definitely out of character for the colony.

"Interesting timing," Marc said. "Since this is our scheduled meeting to review the colony status, I'm guessing this was planned."

"I'd say so."

"Sir, we have security on scene. Should we disperse the crowd?" Major Kobayashi asked.

"Let's find out what they want first," Marc said.

Marc got up and made his way to the door with Major Kobayashi right behind him. When they made it outside, they were confronted with about fifty or sixty colonists standing in a tight group in the street. Several were holding signs that read things like We Want Freedom, We

Signed Up For Opportunity, and the simple and to the point, We Ain't No Communists.

"How can I help you?!" Marc shouted.

"Stop being a communist dictator!" someone yelled.

"That is not my intent," Marc replied in a loud voice so the whole crowd could hear.

"Then how come there's no free enterprise on this colony?!"

"There is some small amount, but I acknowledge your point. We're too young to have much in the way of free enterprise yet," Marc said. "We are still focused on ensuring our survival."

"How come I have to break my back working in construction, and I don't get paid any more than someone who babysits kids all day?!"

"Do you have kids?"

"Sure."

"Do you want someone taking care of them that is malnourished and living in a tent or someone who's healthy and well fed-like you?"

"That's not the point, I should get more for working this hard!"

"You people seem organized; do you have a spokesperson?"

"This is a democracy, ain't it? We all want to have our own say!"

"Okay! First, this is not a democracy; you all work for me. But we want to be democratic about it, so, here's my suggestion. I'll suspend all but critical work for the rest of the week. Everyone needs to figure out who they think best represents their point of view. We'll set up twenty groups, you'll need to select which group you belong to, and I'll meet with a representative from each group to discuss how we're going forward."

"How do we do that?"

"Think of it like a caucus. Everyone, start saying what's important to you. Our DI will collate your issues and start identifying common themes. Once a pattern emerges, the DI will identify groups that share a common set of themes. You can then decide which group you want to represent you. The groups can meet, discuss the issues further, and elect a leader. If necessary, we can go through the process several times until you feel you're being fairly represented. On Saturday, my staff and I will meet with your representatives and look for solutions to your issues."

"How do we know you won't rig the system with your DI?!"

"You can meet with your groups. If you don't like the result, then you can develop a different process. I'll accept a meeting with any group of representatives you come up with as long as it's only twenty. You're also free to utilize your Comms to view the meeting and provide input to your representative."

## Dec 2nd

"Hello, I'm calling for Karl Marc," Blake said when Marc answered his Comm.

"Very funny," Marc said.

"I always knew all that leftist propaganda Mom was feeding you would get you into trouble."

"You grew up in the same house."

"But I was safely ensconced at the Naval Academy before she stated taking you to indoctrination sessions."

"I went to one seminar on 'labor unions as the last bastion against corporate greed,' and only because Mom didn't want to drive at night."

"Yeah, I'm sure your communist handlers taught you to say that."

Marc sighed. "Other than razzing me, is there a point to this call?"

"No, just wanted to take advantage of the situation," Blake said.

"ADI, hang up, and please filter my calls," Marc said.

"Yes, Captain. I'll tell Cer Kal that Cer Blake has used up all the funny lines."

"Oh great, then they'll meet to compare notes."

"They are already arranging to meet at the bar for lunch," ADI said.

"What's the matter?" Samantha asked.

"Oh, this situation. I guess I should have anticipated it," Marc said.

"You can't anticipate everything. You'll figure it out."

"You mean, we'll figure it out."

"*Sure*, we'll be there," Samantha said. "Is ADI giving you an update on their issues?"

"No, they asked for privacy until Saturday," Marc said.

"So, somebody with experience is coordinating this."

"It seems so. I just hope it's not some agent from one of Earth's governments."

"I thought you had ADI filter them out," Samantha said.

"She did, but no filter is perfect."

"Well, even if it's an agent, they can't control all the colonists. They may have started it, but now a democratic process is going to resolve it."

"That's not necessarily a good thing," Marc said. "That's why I'm forcing it to a representative process. We don't want the majority to ride roughshod over the rest of the community."

"Ah, I guess that makes sense. Everyone voting on everything would wash out any input from less well-represented groups. See, you're so smart. That's why I love you," Samantha said as she kissed Marc on top of his head.

## Dec 4th

"Are you ready?" Samantha asked.

"I hope so. This has already cost us three days, I'd like to get everyone back to work," Marc said.

"Well, if you make good progress, maybe they'll go back to work while you finish."

"Maybe, but then I might shoot myself before it's over."

"Just hang in there."

"I'd like to thank all of you for stepping up to provide representation for the colony," Marc said as he opened the meeting with the twenty representatives. They were meeting in the cafeteria; the tables were arranged in a square, with Marc and the six members of his staff on one side and the twenty representatives arrayed along the other three sides. Several servers moved about to provide water and coffee to anyone who needed it. Major Kobayashi had six Marines standing against the walls to provide security.

"Now, if everyone is ready, we can start," Marc said.

"What's to stop us from taking over and just running things the way we want?!" one of the representatives said very loudly. ADI immediately provided Marc with his name, Karl Olsen. He was representing a group of one hundred sixty families, about five hundred people total.

"And how do you plan to do that?" Marc said as he motioned for Major Kobayashi to remain seated.

"There are more of us than there are of you!"

"That may be true," Marc said. "But let me remind you that MacKenzie Discoveries owns this planet, owns the ships that brought us here, owns all the equipment and all the cargo on those ships. In fact, we own everything except the personal belongings you brought with you."

"We could take them with eminent domain!"

"You could try," Marc said. "But let me provide some facts. One, the Marines reporting to Major Kobayashi are committed to protecting all of us and enforcing the law, which currently recognizes said ownership by MacKenzie Discoveries. Two, if you would like, I could take all of our equipment, our fusion reactors, and our supplies, load it back up on the Sakira, and move a few hundred miles away. Taking with me all those who would still like to recognize the contracts that you all signed when you joined this mission. That would leave the rest of you here with just the buildings we've erected so far. The future missions from Earth would bypass you, so there would be no future supplies, no new colonists, and no market for whatever you want to export."

"Shut up, William, you're making things worse."

"What if I don't want to, are you going to make me?!"

"William, if you don't sit down and take your turn, we'll vote to have you removed," a woman said. "And I'm sure Major Kobayashi will be happy to have his Marines remove you from the meeting. Then you can go back and tell the people you represent that you couldn't control yourself and provide them with fair representation."

ADI, immediately informed Marc that the woman was Helena Bachmann. She was representing a large group of colonists, mainly consisting of the ones who planned to live in town, teachers, nurses, and factory workers. She had also been asked to be the main spokesperson for five other groups. Their representatives sat on her left, on the side across from Marc.

"Thank you, Ms. Bachmann," Marc said.

"Cer Bachmann, if you please, or Helena, if you're buying me a drink."

"As if he could buy you a drink!" one of the men said. "There's no damn bar in this town."

"I distinctly remember allocating the space for a bar," Marc said.

"It's a damn coffee bar!"

Marc pressed the 'ADI' button on the keyboard his specs were displaying.

"Captain, he is correct, there were over a hundred complaints about it," ADI said.

'Why haven't I heard about this?' Marc typed.

"They are in the non-urgent complaint file," ADI said. "You asked me to segment the complaints and only inform you of the urgent ones. You *said* you'd check the others on your own."

"I apologize for that oversight," Marc said. "It was always our intention to have a bar down here like the one on the Sakira. We'll allocate space for it right away and get it running. Cer Bachmann, did you have something else to add?"

"I have several points to make," Cer Bachmann said.

"Please proceed."

"Let me say that we're all concerned about pay disparity. Most of us don't actually know what everyone is making, but after talking with my group, I realized we were not all making the same amount. Could you explain the rationale you used for setting pay?"

"Of course," Marc said. "We have essentially three groups of colonists. The first group are the people who work for MacKenzies and expect to continue to work for us long term. The second group are the ones who plan to work for the two-year commitment and then get their land grant and set out on their own. The third group are the ones who plan to work here in town, teachers, factory workers, artisans. Many of them are already performing the jobs they intend to perform. I guess we could add a fourth group, the ones who are doing jobs that are needed while they try to establish their new business. We have two artists who would fit into that category. They're working as teachers now until they have a large enough client base to focus on their art full time."

"And how did you determine pay?"

"For the first group, they're receiving the same pay they were earning before they took this mission plus thirty percent. The bonus percent will decline by five percent per year. Of course, there might be pay raises that will offset that decline.

"The second group is being paid the equivalent of the average factory worker plus the right to select four hundred hectares of farmland or eight hundred of ranchland after they complete their two-year commitment. They also receive a premium based on the difficulty of the job. Construction workers receive a twenty percent premium, miners, a thirty percent premium, fifty if they're working in space.

"The third group is being paid the same salary that they would have earned in Delphi City, with the addition of free housing for the first two years."

"Hey, mining isn't more difficult than construction!"

"It's not only more difficult, it's more dangerous," Paul said. "If you don't believe me, feel free to spend a day on that asteroid out there."

"Ahem," Cer Bachmann coughed to stanch the argument. "Thank you. That is what I surmised based on my contract as well as my discussions with my group, but I thought it was important that everyone know that. I think we all would like some time to talk with our constituents about that before we discuss wages. Might I propose that we address some of the other issues first? Then we can break for lunch. We'll meet with our constituents, who are even now discussing the implications of your information. Then after a two-hour break for lunch, we can reconvene."

"I'm happy to proceed under those terms," Marc said.

Cer Bachmann looked around the table to see if the other delegates were in agreement. Apparently, they had arranged some form of voting since each delegate tapped the table in front of them, and Cer Bachmann nodded and turned back to Marc.

"We're also in agreement," she said. "Now, I'll start on our list. Cer Barone will start."

"I'm representing some of the farmers," Cer Barone said; he had a distinctly Italian accent that made him a bit difficult to understand. "We can understand that we don't have the equipment to have everyone run their own farm yet, but we are concerned about the community farms and how they will impact our farms once we start them."

"First, I want to thank you for your understanding about the equipment," Marc said. "Now to the point about the community farms. Their purpose is to get us to self-sufficiency on food as soon as possible, and then to provide insurance that we have a balanced crop once we shift to private farming."

"But how will we get a fair price for our goods if the community farms are already providing what the community needs?" Cer Barone asked.

"I'm not sure I understand your point," Marc said as he quickly typed some requests to ADI.

"Why would anyone buy our goods if the community farm is already supplying them, and you have very cheap labor?"

"Ah, I see. Let me make this proposal," Marc said. "The produce from the community farms will only be used to fill in the gaps that cannot be met by the private farms."

"What will you do with all your production?"

"We will store it, canning and preserving it for when the supply from the private farms might run out."

"But, what's to stop you from releasing that supply when we want to raise prices and withhold our produce until the price goes up?"

Marc chuckled. "I see. I'll assure you that we will not use the production from the community farms unless the wellbeing of the colony is threatened."

Cer Barone nodded to Cer Bachmann. "We'll work on wording for that agreement, but I think we can live with that commitment," she said. She nodded to Cer Barone, indicating he was free to bring up the other issue that he wanted to discuss.

"We would also like to know why we cannot start working our land now. We could work on the weekends and evenings to make a better life for our family and help the colony become established faster."

Marc paused for a moment to think. "The problem with that is it would require us to allocate the land now. The process calls for each of you to earn points by your good work in order to increase your chance of being one of the first ones to select your land. As you know, we'll be conducting a lottery system to set the order of choosing the land. And your record in the colony will determine how many chances you have to be the next to select. I do not know of another fair way to allocate who gets to choose first."

"I see, but it looks like a lost opportunity," Cer Barone said. "We could increase the diversity of food available as well as increase the supply."

"What about community allotments," Samantha suggested.

"Please explain."

"Each family could be allotted a certain amount of land that they would be able to work on their own time. Like a large garden. When they move to their farm, the land will revert back to the community. But it would allow even our town people to grow something, or just have a piece of land they can go play on," Samantha explained.

There was a flurry of activity as the delegates were listening to their Comms and tallying the response. Apparently, the idea resonated with a lot of the colonists who were listening. It took twenty minutes before the exchange among the colonists settled down.

"We have overwhelming consensus on that idea," Cer Bachmann said. "There are two questions that have been asked. First, could families combine their allotments to make a bigger piece of land? Some of our town's people would like to benefit, but don't feel skilled enough to actually farm the land."

"I wouldn't have a problem with that," Marc said.

"And second, would there be a way for them to utilize the farm equipment from the community farm when it is not in use?"

"I believe we can come up with a process for that. And I'm thinking of two thousand square meters for the land. That's one-half acre per family."

"That brings up another point. When you define it per family, it puts our married couples at a disadvantage," Cer Bachmann said.

"How about one thousand square meters for each colonist over sixteen," Marc said.

"Not two thousand?"

"Fifteen hundred," Marc conceded.

"Thank you."

*"What don't they like about the salaries,"* Marc wondered once they reconvened after the lunch break.

"We're ready to begin this session." Cer Bachmann said.

"We are also ready," Marc said. "I don't see Mr. Olsen."

"His group decided they wanted different representation," Cer Bachmann said. "Cer Morrison will be representing them."

"Okay, then we're ready. Go ahead."

"There is a very strong opinion among the colonists that having pay fixed isn't fair. They would like to see it based on market forces," Cer Bachmann said.

"Ignoring the fact that everyone signed a contract that specified their pay, what market forces are you referring to?"

"The law of supply and demand!" one of the representatives shouted.

"Ahem," Cer Bachmann coughed.

"Sorry."

"You do realize that supply and demand would dictate that wages could go down as well as up," Marc said.

"I pointed that out. I also pointed out that it was likely to hurt the majority of the colonists, who are semi-skilled," Cer Bachmann said.

"Did you also point out that we would provide training to those colonists so that they could start picking up some of the higher paid jobs, thereby increasing supply and bringing those wages down?"

"We wouldn't allow that!" another shouted. "Sorry," he said before Cer Bachmann could cough.

"So you want to form labor unions and negotiate contracts, like those contracts you signed when you joined the mission," Marc said. "And you want to limit the number of workers available in your job, so you can control the supply. What are we supposed to do when the next group of colonists shows up?"

"That is a conundrum," Cer Bachmann said.

"Look, a free market is all well and good. I'm a big fan myself. And my mother would have my scalp if I stood against labor unions. But the economy here is just too small. It has to be managed until it's big enough and has enough momentum that it can adapt without stalling."

"We just want to be treated fair!"

"Okay, then form your unions. I'll be happy to listen to reasonable demands that you present. If your rank and file feel they should be paid more, then show me how they are contributing more to the colony than others. Show me how their current pay is inadequate, and we'll discuss adjustments. But just saying you think you should be paid more doesn't cut it."

"We understand," Cer Bachmann said. "This is really driven by the desire to have a way to make more money so they can get ahead faster. They think the farmers will do better with the allotments than they will, so they want a way to even things up."

"Then ask for extra work," Marc said.

"We discussed that. But the work is limited by the supply of material and is tightly coordinated. There currently don't seem to be any overtime opportunities."

"Oh, you want some overtime, do you?" McCovey asked, sounding almost threatening.

"A reasonable amount would be appreciated," Cer Bachmann said.

"Well, that's not all that easy to arrange. We have to have full work crews," McCovey said.

"Why don't you make that their problem," Chief O'Donnell said. "Tell them what you need and let them chivvy up a crew."

"I could work with that. And we do need to start working on that damn house that Blake came up with. I don't think a façade's going to fool those aliens when they actually show up," McCovey said.

"Excellent," Marc said. "I was wondering when to bring that up."

"That you've waited this long, shows you have more sense than that brother of yours."

"Okay, Cer Bachmann, do you have anything else?"

"I think we'll let the labor unions form up and bring any further issues to you. There was some concern expressed about how you were going to deal with Riley O'Brian and his miners."

"Don't worry, I'll take care of Mr. O'Brian," Marc said.

"I don't think Riley's going to be as reasonable as we were!" one of the male representatives yelled.

"And I don't think another beatdown is going to work!" another added.

"You let me worry about O'Brian."

"Can I come watch?!"

## Dec 5th

Marc had the Lynx overfly the mining town. He was impressed. They'd used local trees for lumber and constructed a pretty nice little town. It was very reminiscent of the towns seen in old western movies. Two rows of buildings separated by a dirt street, with raised sidewalks on each side. In fact, everything was raised to allow the utilities to be run under the buildings without having to excavate. South of the town, they had set up an algae farm to produce diesel. They were using the diesel to run their mining equipment and pumps, and provide electricity for the town.

"Okay, I've seen enough, let's get this show on the road. Please land just outside of town," Marc ordered.

Once the Lynx landed, Marc and Corporal Jenkins, his bodyguard, exited the Lynx. They walked over toward a group that had gathered at the edge of the town. The big Aussie, O'Brian, was standing in front of the group.

"Hey, Nancy-boy, you looking for some gold?" O'Brian taunted.

"I'm here to find out why you've turned away the transport that came to pick up your delivery."

"They didn't offer to pay for our gold, so we told them to get lost!"

"It's not your gold. The mine belongs to MacKenzie Discoveries, and you work for them," Marc said.

"Well, we think this gold is worth more than just wages!"

"Why is that, did you discover it? Did you buy the land? Did you buy and ship all the mining equipment out here from Earth? Did you provide the infrastructure to build this town?"

"We built this town, and we dug the gold out of the ground!"

Mariana Ramsey lay on the deck of the Lynx that hovered above the town. With its stealth technology and being in the sun, it was unlikely that anyone in the town had noticed it. Everyone had been watching Marc's Lynx as it landed.

She watched a man climb out on the roof of a building at the edge of town. He carried a rifle. Back in the main city, hunters had to check the rifle out of the armory before they went hunting, but it had been felt that would be too onerous out here in the boondocks. She'd argued against it, but had been overruled. *"Now, you'll understand why I argued so hard,"* she muttered under her breath.

She lined her shot up on the man as he was lining his shot up on Marc. Unwilling to take a chance that he was just providing cover, Mariana took the shot. The stunner hit the guy in the back, knocking him out. His rifle went off.

CRACK!

"What the hell, Johnny! I told you not to shoot unless I told you to."

"Shooter was lining up on you," Mariana told Marc over their Comm channel. "I took him out with a stunner round."

"That was my sniper, she took your guy out because he was aiming a rifle at me. Don't worry, she was using stun rounds, *this time*."

"So, you're going to come in here with your Jack-booted Marines and kill us all?!" O'Brian yelled.

"No, I wouldn't want to do something like that. But I would like you to honor your contract and start delivering the gold, silver, and copper from the mines. We've invested a lot of time and material to get this town established, and we don't want to lose it."

"Well, we invested a lot of sweat to build this here town. And more sweat to get those mines up and running."

"Everyone here on Artemis can say the same thing. You volunteered to be miners and come out here. You're getting paid a premium for mining and another one for the isolation."

"Well, we don't think it's enough. If you're not going to kill us all, what are you going to do? We've got the gold."

"I'll tell you what we're going to do," Marc said. "We're going to build another town over there about fifty miles. We'll start another mine there to extract what we need. We will not bother you, but we will not pay you or buy your gold. You'll need to start a garden because we will also not be bringing any food by either."

"Someone will buy our gold!"

"I don't think so. We'll apply sanctions against anyone who does. All of the money out here is electronic, so we'll know what they spend it on. And you are a long way off, so I don't think anyone's going to be trekking all the way out here to buy something that there are no customers for."

"That's not fair!"

"And breaking your contract with MacKenzies is? Stealing the gold from the company land and trying to sell it back to us is fair?!" Marc shouted. "Anyone who wants to honor the original agreement, we'll move you to the new town. The rest of you let us know if and when you want to honor your original agreement, until then we'll just leave you alone."

Marc turned and started to walk back toward the Lynx.

"Hold up!" one of the other men yelled. "If I come with you now, will I still get paid?"

"Yes, we won't hold anything against you if you come now. If you wait, then you'll forfeit all your wages from before."

"It's a damn shame to leave this town. We did a nice job on it. But I'm not a thief and I never really thought this was a good idea. Me and mine want to stay with MacKenzies."

"I do too!" a woman called out. "I'm not interested in becoming a farmer."

Marc watched as slowly each member of the group separated themselves from O'Brian. Over half had moved away, and the rest were exchanging nervous glances when O'Brian yelled. "Wait, what if everyone agreed to honor their contracts?!"

"Well, then we wouldn't need to build a new town," Marc said.

"Will you promise not to hold it against any of the others?"

"I'm willing to forgive everyone else," Marc said.

"Then I'll go with you. That way, all these folks won't lose all their hard work for listening to me."

"I really don't want you," Marc said.

"You mean you're going to cast me out of the colony?"

"No, I was thinking you would want to stay here. You've done a good job getting the town built."

"Then what are you going to do to me?"

"You'll forfeit half your pay up until today. But this is your third strike. That's usually all I give anyone, but I'm going to give you a pass on the first one. But you're not going to get another one."

"Okay, that's more'n fair. I won't be causing you no more problems."

"Good, the hauler will be out here tomorrow with a load of supplies, and I expect it to come back full."

"Don't worry, it will."

◆ ◆ ◆

"Boss, is that all?" Mariana complained.

"Sure."

"He called us Jack-booted Marines!"

"Then you have my permission to go down there and kick his ass. He drops his right shoulder just before he throws a jab."

"Thanks!"

# 22 Oh My Gosh

Marc started the board meeting feeling pretty good. It was the first that he would conduct from Artemis, and things seemed to be in hand. The colonists were in general alignment once again; the powers on Earth seemed to be cooperating, and the aliens heading for Artemis were still six months away.

"Thank you for joining me," Marc said. "Catie, are you tied in?"

"Yep, everything's good on my end."

"Then let's get started. I'm sure you've all read the status report on our little strike here on Artemis. We'll have to track things as we go, but I'm optimistic that things will settle down."

"Do you really think it was smart, leaving O'Brian in charge of the mining town?" Blake asked.

"Yes," Marc said with a smile.

"Okay, let me rephrase, why did you leave O'Brian in charge of the mining town?"

"He's a smart guy, he's really proud of what they've accomplished out there. If I took him out of there, where would I put him? And wherever I did put him, he would grow to resent it. Now he's happy, surrounded by people who will be quick to remind him that he almost cost them a month's wages," Marc said. "Seems like a win to me."

"I assume you'll be keeping an eye on him," Kal said.

"Yes, I've asked ADI to keep him under surveillance. Now, Lieutenant Payne, welcome to the board meeting. Can you tell us how the Paraxean Colony is doing?"

"Thank you, sir," Lieutenant Payne said. "They seem to be doing well. They've finished their main street and have some crops in. They have to wait a few months for the season to change before they can plant the rest of them, but they're really working those greenhouses."

"How are their chickens and goats doing?"

"As I understand it, half the goats are pregnant with triplets, the others are being milked. I think the plan is as soon as the pregnant ones drop their babies, they'll put triplets in the other goats."

"Put triplets in them?" Admiral Michaels asked.

"They brought hundreds of embryos; that way, they know exactly what they're going to get," Lieutenant Payne said. "Now the chickens are a different story. The eggs they brought hatched, and they're already laying. They're letting ten percent sit on their eggs, so they get more chickens, and are doing the same with the ducks, by the way."

"Any problems with tigers?" Liz asked.

"No, the tigers are on a different continent, same with that triceratops thing. Here just a few fox-like animals to worry about. They seem to like chicken."

Marc laughed. "Thank you, Lieutenant Payne. Moving on, Admiral, how are our allies behaving?"

"We're still working on the language of the treaties," Admiral Michaels said. "It's a good thing I'm commuting from Nice; I'm usually over my foul temper before I get home."

"I'm sure Pam appreciates it. What is she doing to keep busy?"

"She's still running the hydroponic farms in Delphi city. She's set up a lab at the estate we bought; that lets her do a few experiments there. She does a conference call every day and is constantly on the Comm talking to people. She's going to try to spend one week a month in Delphi City."

"Catie, jumpdrives?"

"We're building the ships. We think the design will be able to move one of the space carriers. Once we've tested that, we'll scale it up to see if we can move an asteroid."

"That sounds promising," Marc said.

"Dr. McDowell actually sounds excited."

"Captain!" ADI interrupted the meeting on a private Comm channel.

*"Yes, ADI,"* Marc messaged, raising his hand to tell everyone to pause.

*"I have received some new data from the Paraxean carriers. It's from their previous battle with the aliens. Based on the scans they made of the aliens who attacked them and the scans we've made of the aliens approaching Artemis, I'm ninety percent confident that they are from the same civilization,"* ADI reported.

"Oh, shit!"

"What?!" Blake asked.

"ADI says that the aliens approaching Artemis are more than likely from the same civilization that attacked the Paraxeans."

"How can that be? Those locations are over two hundred light-years apart!" Catie said.

"I know, Cer Catie," ADI said. "But their ships are nearly identical in construction and configuration."

"Okay, people, we now need a battle plan for when they arrive," Marc said.

"We needed one before we knew this," Blake said. "Now, we're just surer that we'll have to use it."

"Daddy, it's not that bad!" Catie said.

"No? I've brought families out here, and now I find out that we're at risk of a significant confrontation instead of just a minor standoff," Marc said. "This is really bad news."

"I'm sure after a few glasses of scotch, you'll realize it's not that bad," Blake said. "Talk to you later, Karl."

Once the others had disappeared from their HUDs, Samantha walked over to Marc and hugged him from behind. "I don't want to pile on, but I think you probably need to know, I'm pregnant."

"Oh boy!" ADI exclaimed.

"ADI!" Samantha protested.

"I know, private information. But I'm going to start planning a baby shower!"

"I'm *happy* to hear that," Marc said, trying to keep the shock from showing on his face. "Why didn't you tell me before?"

"I was waiting for the right time," Samantha said. "This isn't exactly the right time I envisioned, but it does seem to be the right time, anyway."

Marc sighed, "Why is it that every time we think we're cooking, someone throws a handful of chili pepper into the pot?"

# Afterword

## Thanks for reading **Delphi Colony!**

I hope you've enjoyed the eight book in the Delphi in Space series. The story will continue in Delphi League. If you would like to join my newsletter group go to https://tinyurl.com/tiny-delphi. The newsletter provides interesting Science facts for SciFi fans, book recommendation based on books I truly loved reading, deals on books I think you'll like, and notification of when the next book in my series is available.

As a self-published author, the one thing you can do that will help the most is to leave a review on Goodreads and Amazon.

The next book in our series is Delphi Challenge.

# Acknowledgments

It is impossible to say how much I am indebted to my beta readers and copy editors. Without them, you would not be able to read my books due to all the grammar and spelling errors. I have always subscribed to Andrew Jackson's opinion that "It is a damn poor mind that can think of only one way to spell a word."

So special thanks to:

My copy editor, Ann Clark, who also happens to be my wife.

My beta reader and editor, Theresa Holmes.

My beta reader and cheerleader, Roger Blanton, who happens to be my brother.

Also important to a book author is the cover art for their book. I'm am especially thankful to Momir Borocki for the exceptional covers he has produced for my books. It is amazing what he can do with the strange PowerPoint drawings I give him; and how he makes sense of my suggestions, I'll never know.

If you need a cover, he can be reached at momir.borocki@gmail.com.

## Also by Bob Blanton

Delphi in Space
*Starship Sakira*
*Delphi City*
*Delphi Station*
*Delphi Nation*
*Delphi Alliance*
*Delphi Federation*
*Delphi Exploration*
*Delphi Colony*
*Delphi Challenge*
*Delphi League – coming in April 2021*

Stone Series
*Matthew and the Stone*
*Stone Ranger*
*Stone Undercover*

Made in the USA
Middletown, DE
22 October 2023